SCARLET

OATH

THE CRIMSON LEGACY
BOOK TWO

SCARLET
OATH

MICHELLE BRYAN

Published by Aelurus Publishing, March 2020

ISBN 13: 978-1-912775-44-6

www.aeluruspublishing.com

For my boys. Thank you for all your support.

CHAPTER ONE

The Return

———❦———

The knee pressing painfully into my back and pinning me to the floor is pissing me off something fierce. I want to scream. I want to reach up and tear Mack's flesh right from his face. Maybe gouge out his good eye or something. Instead, all I do is hiss at him like an angry cat as he taunts in my ear, "Come on, girlie, that all you got?"

Slamming my head back hard into his, I hear his muffled cussing as he loosens his grip. I roll from underneath his confining weight, sweep out with my leg and smack my boot to the back of his knee, taking him down. He hits the ground with a satisfying thud, and I take advantage of besting him to scramble back to my feet. My tunic sticks to my back and wisps of hair cling to my forehead. I'm drenched in sweat. But I don't dare take the time to wipe it out of my eyes since he's already back on his feet and circling me like some hungry wolfling. His eye mocks me, daring me to try something else.

"Oh, so the baby New Blood has learned something after all."

He raises his fists in front of his face and continues to walk around me, grinning at me like some crazed fool. Opening one of his hands palm up, he waggles his fingers at me. Beckoning me to come at him.

"Come on then. Try to take me down."

I grit my teeth and attack, throwing a punch at Mack's face. He deflects it easily and wallops his fist into my shoulder, sending pain searing through my arm. I bite my lip to stop from crying out, refusing to show him any weakness by cradling my injured arm like I so want to. Instead, I remember his words from yesterday.

"You have long legs, Tara. Use them. They can be your strength."

Before he can predict my next move, I pivot on my left heel and swing with my right leg, my foot hitting him just below the ribcage. He stumbles backward with a loud "Omph!" He bends over, winded, but the kick doesn't take him down. His grin just widens as he growls, "Good. Now try that again."

Seriously? I don't want to try it again. I don't want to do any of this. I'm tired and sore, and I ache in muscles I didn't even know I had. But I know Mack isn't anywhere done with me. This "training" as he calls it has been going on for weeks now. I can't understand what he hopes to come from it. There's hardly been any sign of the Chi, the bio-energy that he and Lily insist I possess. There's no sign of any New Blood powers that the rebels think I have. All this sparring does is leave me sweaty, stinky, and achy. A total waste of time as far as I'm concerned. I'm truly starting to believe the strange things I'd done during my travels had been flukes. Just random chance occurrences. There's certainly no reason to believe the weird strength I'd mustered when fighting the raider girl and the crazies in the dead city could ever be summoned at will. And as for raising that dust devil to fend off the Army, well, I still find it hard to believe that was my doing. Maybe it had been just a freak dust storm after all and nothing to do with me.

Yet Mack and Lily still insist I'm the cause of it and I can control this power, and that by training every day, I will control it. So they keep me here, wasting my time while Ben is still in the hands of the Prezedant and going through the gods only knew what. We should be on our way to rescue him. We should be doing something instead of just sitting on our arses. What were they thinking?

Whack! Mack's open-palmed hand slaps me hard on the side of my head, making my ears ring.

"Ow," I cry in shocked surprise. Did he just bitch slap me?

"Pay attention," he scolds me. "This time it was just my hand. Could have been a shot of serum. What would you have done then, eh? You have to learn to keep your opponent at arm's length. You can't let the soldiers get close enough to you to jab you with that. Now, try coming at me again."

Mack is right. I'd already encountered the serum once,

when we'd been captured by the Army, and it had knocked me off my feet and then some. Even though Lily tells me this serum is a medicinal thing, similar to Grada's healing herbs, I still think it's dark magic. I've never heard of being able to pass herbs through a metal needle tube. Although since I'd been in Littlepass, I'd seen some real strange things.

Whack! He slaps me again, and I cover my head with my arm.

"Stop doin' that," I cry out.

"Well, pay attention then. Fight back. You have to learn to protect yourself. You have to learn to control your Chi. Discipline your mind," he yells. "How do you expect to face the Prezedant when you can't even summon your Chi at will?"

"I'm tryin'," I snap back, fed up with this whole training shite. "But it just ain't happenin'. I told you I wasn't the New Blood y'all think I am. I don't have the power."

Before I can recover from the second slap, Mack lunges at me. He moves so fast I don't have time to prepare for his attack. He's on me like some wild wolfling on its prey. I'm spun about and shoved face-first against the rough, stone wall, my arm twisted behind my back. I can't help but cry out this time at the jolt of pain. His solid frame presses me firm against the wall, and I can feel his hot breath on my neck.

"What you gonna do then, girl? If you can't even save yourself from me, how you gonna save Ben? I guess he's as good as dead then if it's up to you to save him. How do you feel about that? Do you think we should all go to Skytown to watch him get beheaded? Because that's how he likes to do it: chop their heads off right in front of their families.

How do you feel knowing that Ben is going to die at the Prezedant's hands just because you're a weak, sniveling little coward?"

The cruel, cold words snarled into my ear fill me with utter shock, but anger quickly replaces it, rushing in and forcing away my surprise and pain. Mack's harsh words are drowned out by the familiar buzzing. The fire rises in my blood, spreading rapidly through my veins, from my toes to the top of my head. Every fine hair stands on end. Every part of my flesh sparks with awareness of the Chi. My body braces itself for the overwhelming surge of energy.

My power fills me now, and I twist easily from Mack's hold, grabbing his throat in a vise-like grip. I stare into the familiar face, but the knowledge of who he is and the fact that he's my friend, doesn't make one lick of difference to me. The need to make him pay for his cruel words is the only thought in my head.

I push him away from me and he flies across the room, crashing into the stone wall. A grunt of pain escapes his lips as he hits, before sliding down and crumpling on the ground. His hands encircle his neck like he's not able to breathe. Like there's something there preventing the very air from entering his body. His gasps echo around the room and although it doesn't show on his face, I smell his fear like an underlying rot.

"Control … it …," he croaks, and his plea breaks through the ice-cold barrier encasing me.

He can't breathe because of me. Shizen, I'm doing this. I'm choking him! The fear jolts my brain into understanding. I need to pull back my Chi. *Think, Tara. Think.*

Ignoring my own panic, I close my eyes and concentrate hard. I force every other thought out of my head and imagine my Chi—my aura—as a brightly lit flame growing dimmer and dimmer, just like Mack has been training me to do. I will it to draw away from Mack and back into my body. I can actually feel the energy pulsing through my blood, and I force myself to slow my breathing, slow my heartbeat. Calm myself down. I picture the lit flame going dark, and just like that it's over. My Chi retreats, leaving me slumped over and exhausted, hands braced on my knees to keep from falling.

I finally raise my eyes, afraid of what I will find. But Mack is back on his feet, standing still as a statue. His neck bears the marks of the unseen force holding him down, throttling him. His one eye bores into mine, and I wait for the scathing reprimand. But he doesn't seem the least bit upset at what I've done. If anything, he looks pleased. I almost killed him, and he's pleased?

"That was … impressive. Now, we're finally getting somewhere. Seems like pissing you off is the trigger. Should have done that to you weeks ago," he says, his raspy voice evidence of what he'd just endured at my hands.

Anger starts flickering again in my gut like some re-lit ember, but I squash it back down. I don't want a repeat of what just happened, but I'm so damn pissed at him for pushing me that far.

"Why did you do that, Mack? I coulda hurt you … coulda killed you." I glare at him in accusation.

He merely shrugs at me and grins. "Coulda … shoulda … didn't. You controlled it, Tara. You stopped it. That's great progress."

My anger dulls as his words finally dawn on me and elicit an unwilling grin. He's right. I'd controlled it. For the first time ever, I'd stopped my Chi on my own terms.

"I did, didn't I?" I say in wonder. "How did you know, Mack? How did you know I'd be able to stop it?"

He shrugs at me. "Your Chi is controlled by you, not the other way around. It's your power to do with as you will. Your gift, not the curse you believe it to be. I just had to make you come to that understanding." He smiles ruefully and rubs his neck. "Although, you were a little slow on the uptake. I was starting to worry. Thought I was a goner there for a bit."

"I'm sorry," I say, as my grin fades. "I've never done anything like that before. It was a little, well, it was a lot scary. How *did* I do that?"

He shrugs again.

"That, I can't answer. A New Blood's power is multifaceted. Not even Lily is sure of the things you may be capable of. And if I'm to guess, I'd say this is only the tip of your abilities. We still have quite a ways to go. To go up against the Prezedant, you have to be able to use your Chi like a weapon and use it well. He's had lots of experience dealing with New Bloods. You are going to have to learn to anticipate his every move. It's the only way to save Ben and everyone else."

I sigh as I wipe the sweat from my face with my forearm. I know Mack's right. What he and the others are asking me to do still truly does terrify me, but not as much as it terrifies me to think of what the Prezedant will do to Ben if I fail. My heart rate spikes again as I recall Mack's earlier words.

"Were you being truthful about how the Prezedant … kills his prisoners?" The words stick in my throat because the thought of it makes my stomach sick, but I need to know.

His nod is stiff. "It is his preferred method of dealing with prisoners, yes, but no need to worry. Ben's head will remain safely attached to his shoulders for now. He won't destroy the bait when he hasn't yet caught the fish."

Hmm. I narrow my eyes at him. That sounded suspiciously like something Tater would say. If I were to guess, I'd say Mack has been spending way too much time in the half man's company. In the three weeks Tater has been underfoot at Sanctuary, he's obviously made an impression on its occupants. And an impact on their supply of ale, too, no doubt.

These past two weeks though, he's been gone on a trading mission, and I never thought I would ever say this, but I kinda miss the little guy. Sanctuary is certainly a lot quieter without him around. Mack's Tater-ish words don't put me at ease though.

"How do you know for sure? How do you know he won't tire of waitin' for me to show up and just kill Ben anyways? We should be doin' something. Anything is better than just sittin' here waitin'. I don't understand why we're not doin' anything," I say, my frustration making me sound like some whiny child.

"Tara, I understand your impatience, but you have to trust that we know what we're doing," Mack says calmly. "We cannot rush into this headstrong. When you're ill-prepared, mistakes happen. We can't afford that again."

He doesn't elaborate, but I have a gut feeling he's referring to my ma. I never knew my ma. Although she was a New Blood too—and a reportedly strong one at that—she had perished long ago in this ongoing fight against the Prezedant. Lily had promised to tell me the whole story when "the time was right," but it hasn't happened yet no matter how much I nag her.

"Go now," he continues. "Rest up for tomorrow. Keep in mind what you did today. We will focus on that, see if you can make your Chi appear as easily as you stopped it."

I give him a withering, sidelong glare. *That's* his definition of easy? But I don't say anything. I'm happy enough to be quitting early since there's someplace I need to be, so I don't want to say anything to make him change his mind. I leave without even so much as a goodbye.

I shuffle my way slowly through the long, white hallway of Sanctuary. My body protests with each step I take, and my arm throbs something fierce. But considering that I'd thrown Mack across the room and nearly choked him to death, well, I guess I got the lesser of it today.

Now that the shock at what happened back there has worn off, I'm left with a mixed bag of emotions. What I'd done to Mack pleases me in some twisted way, but it also scares me shiteless. Every time my Chi shows itself, it seems bigger and more terrifying. And what I'd done today, well, that's the most terrifying of all. I'd actually used my Chi on a friend, an ally. What if the next time it happened, it was to Tater or Lily or Finn? What if I can't stop it the next time? Regardless of what the others believe, I still don't think this curse of mine is controllable at all.

It's moments like this that I question what I'm doing here with this bunch of rebels. I'm not a rebel or a fighter. And even after all Mack has taught me, I still feel utterly useless.

Like what they expect of me is impossible and that deep down, I'm still that scared little girl who just wants to run and hide. But it's the thought of Ben at the mercy of the Prezedant that keeps me going. So like yesterday and the day before that, I will do it all over again tomorrow. Lily and Mack and Finn—they believe in me. Now if only I can believe in myself.

As if thinking of Finn conjures him up, he and Cat barrel around the corner of the long hall at break-neck speed. Both boy and beast are heading away from the kitchen, scrambling like there's a starved wolfling on their heels. Since Zoe and I had snuck the black devil cat into Littlepass weeks ago, much to Finn's delight, it wasn't an uncommon sight to see the two of them running through the great halls or yard of Sanctuary. But this time, something doesn't seem quite right about their mad dash.

I notice Finn's carrying a couple of those orange ball things that, I've come to understand, are actually called oranges. Go figure. He has one in each hand, and Cat has something hanging out of her mouth. I can't quite figure out what it is, but its drippings are left down the entire length of the hallway. I look closer. Is it a rabbit? The boy keeps glancing over his shoulder every two steps, but draws up short at seeing me.

"Hey, Tara. We ain't doin' nuthin', I swear," he says, his eyes shifting about and looking at everything in the hallway but me.

"I didn't say you were, now did I?" I drawl. "Though I wouldn't exactly call that rabbit hangin' outta Cat's mouth nuthin'. I gotta bad feelin' that's supposed to be part of tonight's supper. I'd be willin' to bet Cook's not gonna be happy about that." And then as if on cue, I hear the outraged bellow coming from the kitchen.

"BOY! I know this is your doing, boy. You and that gods' dang cat."

Finn's face drains of color at the angry scream, and his eyes finally connect to mine with the frantic look of a trapped animal.

"I swear, Tara, I didn't mean for this to happen. I was so hungry, and I went to the kitchen to get one of these." He holds up the orange. "They're just so dang good. And the rabbit was just sittin' there fresh cooked and all, and it smelled so good. I figured just a little bite, but then Cat, well, she figured she could have a bite too, and the next thing I knew she has the whole thing in her mouth, and then we hear Cook comin' back, and we ran and …," he finally stops to breathe as his fear shifts to pleading. " A little help? Cook's gonna kill me," he moans.

I nod, trying seriously hard not to laugh.

"Yup, he's crazy enough, that's for sure." I hear the heavy thud of footsteps coming dangerously close, and I jerk my thumb upward.

"You'd best go hide up in the loft," I say, feeling bad enough for him to give him a way out. The loft above the sanctuary is huge. All of my Rivercross kin could have lived there easily with room to spare. It's probably Finn and Cat's safest place to hide in right now.

"Marcel cain't make it up those steep steps. It's your best bet."

"Thanks, Tara," he blurts, his face filled with gratitude as he starts running in the opposite direction of the approaching mad man. He isn't outta sight long before Marcel's massive bulk comes lumbering around the corner. He stands in the long hall and his head swings back and forth on his wide shoulders like some mad dog until his anger-filled eyes come to rest on me. He stomps toward me, and I swear the floor shakes underneath me with each step he takes.

"Where is he?" he wheezes, his nostrils flaring with each word.

I look up at him with all the wide-eyed innocence I can muster. "Who?"

His already narrow eyes shrink to mere slits. "Don't play dumb with me, girl. That dang boy and his damn beast. Where did they go?"

"You talkin' about Finn? I ain't seen him all day. I've been trainin' with Mack. Nope, haven't seen no sign of Finn," I shrug my shoulders at him.

"Is that so?" He scoffs and I get the feeling he doesn't believe me. "And I guess that is not the delectable smell of my perfectly cooked rabbit hanging about in the hallway? You're lying. I know he came this way."

I raise my nose in the air and take a big sniff. "Nope. All I can smell is me. But if you're sayin' you cooked rabbit for tonight, well, I'm pretty sure I heard Lily mention she wanted wildfowl for tonight's evenin' meal. I could go to the market and get 'em for ya if you like."

I can tell he doesn't want to be taken in by my obvious attempt to distract him, but as angry as he is, he knows I'm Lily's "honored" guest. I swear I even see him biting his own tongue to stop from spewing out what he's thinking. Instead, he gives me a stiff nod.

"So be it. Go get them, and make sure to tell the butcher they are for Marcel. He will give you the best he has."

I nod and start to walk away, but he grabs my arm with his meaty fingers.

"Give the boy a word of advice. Tell him to keep that damn beast out of my kitchen, or I swear on all that is holy I will serve that cat's head on a roasting platter."

I watch him stomp away; still muttering under his breath and knowing that he isn't exaggerating. Not in the least. Finn's definitely going to have to stay away from the kitchen for a bit, at least until Marcel calms down. Lily says the cook's bark is worse than his bite, but that man has a sharp set of chompers, and I don't want Finn finding out otherwise.

I head to my room to collect my wrapper, the fleeting idea of a shower pushed outta my head as I realize I don't have time. I do take the time to hide my knife in my boot though. Since I can't very well walk through the market with my iron shooter, the knife is my only source of protection, and I never leave Sanctuary without it.

As much as Lily hates my trips to the crowded marketplace, it's necessary for me to go. I always take care not to have anyone notice me, and I make sure to keep the white in my hair covered at all times. The last thing I need is someone tying the telltale white stripes together with the wanted New Blood fugitive. But the trips to the marketplace have an ulterior motive; one that I haven't told her about because I know she won't like it.

Ever since I'd found out that every middle of the week they sold the captured outlanders there, I make a point of being there. Not that I could ever afford to buy the poor people put on display. As much as I want to just to set them free, I don't have two pieces of iron to rub together. But I go on the off chance that I may come across Jane or young Thomas or at least hear news of my missing kin. As troubling as it is to watch the sordid selling of the young'uns, I force myself to go and study every face in the crowd. I need to understand what kind of people can do this to others and not think twice about it. Oh, not everybody there agrees with what's happening. I know that. I can see some of the people look away in disgust and anger. Others hold their own young'uns tighter; the relief that it isn't their own children up for sale clearly written on their faces. But they don't say or do anything about it, too terrified to take a stand.

Then there are the rest. The ones that watch in amusement and excitement, enjoying every bit of the debacle. Hollerin' and hootin' as the bidding goes up. Grading each young'un like they're livestock instead of people. Buying them like they're buying meat for whatever brutal purpose they have in mind for them. Those are the people I truly hate. Those are the people whose hearts I want to rip out and feed to the wild wolflings. But like the cowering villagers, I don't do anything. There's nothing I can do but add that hatred to the growing pile of shite I already harbor against the Prezedant and his true followers. Maybe someday, I'll be able to do something about it and make him pay for their suffering. But today isn't that day.

I head for the front entrance, content in the knowledge I won't run into Finn this time. I reckon Cook had scared him plenty today. He won't come out of hiding for a while yet.

My last few trips to the market he'd pleaded to tag along, but I never let him. We can't be seen together. It's still too risky even if Tater and Jax are no longer an everyday part of our little group. Tater may have been cleared in the eyes of the Army with his fake betrayal of us, but the rest of us are still wanted fugitives.

Jax. I still can't think of the name, of the man himself, without feeling an overwhelming sense of guilt and remorse. The last words I'd said to him was to blame him for Ben's capture. For the deaths of all those innocent prisoners. I know it wasn't his fault, truly. I know that now. But at the time, there'd been so much anger and hurt and pain, and Jax, well, he got the brunt of it.

I'd looked for him after Mack brought me back to the Sanctuary. After I'd stewed in my anger and self-pity for days in my room, just hating the world and the gods for allowing this to happen. But I was too late. I was too late to take back the terrible accusations I'd thrown at him. He was gone. Back to Gray Valley, back to Sky. It was probably for the best. We were a volatile combination. Him with his hatred of New Bloods, his sarcastic nature, and his unwavering belief that he was always so right. And me ... well ... just being me.

I think about him often, wondering how he's doing. If he and Sky are wedded by now. If they already started a family of their own. A bunch of little Jaxes with those light blue eyes and the black, spiky hair, and that odd little dent in their chins. I don't know why I think about him, but I can't seem to help it, or the sharp pain in my gut that always accompanies thoughts of him and Sky together. So I do what I always do when I don't want to face something, I push it away. Bury it.

If I don't think about it no more, then it can't hurt me. I'm becoming real good at doing that.

—◆—

The afternoon heat wallops me in the face as I step from the cool interior of Sanctuary's stone walls to the outer courtyard. Passing through the graveyard of a garden, I pause for a bit at the massive iron front gate and nod a greeting to Flip. To any passerby, he looks like a simple, filthy beggar sitting against the gate. His head wrapped in dirty rags and his tunic no cleaner. For the longest time, I believed the same. I actually felt sorry for him the first couple of times I'd seen him and proceeded to sneak food from the kitchen to bring to him, much to his delight. He never told me any different. But then I finally found out he was actually Lily's top guard and one of her most loyal. He watched the comings and goings of Sanctuary like a hawk. If anything suspicious was going on, Flip would know. The knowledge hasn't stopped me from sneaking him treats from the kitchen though.

He nods back and smiles, showing me his broken, yellow teeth.

"Afternoon, Mistress. You off to the markets again?" he says.

"Aye. Cook needs some wildfowl for the evenin' meal," I say.

"And I'd be willing to bet that's your only reason for going, eh? Ain't got nothing to do with the fact that there's some flesh trading going on again today?"

I stop in my tracks and stare. How did he know what I'd

been up to in my time at the market?

Flip laughs at my undisguised look of surprise.

"You should know by now, Mistress, that nothing happens in Littlepass without Flip knowing. But don't worry. I won't tell Lily, not as long as you promise to stay unnoticed by the Army."

"How did you know what I was doin'? Have you been followin' me?" I say, a little put out by this. I never noticed anyone following me on my trips to the market. Some sense of awareness I had. If I hadn't noticed Flip, how was I supposed to notice the Army on my tail?

"I have my little birdies watching out for you, girl. Can't be too careful when it comes to the Army—foul-smellin', black-hearted, lice-ridden bastards that they are."

I bust a gut laughing at his words.

"Shizen, Flip. Why don't ya tell me how you really feel?" That's the thing I like about Flip. He doesn't beat around the bush. He just says it as he sees it.

"Aye, and why don't you just get your smartass attitude outta here," he says with a scowl, but I know he's just teasing. I wave goodbye and head down the hill toward the bustling marketplace.

I hurry my stride and it isn't long before my senses are assaulted by the mixed odors of freshly baked goods, animal droppings, and unwashed bodies all rolled into one. The sun-bleached buildings crowding the road to the market soon give way to the dizzying array of colorful market stalls all stuffed to overflowing. It still amazes me at the amount of stuff available here. I was used to scavenging for every meal in the sand lands, yet here in the Prezedant's domain, there's just so much. Meats and greens and fruits and baubles, all available for the right price. The fact that it's ill-gotten from the blood and sweat of the outlanders and sandlanders didn't seem to matter much to the crowd flocking happily about in the streets. That or they simply choose to turn a blind eye. Either way, as far as I'm concerned, they're all just as bad as the Prezedant himself. I keep my eyes downcast, avoiding eye contact so as not to make anyone aware of my obvious disgust.

The constant barrage of people yelling is like a roar in my ears, so loud you can't even hear yourself think. I get jostled and shoved about as I fight my way through the crowd, that familiar feeling of panic I feel every time I come here threatening to overwhelm me. But I push the panic down. I need to do this.

Elbowing my way through the wall of people, I finally reach my destination; a massive statue situated in the middle of the town square. The ugly, golden monstrosity of a robed man sitting on a throne, his subjects kneeling at his feet, raises my ire every time I see it. It was supposedly erected in honor of the Prezedant, a benevolent ruler loved and worshiped by his people. What a bunch of hokum. It reminds me more of some threatening master towering over his terrified servants. I hate the very sight of it. And I take way too much pleasure in seeing how the birds have defaced the statue, almost on purpose you would think. Their shite is splattered everywhere over the Prezedant's head and face. It's fitting.

I climb the statue, careful to avoid the bird splatters, and settle out of sight behind the gold throne. I figured out on my earlier visits that this is the best spot to overlook the traders and the crowd without being seen. As usual, the flesh trading has attracted a large crowd today. They gather around the raised wooden platform like an audience around a stage. I'd only ever seen flesh trading carried out on the platform, but the rust-stained stone situated in the center of the structure tells me it has another purpose. An executioner's block. I hope I never have to see it used for that.

I arrive just in time. The crowd erupts in a huge roar as today's goods are herded up the platform stairs, some of them stumbling as they're shoved and pushed about by the guards. I hold my breath and count them as they're forced to line up. There are eight today: six young'uns and two muties. I study their terrified faces, but eventually my pent-up breath releases in a big sigh—part disappointment, part relief, since none of them are my kin. They're just eight more poor, innocent souls being sold off like they're nothing. Like they aren't people. Like they don't even matter. They matter to me. As always, I feel my hatred growing. I want to run right up there and put my knife through the hearts of every guard standing there and set the prisoners all free. But I'm not that stupid. I stay on my perch, chewing on my bottom lip in frustration as they bring the first prisoner up front for the bidding.

The boy is all skin and bones, probably no older than Finn. His tunic is ripped from the neck down, and there's a big bruise on his cheek. Looks like he'd put up a fight. *Good*, I think. I hope the soldier that had done this to him is sporting bruises of his own or at least is unable to walk from a good, swift kick between the legs.

As terrified as he must be, he stands with his head held

high, refusing to drop his defiant gaze from the mocking crowd. I watch as the soldier leading the trading praises his virtues to the gawkers: good, strong teeth, pox-free skin, scrawny but muscled arms, and used to hard work. A good buy for any house or trade. A good buy.

How did it come to this? I think. How can people believe that selling young'uns is acceptable? Had the old settlers believed in this, too? Had they once done the same? Or is this evil the Prezedant's doing? But as usual, I have no answers to my own questions.

The boy's rebellious eyes scan the crowd, and then seem to stop on me. I sit up straighter. Did he really spot me sitting here, or is he just eyeing the statue and trying to shut out the crowd? No, it's me he's staring at no doubt. His eyes bore into mine with a fierce plea. "Save me," he seems to say. "Help me."

My stomach churns, but I can't look away from his pleading stare. I watch in horror as he's looked over by a fat-bellied man in a stained smock, probably from one of the numerous butcher houses or taverns in Littlepass. The boy ignores the man's probing hands, refusing to drop his gaze from me, and I suddenly can't breathe. *Help me!* The scream echoes in my head, and I jump at the invasion. What the hell new kinda thing is this? The boy's lips aren't even moving. Is he really speaking to me, or am I imagining the whole thing? My eyes scrutinize his shaved head, wondering—if there was hair growing there—would it be black as crow feathers and streaked with white?

I'm sorry, I think, dropping my eyes in shame from the boy's, unable to look at him anymore. *I'm sorry, but I cain't help you.*

I don't want to be here anymore. I don't want to see anymore. And to be honest, the way the boy seems to be in my head, well, it's freaking me out. Eyes averted, I climb down from my perch, not waiting to see the sale, to see the boy led away to his new life of servitude. I push my way through the suffocating crowd, my anger intensified by their laughter and uncaring attitudes to what's happening around them. Unfeeling, callous, cruds, all of them.

I stop long enough to get the wildfowl from the butcher, wanting to get away from the market as quick as I can. I'm totally unsettled by my experience. Did I truly imagine the boy's voice in my head? Is the connection real, or is it just a manifestation of my anger and guilt at my inability to help? Is this a new aspect of my Chi, or am I truly losing my mind? I hurry my steps in a rush to get back to Sanctuary. I need to talk to Lily. I need some answers.

Keeping my eyes down, I scurry along the sides of the street, sticking close to the stone buildings. The sea of people isn't as heavy in here, and I don't have to watch everywhere I step.

I hurry by a dark alley, but a slight movement in the gloom catches my eye as I pass, and I halt in my tracks. I blink into the dimness, wondering if maybe I'd finally spotted one of Flip's little "birdies" following me. Nothing else moves, and I start to think my mind is playing tricks on me when a soft cry wafts from the darkness. A tiny cry for help. My heart skips a beat. Maybe it's the boy. Maybe he's escaped from the fat-bellied man somehow and is asking for my help again. I keep peering, but I don't see nobody. I hesitate, debating if maybe I imagined it when I hear it again.

"Help me."

It's real enough all right. It sure sounds like a young'un. I look around, trying to see if anyone else is hearing this, but they're all passing me by, not even giving the alley a second look.

"Hey, did you hear that?" I say to a scruffy-bearded man as he passes, but he just growls at me and pushes me outta his way.

"Jackass!" I yell at his retreating back, but he doesn't even bother to turn back. I take a step, but falter. The alley is dark and just reeks of trouble. Probably shouldn't go in there. Maybe it really is all in my head. Wouldn't be the first time. But then that little cry comes again, and my feet start down the lane on their own before my mind even decides. I can't ignore it anymore.

About halfway in, I stumble to a stop. A shape huddles on the ground, sitting underneath a rotting, half-crumbled stairway that occupies most of the narrow passage. *This ain't a wise decision,* the little voice in my head nags at me, but another whimper overrides the voice. Closer now I can see that it's a small person for sure, hunched over with its head on its knees.

"Hey," I say in a quiet voice as I approach, not wanting to startle him or her. "You okay?"

There's no answer. I reach out and touch the bony shoulder. Suddenly the kid's head pops up, and his hand grabs my wrist with alarming strength. I gasp, immediately realizing my mistake. It's no poor, innocent child at all but a young man, his pockmarked face twisted with a leering grin.

I try to jerk my hand back, to get away, but his strength belies his scrawny frame, and he just keeps grinning at me.

"Well, well, and what did you entice into our alley this time, Nud?"

The voice comes from behind me and panic sets in. Being stuck between two unknowns in a dark alley is not good. Are they Army? I try again to yank away, but the skinny runt holding my wrist scrambles nimbly to his feet, almost pulling me down on top of him with his effort.

"Let. Go. Of. Me," I demand, tugging hard on my wrist.

"And look at this. She brought us supper." The wildfowl is yanked out of my other hand, but I kind of think that's the least of my worries at the moment. The owner of the voice walks into view. He's much older and bigger than the runt with the iron grip on my arm. He's dressed in rags with a long, scraggly beard hanging nearly to his chest. The parts of his face not covered in hair are crusted with dirt, and the stench that's wafting off him overpowers the rotting garbage of the alley. He's definitely not Army like I'd first thought. My panic lessens some as I realize I'm not being captured. I'm just being robbed.

"Let me go," I say again, glaring with all the fierceness I can muster at the dirty thief in front of me. "I got nuthin' you want."

He raises one eyebrow in surprise.

"Well, I don't know about that. You have these delicious-looking, fat birds in your possession. And you have this." He bends over and snatches my knife from my boot before I even realize what he's up to. He's quick, I'll give him that. He studies the blade, turning it over in his hands before his eyes come back to rest on my face.

"This is a beauty. Tell me where a young thing like you got such a nice knife?" He doesn't give me a chance to answer before those beady eyes leave my face and travel slowly down my body with a look that makes every inch of my skin crawl. "And you'd be surprised at what else I want from you, girl."

The runt holding me laughs then, a twisted sound that makes the hair on the back of my neck stand on end and leaves me no doubt as to what he means. Enough of this shite. I open my mouth intending to scream for help, but a hard punch to my gut leaves me gasping for breath instead. I hunch over in pain. That little shitehead just punched me! Furious now, I wait for my Chi to rise and overtake me. Serves them right when it does and I make mincemeat out of them. So I wait for my blood to be set aflame and for the buzzing to fill my head, but it doesn't happen. There's no surge of power like I'm expecting. What the hell?

"In here, Nud." The older one stands by a door I didn't notice on my way in, motioning with my knife and whispering in excitement. The runt gives a tug, pulling me off balance and starts dragging me towards the entryway. Fear festers in my innards, tying them in a knot. I know I sure as hell don't want to be inside there with these two crazy bastards. Where is my Chi?

The knot in my gut tightens the closer I get to that doorway. I know if they manage to get me in there, something real bad is going to happen. I dig in my heels, still waiting for that familiar heat. Nothing. Panicking now, I frantically try to disengage my arm from the young man's grip, but he isn't letting go. I have to do something and quick.

Suddenly, Mack's voice fills my head. His weeks of yelling at me start to make sense. I dig in my heels and yank hard, spinning the runt around with this change in balance.

"Oh, hell no," I snarl as my free hand shoots out, and my fist rams into the runt's throat. Immediately, he drops my arm and begins choking and gasping for air. I take advantage of his inability to breathe and kick my boot hard into the side of his knee, causing his leg to buckle and him to drop to the ground. Once he's down, I deliver a bruising kick to his face, and he flies back with the force of the blow.

With him down for the moment, I whirl on the bigger one. Stinky quickly overcomes his surprise at this turn of events, and his eyes dart between me and his gurgling partner in crime, bulging with rage. He holds up the knife he'd taken from me earlier, threatening me. He moves at me sideways, looking to slice me open.

"Don't matter if you fight back, girl. Dead or alive, you'll still serve us your purpose."

He slashes at my belly then, and I twist back just in time as the knife misses me by a hair and slices at nothing but empty air.

Having missed his intended target, his momentum throws him off balance and he stumbles forward. I don't hesitate. My foot comes up hard, aiming for the vulnerable spot between his legs. Realizing my intent, he swerves at the last second, causing my foot to connect with his thigh instead, and he catches my leg in a death grip.

He twists my leg hard, and I start to fall, but the runt has recovered somewhat and grabs both my arms, pinning them behind my back. I can hear his raspy breaths behind me, and

I know he's gonna have trouble talking for at least a few days. I struggle against him, but for such a skinny piece of shite, he has a strong grip.

The older one drops my leg now, breathing heavy with exertion. Hate radiates off him in waves. Before I can brace myself for his attack, he backhands me hard across the face with his hairy knuckle. I swear I actually hear my teeth clatter as my head snaps back from the blow. I shake my rattled noggin, trying to clear away the stars and the unwitting tears. I try to focus on the ugly face in front of me. I need to see what he's about to do. He looms over me, so near I can smell his sour breath and it makes me gag. He holds the knife dangerously close to my chest, his eyes filled with burning anger.

"You little bitch. You're going to pay for that."

"Hey! Let her go!"

The yell from the mouth of the alley draws Stinky's attention, and that moment is all I need. I don't miss this time as my boot delivers a punishing blow to his private bits. A stupefied expression of agony replaces the hateful sneer on his face as he drops the knife and falls to his knees with a loud moan.

No time for hesitation, I bring my boot down with a crushing force on the runt's instep. He cries out in pain and releases my arms. I whirl around, not giving him time to recover, and bring my open-palmed hand up hard into his nose. I hear the sickening crunch of broken bone and his screams as crimson liquid spurts out. He staggers a couple of steps and then crashes to the ground in a crumpled heap, his hands covering his smashed face. The bigger one is still on the ground, curled up with his knees almost to his chest. I lunge at him, my boot kicking him again and again in the stomach, the leg, the arm, any place I can. I'm screaming at him now, but I can't help it. I'm filled with fury. He'd tried to kill me.

I kick him in the ribs, and he screams as I hear them crack with the contact.

"That's for hittin' me!"

Another kick to the ribs.

"That's for tryin' to gut me with my own knife!"

I pull my leg back for another kick.

"Tara. Stop."

One of my arms is caught in a tight grip as I swing wildly with the other fist, but I don't get a chance to connect. My fist is grabbed in mid-air before the punch can land, and I stare furiously into a set of sky blue eyes. Eyes that I know so well. Confusion sets in, stilling my attack.

"Jax?" I say stupidly. How can Jax be here when he's in Gray Valley?

"Yeah, it's me. Now, let's get the hell out of here before the Army shows up. Those screams are sure to have attracted attention."

Still in total shock at what had just gone down, I allow him to grip my hand and start leading me away. But then I remember my knife. Vi, Jax's ma, had given me that knife. I'm not leaving without it. Against Jax's colorful objections, I pull away and head back, grabbing the wildfowl laying on the ground and my knife, ignoring the two moaning bodies lying there. But suddenly my anger rears again, and I give Stinky another swift kick as I pass by.

"And that's for callin' me bitch ... *bitch!*"

I follow Jax out of the alleyway, not bothering to look back. They're in no condition to follow after us.

Too bad the same can't be said about the Army. As soon as we exit outta the alley, we spot five or six of the brown-robed soldiers making their way through the massive crowd. It's the same bunch that had been doing the flesh trading earlier. Jax is right. Even in a place as corrupt as Littlepass, the thieves' screams still garnered their attention. The moment they see us coming outta the alley, shouts of "Halt!" pierce the air.

We do just the opposite. Jax grabs my hand and grunts, "Run," in my ear, and we do just that. I hang on to him for dear life as he bowls over the people in our way. For once, I'm grateful for the massive sea of bodies in the market slowing down our pursuers.

Trying in vain to lose ourselves in the crowd, we take advantage of a break in the flow and change direction, veering up a side street. An old man, arms laden down with a basket full of oranges, unfortunately turns out from the street at the same time we turn in. Jax swerves at the last minute narrowly missing him, but I'm not as lucky. My shoulder rams the basket and he loses his grip on it, the oranges flying out everywhere. We don't stop running or even look back, but I'm pretty sure from the cussing hurled after us, my children and their children are now destined to be cross-eyed and pox-ridden. Great. Just what I need; another curse.

We run blindly through the narrow alley, my heart beating out of my chest as I pray in my head it isn't a dead end. It's not. Instead, we stumble out onto another crowded square. We circle around the maze of stalls, no clear destination in mind, just desperate to get away from the pounding footsteps echoing behind us.

Another shout of, "Stop! In the name of the Prezedant," reaches my ears, but it only makes me run faster. *Fat chance of that happening,* I think.

I quickly lose track of where we are. I've no idea. The streets are all starting to look the same. The sweat rolling down into my eyes is making it hard to see and the stitch in my side hard to breathe, but still we don't slow down.

Suddenly Jax yells over his shoulder, "In here," an instant before my arm is almost yanked out of joint, and I'm dragged into a crevice between two buildings. It's so damn narrow we have to shuffle through sideways. The alley angles at the back of the building and leads us to a set of stone steps heading down to lower ground. Not quite sure where this is gonna take us, but we don't have much choice. Taking the steep stairs two at a time, we end up on a narrow platform underneath, what I recognize as, the crumbling stone bridge connecting east Littlepass to west. Taking care not to fall into the brown, sluggish excuse of a river, we press ourselves into the moss-covered wall, hidden from anyone passing by overhead.

Our wheezing echoes in the small confines of our refuge. I bend over, trying to catch my breath and listening intently for any sign of our pursuers. We don't hear any tell-tale footsteps or shouts. It doesn't sound like anyone is following us anymore. We lost them.

"You're bleeding," Jax whispers, and I finally look up into the face I thought I'd never see again.

Like me he's sweating from our run, the rivulets mixing

with the layers of dust, causing brown streaks of dirt to blend with the stubble covering his lower jaw. He's dirty, sweaty, and looks like he hasn't slept in days. To me, he never looked so good. I find myself itching to reach out and touch his face and wipe the dirt away, but I clench my hands tight at my side and flinch as he gently tries to wipe the blood from my lip. The touch shoots a spark through my lip, and I jolt upright.

"I'm fine," I say, my words sharp as I knock his hand away. "It's nuthin'. I'll heal quick enough. What the hell are you doin' here?"

He responds to my harsh question with a halfhearted grin. "Nice to see you too, freak."

"Seriously, Jax," I say, still baffled by everything that just happened. "Where did you come from? I thought you went back to Gray Valley weeks ago."

"I did," he says simply. "And now I'm back. Just in time to find you beating the shite out of two thieves like some warrior princess and get chased by the Army. I'd almost forgotten how there's never a dull moment around you."

Just in time to find me? Had he been following me? And did he really just call me a warrior princess? What the hell is that supposed to mean?

"How did you find me?"

"We just missed you at Sanctuary. The guard there told me you'd be at the flesh trade in the market. I caught sight of you at the butcher's stall, but then I lost you in the crowd. Not until I heard the screams did I track you down to that alley. I'm sorry I didn't get there sooner," he says, the anger on his face directed at himself. His concern for my safety reflects in his azure eyes as they stare into mine, and it sends warmth flooding over me.

Tearing his gaze away, he runs his hands over his face, wiping away the sweat. "Look, I know you must have a hundred questions, and I know I'm probably the last person you want to see right now … but something's happened."

My heart jumps into my throat. What now?

My fear must be evident since he rushes to reassure me. "No, not to any of your kin but—"

A loud thumping on the bridge above our heads silences what else he's about to say as he pushes me back against the wall. We don't move, not even to breathe, but whatever caused the ruckus passes on without incident and I suck in air.

"Tell me," I whisper once I know we're alone again, but he shakes his head.

"We need to get back to Sanctuary. It's not safe out here. I'll explain everything there."

I know he's right. We have to get off the street. The Army won't give up the chase that easy. So I follow him again, not pestering him with a word, although there are a thousand thoughts running through my head right now. But the one that screams the loudest? *Jax is back.*

CHAPTER TWO

The Plan

———◆———

Flip meets us at the gate, the relief in his eyes evident at our appearance.

"Good, you found her all right then. The others are waiting for you inside."

What others? Who's here? What's going on? There's no time for questions as Flip hurries us both inside and closes the gates behind us with a resonating clang. It spooks me something fierce. I've never seen the gates locked since I'd been here, and the sound reminds me of some death toll. Even though the day is still very warm, a cold shiver passes over me causing my skin to pebble. I have a sinking feeling that what I'm about to find out is not going to be good news.

We don't see anyone as we enter; the white hallway is completely empty. But I know that if something big is going on, they would gather in the book room or library as Lily called it. I'm right. We find a whole crowd of people waiting for us in there. Lily, Mack, Zoe, Riven, them I expected. But I'm thrown for a loop to see the two crazies from the dead city there as well. What were their names again? Talbert and Beanie. That's it. What the hell are they doing here? And is Orakel here too? I scan the room, but there's no sign of the withered old woman.

"Mistress!" Talbert flies across the room at my entrance and falls at my feet like he hasn't had a drop of water in weeks and I'm a full waterskin. Embarrassed to have everyone witness this, I nudge him with my boot.

"Get up, you idiot," I hiss at him, but he just does as I ask, bowing to me like my every word is his command. It makes it even worse when Beanie joins him and plants a big, wet kiss on my hand. It takes all my willpower not to gag and wipe the back of my hand against my thigh. Instead, I choose to ignore their adoration and zone in on Lily.

"What's wrong?" I direct her way. Her usually placid face is a mask of concern. "What's happened?"

It's Talbert who answers me. "They found us, Mistress, the Army. They found us. Most everybody is … gone …," he trails off as big, fat tears start splattering down his boil-encrusted face, and I immediately feel ashamed for calling him an idiot earlier.

"Orakel?" I question quietly, but he just shakes his head at me and keeps blubbering.

Beanie picks up the story since Talbert can no longer talk,

his eyes glistening with his unshed tears. "She told us to find you before … before they got to her. Find you and let you know that they know the truth."

"The truth about what?" It comes out as a whisper because I honestly don't know if I want to hear the answer.

"We followed 'em, the Army. They came through the city." Talbert wipes the tears from his face, sobs breaking his voice as he speaks again. "First, we let 'em be. We didn't want to draw attention to ourselves, see. But then we 'ears 'em speak 'bout you Mistress, so we listened in. They wuz talkin' bout 'ow they wuz followin' you to this safe 'ouse an 'ow they wuz gonna capture you an get the big reward from the Prezedant. We thought it wuz really you they wuz gonna capture, so we followed 'em. We couldn't 'ave anything 'appen to you, now could we? We followed 'em to the safe 'ouse an watched … watched 'em kill everybody there when they didn't find ya like they wuz expectin'. Then, we 'igh tailed it back. We needed to let Orakel know. But they pulled a switch-a-roo, they did, an followed us instead. They found us. We didn't know they wuz followin' us … an we lead 'em right to …"

He shakes his head, not able to tell me anymore, but he doesn't have to say much else. I know firsthand what they did to the people they found.

Beanie lays a comforting hand on Talbert's heaving shoulder, causing his wails of grief to pierce the air.

"Orakel made us take the young'uns and run through the back tunnels. The others stayed behind and held off the Army while we got 'em out." Beanie does the talking again. "She said we had to keep 'em safe and to get to you. You had to know that they wuz comin' back to Littlepass to search for ya. That they knew you wuz still here in the city. But we knew we wouldn't be able to sneak into Littlepass, not with all the young'uns, so we went to find him." He points at Jax. "We knew he wuz gone back to his village. We seen him passin' through weeks ago. So we found him, and he bought us passage into town so we could warn you, Mistress."

My eyes find Jax, silently questioning if what they're saying is true. He nods at me.

"We left the children in Gray Valley with Ma and rode day and night to get here. You have to leave, Tara. Sanctuary's not safe for you anymore."

"I'm afraid Jax is right." Lily's face is tight with concern and grief, and I reckon I know why.

If these two are to be believed, then her people had been killed along with the occupants of the iron bones. The young girl and the boys pretending to be us to lead the Army off our trail, all snuffed out just because of their connection with me. Orakel and most of the others in her care also dead. I'm like some magnet to this evil, drawing it in, tainting everyone I come in contact with. Jax's words at our first meeting echo in my head. "Carrier of death," he had called me. It's true. I close my eyes, lost in my own grief and horror at everything I've just heard. But then another realization hits me and I open my eyes again, staring at Lily in panic.

"If they know I'm still in Littlepass, then I have to get away from here as soon as possible. I cain't lead them here to you and Finn and everybody else. Shizen, I have to go now!"

Lily grabs my arm, stopping my frantic rush for the door.

"Tara, calm down. If my people had talked, the Army would have been here by now. They would have found us already. No, they took our secret to their graves. The Army may now know you're still in the city, but they don't know where yet. If I know them, they'll carry out a quiet, low-key search. They won't want to tip you off and spook you away. It's only a matter of time before they find us, however, so I'm afraid Jax is right. You have to leave Sanctuary. While Jax was out searching for you, we were making arrangements for Mack to take you to his home in Skytown. They'll never suspect you to be right under the Prezedant's nose and in the home of one of his elite. It will be the perfect hiding spot."

"No," I say, shaking my head adamantly. "I cain't put anybody else in danger. I have to get away from all of you. I don't want any more blood on my hands."

"And go where?" Mack says, his words harsh. He steps in front of me and peers at me with that one beady eye. I almost back up from the intensity of that stare. "There's no place to run where he won't find you. Your Grada and Orakel have proven that. Come with me. Learn how to deal with this once and for all. End it, Tara."

I open my mouth to protest. I want to scream at Mack that I don't know how. I want to scream it at all of them. But then I look around at the faces staring back at me. Some are marked with pity, some marked with grief, but all of them are marked with something else. Hope. I see hope in their eyes as they look at me, like maybe I really could fix this. I shut my mouth with a snap. There's nothing I can say that will convince them otherwise. I know that. *Oh gods,* I think. What have I gotten myself into? I don't want or need this much trust, but I just nod my consent at Lily. She's right. Skytown is the perfect hiding spot, and at least I will be that much closer to Ben.

"Fine. Let's move then," I say, keeping all of my doubts and fears hidden inside. From the looks I just witnessed, I reckon they would fall on deaf ears anyways. "Jax, I'm askin' you to step up with Finn again. I need him taken to Gray Valley and kept safe. Can you please do that for me this time?"

"No can do," he says, and I narrow my eyes at him.

"Why not?" I say, and he raises a dark brow my way.

"Now, why you asking such a stupid question? I promised to look out for you and help you find Ben. I'm not leaving again no matter what blame you lay on me this time."

In all my years, I've never met a man as stubborn as this jackass in front of me. Anybody in their right mind would run from the danger and death that surrounds me like a black cloud, but what does he want to do? Stay by my side. And for the life of me, I can't figure out why. When I first met him, he could barely look at me without contempt, and now he wants to protect me. Why had he changed his mind about me? I open my mouth to argue more, but Talbert steps in front of me, blocking my view. His face is still swollen from his crying, but the earlier grief is gone now, replaced by a look of determination. It shocks me into silence. He bows his head to me in complete respect.

"Beggin' permission to go with ya as well, Mistress. With Orakel gone, my life is now yours."

As crazy as I know Talbert to be, his words scare me to death. I know he means every word of what he's saying, and I sure as hell don't want any of them swearing any allegiance to me.

"No, it ain't," I snarl at him. "Your life is your own. It doesn't belong to me or nobody else. Don't ever say that to me again."

His wounded expression at my harshness fills me with guilt, but I don't apologize. I mean what I say.

"But I don't unnerstand. Ya don't want our 'elp?" he says.

"No. I mean yes, I appreciate that you wanna help, but I cain't … I don't wanna be responsible for anybody else gettin' hurt. And y'all are too dang stubborn to see that." I don't mean to be yelling at them all. I'm just so frustrated at their blind faith. I just don't get it.

"We have to go with ya, Mistress." Beanie's words sound so serene and calm in the face of all my yelling that it's hard to believe that outta the two of us, I'm supposedly the saner one. "Orakel said we have to play our part. It is foretold."

He sounds so sure that I almost believe him. Maybe it is our destiny to cross paths again. But then that small twinge of laughter comes bubbling to the surface, and even though he tries to hide it behind his hand, it sneaks out. Yup, he's just as crazy as I remember.

"Enough talk," Lily says briskly. "With every moment we waste, the Army gets closer. Tara, go pack your things. You will be leaving as soon as we get the wagons ready to go. The Army may be looking for you, but at least we have the advantage of them not knowing we're aware of their search. It may be our only chance of making it out of the city undetected."

"Finn and Cat?" I say, and she tilts her head.

"They will be accompanying you on your journey. Sanctuary is far too dangerous for anyone to stay right now.

Mack will take good care of you all."

"But if they're looking for us, how will we get past the guards at the gate?" I say.

"Ah, that's where Riven comes in." Mack points to the big, burly man I remember from the night of Ben's attempted rescue. Riven winks at me as he absently rubs at his face of whiskers. "He has a very prosperous fleet of caravans that transport goods to Skytown all under the orders of the Prezedant himself. Sometimes, he helps us transport 'goods' the Prezedant is unaware of. He has proven very useful in the past."

I don't know how I feel being referred to as "goods," but as long as their plan works, I'm not about to argue the small stuff.

"We all know what has to be done," Lily says, waving her scarred hands at us. "Let's move."

"Lily," I try to catch her attention before she leaves the room with the rest of them. I want to talk with her alone. She stops and looks at me, her brown eyes filled with sadness, and I realize this is the first time I've seen her look defeated. That's the only word I can think of.

"Tara, can this not wait? We don't have time—" she starts to say, but I cut her off.

"Then we gotta make time," I snap, my patience wearing thin. "Are you sure this is the right thing to do? Going to Skytown? Seems like wherever I go, I place people in danger. Maybe my best bet is to get away from y'all and wait until the search dies down."

The ghost of a smile flits across her face and I'm not positive, but I think I see tears fill her eyes before she averts them to look down at her clasped hands.

"I'm not sure of anything anymore, child. But this much I do know. The Prezedant will never stop looking for any New Blood, especially not one as powerful as you. You can run all you want, but someday he will find you, and kill you. And it won't matter how much distance you've put between yourself and those you care for, he will destroy anyone who stands in his way. If we don't fight against him now, then all the deaths that have already happened will have been for naught."

Her words don't surprise me. I knew she wouldn't see it my way, but I have to let her know.

"But something happened today, Lily, that makes me think I ain't strong at all. That I'm not the New Blood y'all hope I am. When I was at the market, I was tricked by these thieves and, well, my Chi … it wasn't there. It failed me. How can I fight for any of you—how can I keep Finn safe—when I cain't even protect myself?"

She stares at me in silence and I think my words have gotten through to her, but then she speaks.

"Tara, do you know how your mother died?"

Her words stop me cold in my tracks, anything else I'm about to say forgotten. She's going to tell me that *now*? After all my persistence and nagging, she feels that now is the time to give me that little tidbit of information? Not waiting for my answer, she just continues on.

"We were so close to defeating the Prezedant. All of our planning and our hard work—all of our sacrifices—it was going to be worth it. We were finally going to end his reign of terror. The bloodshed and death would be stopped." Her voice drops almost to a whisper, and even though she continues talking, I don't think it's to me anymore.

"She could have ended it. Rease, I mean. She could have ended it right then and there. She had beaten him. As strong as he was, she had proven herself stronger. All she had to do was drive that blade through his foul heart. But she faltered … she hesitated. She showed weakness. And do you know what that weakness was?"

I feel rooted to the spot, and I want to yell at her, "No! I don't wanna know," but I'm helpless to stop her admission.

"It was you. Given the choice between taking his life or saving yours, she chose you." There's no blame in her voice, no accusation, yet her words cut me through to my core like she's just told me I'd killed my ma with my own hands. Her voice catches then, and I think she may cry. But when she raises her eyes back to me, they're as cold as ice.

"He, on the other hand, showed no such weakness. He saw his opportunity, and he took it. They say it took her days to die. Days of her being strung up like an animal at slaughter while he drained her of her blood, her power. Days of torture and suffering because she showed weakness. You cannot afford that, Tara. You cannot afford doubt or weakness or uncertainty."

Her fingers bite painfully into my arm, but I don't cry out. Her words have numbed me completely.

"You are a true New Blood in every sense of the word, and you must believe that. When the time comes, you must act with decisiveness and trust in your power. No one is more important than your purpose, and that includes me or Finn or Ben. Do you understand?"

I understand with cold clarity. She's telling me that not

even those I love should stand in the way of what she thinks I'm capable of. How can she even think that?

"Lily!" The yell from the hallway interrupts anything else she's about to say, and her eyes flit to Mack as he barrels into the room. His face is a mask of despair and I know something dire has happened, yet I'm glad for his presence because Lily's words are scaring me something fierce.

"What is it, Mack?" she questions. He looks at her with true sadness, hesitant to impart the news. He swallows hard before running a hand over his chin.

"Flip just received word that the Army captured Critch this afternoon."

"And?" she says.

"He's dead," he answers bluntly.

Her slight intake of breath is the only reaction to this bit of news. I have no idea who they're talking about, all I know is it's just more death.

"They know more than we suspect," she says in a quiet voice. "Are the caravans ready? We have to get Tara out of here and now. If they found Critch—"

"We're ready to move out as soon as possible. The boy and the cat are already in place. We're just waiting on the girl." Mack points his chin at me.

Lily whirls on me. "Tara, go with Mack."

"But I ain't gathered my things yet—"

She cuts me off. "No time. You must go now."

I stare into her face. "You're comin' too, right?" As much as what she told me scared me shiteless, I still need to hear more.

She shakes her head. "I must stay here and keep things as

normal-looking as possible, keep them from being suspicious of the caravans."

"But—"

"Go, Tara."

I don't want to leave her. It took me so long to find her, my last remaining link to Grada, to my ma. As if she can read my mind, she smiles at me and touches her hand to my cheek, causing the familiar tingle of our New Blood connection.

"Trust me, child; this is not the end. You will see me again. Without proof of you being here, they have no reason to harm me."

I grab her hand tight. "You bein' truthful? You ain't lyin'?"

She squeezes my hand back in confirmation.

"Thank you for everything," I whisper to her.

"You have to leave now," she murmurs and without another word or even a look back, I follow Mack out of the book room. I know in my heart that Lily would sooner die then give me up to the Army, but I refuse to even think about what that could mean.

We hurry through the white hall, towards our stone training room. With every couple of steps, I glance over my shoulder, expecting at any moment for the hall to be overrun with Army. But we make it to the stone room unimpeded. The hay and stink that usually fills the room is now accompanied by two huge, wooden caravans; the words "Riven's Runners" painted in bold, red letters on the side. I scan the room looking for any sign of Finn and Cat, but fear clogs my throat when all I see are the brown robes of the Army standing between the wagons. Shizen. They'd already found us. I turn to bolt, but Mack grabs my shoulder.

"Easy, girl. They're just some of Riven's men dressed as Army. We find no one questions us when we're being accompanied by the Army, real or not."

I release my pent-up breath and take a couple of calming gulps of air.

"Where are Finn and Cat?" I manage to croak.

Mack points to the wagon on the left. I peer through the open doors, but all I see are barrels and baskets of goods piled to the top of the wagon.

"Behind all those supplies is a false wall with just enough room to smuggle a few people or one boy and a gigantic cat. It was no easy feat getting that beast to succumb and get in there. But the boy talked her into it. I swear on all that is holy I've never seen an animal listen to a human like that. It's almost as if she understands the boy."

I kinda give a weak smile at that. Trust Cat to put up a fight, but if Finn had asked her to do it, well, she'd follow that boy to the ends of the Earth. They shared a bond that even I can't understand.

Mack motions to the other wagon. It's not as full as the one holding Finn and Cat, and I realize most of the supplies are still waiting to be loaded. I guess I had to go in first.

Mack hoists himself into the wagon and then gives me a hand, pulling me up to join him. Making our way to the rear, I watch as he runs a hand down the crease between the wall and the back of the wagon. There's a tiny click before the back pulls slightly away from the side, forming a gap. I look a little closer. There are hinges hidden in the knots and natural grain of the wood. Camouflaged if you didn't know what you were looking for. Very clever.

Mack steps aside, motioning for me to enter the crawl space. Expecting it to be dark and dank, I'm surprised to see light filtering in through little holes cut at the top of the wagon, unnoticeable from the outside since they sit just below the roof's overhang. I heave a sigh of relief. If I'm to be stuck in this crawl space, at least I'd have light and air. It's only about an armspan long, but it's the width of the wagon itself, so I can sit with my back against the side of the wagon and at least stretch out my legs. And I'm real glad to see someone has thrown a couple of blankets on the floor as padding for me to sit on. I squish them against the wall and settle down as Mack gives me a little nod.

"Okay then, stay quiet, and don't come out unless I come to get you no matter what you may hear, understand?"

"Aye," I say.

He pulls his head out, and I wait for the fake door to close, but then another body squeezes through the opening. All of a sudden, it feels like the crawl space shrinks in size as Jax fills the compartment.

"Hell, no," I say instantly, shaking my head. I'm not being cooped up in here with him.

"No choice, mutie," he says as he looks around for a bit then decides the most comfortable spot for him to sit would be directly on the blankets beside me. I'm crushed into the wall as he falls next to me, our shoulders and arms squeezed together. I try to stand, but I'm stuck like a hog on a spit between Jax and the wall.

Mack," I yell. "Mack, switch me and Finn. I'll travel with Cat. Mack."

The only response to my plea is the slight click of the fake wall as it closes shut. Shizen. What have I done to the gods to deserve this?

"Mack," I yell again but to no avail.

"May as well stop your belly aching, Tara. Mack's not going to take the time to unload Finn's wagon just so you two can switch places," he says.

I glare at him the best I can, but our noses are only inches apart, so I don't think he quite appreciates my frosty stare.

"You did this on purpose," I say. "You could have gotten in the wagon with Finn, but you planned on being in mine."

He arches a brow at me.

"Actually, I did consider traveling with Finn at first, but then I realized to keep Cat calm and quiet, they couldn't put anyone *but* Finn with her. Still, it's good to know you think yourself so irresistible that I would 'plan' to be stuck in a tiny crawlspace with someone who …," he wrinkles his nose up at me, "I don't think has seen a bath in quite a while."

I can feel heat flooding my cheeks as I remember the shower I had forgone earlier so I could go to town instead. Jax is right; I'm ripe. But serves him right to be stuck in here with my smell. I flap my armpit at him trying to enhance my stench, but he just laughs and bumps me into the wall.

"May as well get comfortable, freak. It's gonna be a long ride."

—◆—

Not as long as we thought. We've barely gone four leagues before we're unexpectedly stopped and from the shouting I overhear, I reckon it's guards. We must be at the city gates.

My earlier irritation forgotten, I stare nervously at Jax. I thought Mack said the pretend Army riding with us would guarantee safe passage?

The guards are yelling at Mack and Riven, inquiring as to the nature of their business. Riven's deep growl answers back, but I can't quite make out what he says. I do hear the order to open the wagon doors though, and my gut clenches tight. Terrified to make the slightest movement, we listen as the guard rummages through the back of the wagon. Sweat beads my neck and trickles down my back as the footsteps shuffle closer to our hiding spot. Nothing but a thin sheet of wood separating us from certain capture. I can't help the images popping into my head of the fake door opening and the soldier finding us cowering here. *Stop it!* I scold myself, but it doesn't seem to work. The images stay in my head like some bad night terror.

After what seems like an eternity of baskets being tossed about and faint cussin', we hear, "All clear. It's just like they said, more supplies meant for those spoiled cruds in Skytown."

"Move along!" I nearly jump from my skin as the yell bellows right at our heads, and a fist bangs the wagon wall, giving us permission to move. Jax holds a finger to his lips in warning. I know the message he's sending. Don't make a sound. I can only hope Finn and Cat know to do the same.

The wagon starts moving again. The intense wobbling causes my stomach to flip flop before we finally seem to level out and move into the flat plains of the outerlands beyond the gate. I exhale the air trapped in my chest. We did it. We made it through.

"Can I have my hand back now before you crush it?" Jax's words are whispered so close to my ear his breath stirs my hair. I look down, shocked to find his hand wrapped in mine. I'm holding it so tightly his fingers are actually turning purple. When had I done that? I don't remember grabbing his hand. I drop it like it is a red-hot ember and fold both my own hands in my lap so as not to touch any part of him, my cheeks flushing from our contact.

"Sorry," I mutter.

I can feel his body shake with his quiet laughter as he flexes his hand. "It's okay. Glad to be of assistance. I didn't really need that hand anyways … other than for feeding myself. And dressing myself. Shooting. Hunting. Harvesting maybe. Useless stuff really."

I choose not to respond to his sarcasm, and we continue on in silence, the only sound the creaking of the wagon as it moves over the broken trail. My heartbeat slows to normal and the fear in my gut fades as we don't meet any more obstacles. I finally relax my head back against the wall. Shizen, it's so hot in here. Wiping the sweat from my face with my sleeve, I try to fan myself with my hand. What I wouldn't give to feel just a little breeze right now.

"How long you think they're goin' to make us ride back here?" I say, the heat getting the better of me. "Not all the way, surely?"

"Long enough to make sure we're well away from prying eyes," he says.

I glance sideways at him. He's not sweating at all, the heat not bothering him in the least. It adds to my irritation. "How come you let Talbert and Beanie leave their young'uns in Gray Valley? When me and Finn and Tater were there, you couldn't wait to get rid of us you were so scared we were gonna draw the Army, yet you're helpin' them?"

He gives a little sigh. "I should have ridden with Finn," he mutters to himself before he turns his head to look at me. "It was Ma's choice, not mine. As you well know, she is a very mule-headed woman. Most stubborn woman I ever met … until now." I narrow my eyes at the insult. "She took one look at those bedraggled children and insisted they go no further. They were still in shock and dehydrated and in no condition to go anyplace else. I'm surprised they even survived the trip to us."

Immediately, I regret asking him to explain his reasons for helping. Sometimes I could be a real, unfeeling jackass.

"How many of 'em survived the attack?" I ask and it comes out as a whisper.

"Including Beanie and Talbert? Fourteen," he says.

Fourteen. Shizen, there had to have been well over fifty or sixty people living there and only fourteen survived. His words make my heart feel like there's some kinda binding around it, drawing tight and squeezing the life outta it.

"Your ma is a good woman," I say. "Those young'uns are in good hands. The girl who collected our bowls that night, the marked one, was she one of the survivors?"

Jax nods at my question, and it makes me feel just a tiny bit better knowing that she, at least, had made it out alive.

"When I left home, Ma and Sky were taking good care of them all. No need to worry about them."

I swallow the lump in my throat, and look away from him back down at my folded hands.

"Good," I say. We fall quiet for a bit more while I ponder what he's told me. Finally, I sneak another sidelong glance at him. "Sky musta been real upset at you leavin' again since you only just got back and all …," I trail off, wondering if he'll answer the unspoken question that's been gnawing at me these past few weeks.

"If she was, she didn't say as much. She knows our wedded day will come eventually. She doesn't harp about it. She's real good like that," he says.

The little twinge of relief I feel at knowing they're not wedded yet is followed by immediate guilt. I just found out only fourteen innocent souls survived a massacre, and here I am feeling relief that Jax isn't wedded. I truly am an evil soul.

"Well, thank you for comin' to warn us. If you hadn't come …," I stop talking, not wanting to say out loud what would have happened to everyone involved if I'd been found at Sanctuary.

"You should thank Talbert and Beanie for that. They were determined to get to you with the warning, to keep you safe. I've never seen anyone believe in your ability to stop the Prezedant as much as those two. I truly believe they would just lie down and die if you asked them to."

I know he's only half teasing, but it doesn't sit well with me. I can't stand the thought of anyone having that much faith in me. I don't deserve it. If only they knew the fear and cowardice that lives in my heart. The desire to just run away from it all. Nobody should risk their lives for someone as yellow-bellied as me.

"I wish y'all would stop treatin' me like I'm some kinda savior," I say, irritated again. "Don't know why any of you think I can make a difference to anything. There's only one reason I'm involved in any of this shite, and that's just to find my kin."

Instead of being pissed at my words like I reckoned he would be, Jax just busts out laughing. What the hell is so funny?

"You are a piece of work, you know that? In one breath, you're showing your grief and concern over a bunch of people you hardly even know, and the next you're pretending you don't give a damn about anybody but your kin. Cold-hearted snake or mistress of the light? Decide for yourself who you truly are, Tara, because the rest of us already know."

I glare at him. "You think you know me?" I question softly.

"Yup, not much to figure out really. You're pretty simple."

I raise a brow and scowl, not quite sure if I should be angry at him. "Are you callin' me a simpleton?"

He laughs softly. "No, I mean simple in the fact that there's nothing deceitful about you, Tara. You're honest, straightforward, even abrasive at times, but you're basically good. It didn't take me long to see that about you as much as I didn't want to admit it." He pulls his knees up and rests his forearms on them, staring at me so intently with those light eyes that I forget to breathe. "The way you look out for Finn and Cat and Tater, hell, even me. Your determination to save Ben and the rest of your kin without a second thought to your own safety. The way Talbert and Beanie would follow you to the ends of the Earth and bow to your every command. It makes me believe Orakel may have been right. Whether you like it or not, Tara, you've become a symbol of hope to many."

His words only add to my unease. And why is it so damn

hot in here? I can't catch a breath, like the very air itself is scorching my lungs. I feel the sweat dripping down my temple as Jax keeps staring at me like he's expecting some sort of answer, so I say the very first thing that pops into my jumbled head.

"I was glad you ain't wedded yet."

"What?" The puzzlement in his voice matches his furrowed brow.

"That was the only thought in my head … even after you told me about the terrible massacre and the fourteen survivors and the poor young'uns, all I could think was how glad I am that you ain't wedded yet. That's not something any good or noble person would think, Jax. I'm selfish and stubborn and … and a scared coward at heart. You don't know me at all."

I watch as his puzzlement quickly turns to amusement.

"You're happy because I'm not wedded?"

I stare at him in disbelief. *"That's* all you got outta that whole confession?"

A huge grin splits his face, causing the blue eyes to sparkle brightly. "Why, Tara, if I didn't know any better, I'd say you actually like me."

"I didn't say that," I snap, mortified now at what I've let spill.

"Yes, you did. Not in so many words, but that's what it means," he says.

"No, it don't," I say, shaking my head at him.

"Well, why else would you care if Sky and I are wedded yet?" he asks.

"Oh, geez, I dunno. Maybe it's because I'm glad that the

poor girl ain't stuck for a lifetime with a jackass like you," I say, his grin pissing me off. He's such a cocky bastard.

"Too late, I know how you really feel now." He grabs a strand of white hair that has fallen out of my braid and twirls it around his finger, the music of his laughter filling the air. I knock his hand away, but it just causes him to laugh even harder. Ignoring his laughter and refusing to even look at him, I stare straight ahead at the other side of the wagon. The damage is done. I can't take back what's already said, but I sure as hell won't give him any more reason to taunt me, so I clamp my lips shut. Let him stew the rest of the way in uncomfortable silence because I'm not saying another word to that mule turd.

The lack of movement is what awakes me. I open my eyes and look around in confusion. I'd been dreaming. Dreaming about cattle hung in a line for bleeding out, only none of them had normal heads. Instead of cow heads, they all had human heads with long, black hair and white stripes. I was glad I hadn't seen a face, though, since I have a sinking suspicion the face would have been my own. I blink my eyes a couple more times and shake my head, trying to clear away the remnants of the lingering dream. I squish the pillow underneath my fingers. Why is my pillow so hard? I poke at it a bit more, and it starts moving up and down in laughter.

"Stop tickling me," it says, and instantly I know it's no damn pillow I'm laying on.

Horrified, I realize the rough cloth underneath my fingers

is Jax's tunic. I'm lying against his chest. Pushing myself upright, I snarl at him, "Get offa me!"

"Get off of you? Beg to differ, but you're the one sprawled all over me like some wet blanket. Well, actually, I'm the one who feels more like the wet blanket since you were snoring and drooling so much."

He points to the wet spot on his tunic, and my flushed cheeks get even hotter. Instead of rising to his bait, I change the subject. No point in arguing what I can see to be true though he didn't have to be such a jackass and point it out to me.

"Why have we stopped movin'? Is anything wrong? How long have I been asleep?"

"A few hours at the most. And no, I don't think anything's wrong. I heard Mack and Riven laughing earlier. I think we've just stopped to make camp. They should be letting us out soon."

As if in response, I hear movement just outside the false door. *Thank gods*, I think. I can't stand to be cooped up in here any longer. I wait with growing impatience as the goods get shifted around to let us out.

Mack's voice calls out, "All is well. Time to come out."

Jax don't get the opportunity to move. As soon as the false wall opens, I crawl over him in my frantic attempt to be free. Ignoring his winded "omph" as my knee comes into contact with a tender spot, I literally fall out of the crawlspace at Mack's feet.

"Up we go," Mack says gently, hoisting me to my feet.

My whole body feels like it's seized up, and I shuffle my way out of the wagon, the wind a welcoming relief on my flushed face as soon as I step outside. Oh gods, that feels good.

"Tara," Finn spots me as soon as his feet hit the ground, and his short legs fly the distance between us. Cat follows him out the wagon, but she hightails it in the opposite direction, straight to the low brush on the other side. Her intentions quite obvious as she squats in the brush, oblivious to anyone's eyes watching. Kind of jealous really since I'm wishing I could do the same right now.

"What's goin' on?" Finn's head swivels as he takes in the Army get ups surrounding us. "Are we being captured by the Army again? Nobody told me nuthin'. They just said there was danger and herded us into that wagon. I didn't know if you were okay, but I figured I could believe Mack, and is that Jax? What's Jax doin' here?"

"I don't quite know," I sigh as I watch Jax jump down from the wagon and stretch, his toned body moving fluidly with cat-like grace, like he didn't just travel for hours in a cramped position with me drooling all over his chest. He doesn't seem the least bit stiff like I am. It makes me hate him even more. He gives Finn a cheery wave and the boy waves back, all smiles. It irritates me to no end.

"Ya be needin' water, Mistress?"

One of Riven's fake soldiers approaches me with a water skin, but I don't need to see the face underneath the wrapper to know who it is. I'd recognize that voice anywhere.

"I thought I told you already I don't want you followin' me," I say in annoyance as I yank the water skin from his hands and take a deep drink. Talbert merely shrugs as he pulls the wrapper away from his face and grins ghoulishly at Finn with his black lips. Finn's smile falters, and his gaze flickers uncertainly back and forth between me and Talbert. The look of confusion on his face would've been almost comical if I didn't know it was soon to be followed by a hundred more rapid-fire questions.

"And I suppose Beanie's here as well?"

"Oh, aye," Talbert says and points with his chin to the soldier unhitching the horses from one of the wagons. "We's sworn brothers; one ain't never far from the other. An' now we's sworn protectors to you, Mistress."

Great. Just what I need. An offer of protection from those two. Sighing loudly, I hand Finn the water skin, hoping to delay the inevitable questions from blubbering out. It doesn't work.

"Why are *they* here, Tara? What's goin' on? Why did we have to leave Sanctuary? Where are we goin'? Why are they dressed like the Army?"

Finn's questions are making my head spin, and honestly, I just don't have to gumption to answer any of them right now. Thank gods I'm spared the ordeal as a shout from Beanie interrupts.

"We got company," he yells, and I follow his pointing arm to the glow of the low setting sun. He's right, sure enough. There's a cloud of dust approaching from the west. Something is moving and coming straight for us.

"Mistress, 'urry, git back in the wagon!" Talbert pushes the baskets of supplies aside, as I grab Finn by the scruff of the neck and toss him unceremoniously into the wagon.

"Cat, hide," I yell at the beast as I quickly follow Finn. There's no time to get her back into either wagon. She's too far away, so I hope she heeds my warning.

"Tara?" Finn tries to question me but I shush him with a finger to his lips and pull him behind a pile of baskets. A sliver of light pokes its way through some cracked wooden slats on the wagon wall, and I kneel at the spot, peering through so I can watch what's happening outside. I can see Mack and Riven. They're standing casually, watching what appears to be two horses approach, but Mack's hand is hovering above the shooter hanging at his side. The setting sun provides too bright of a backdrop for me to pick out the features of the riders or even tell if it's Army or not. Maybe they weren't fooled by us at all. Maybe they've been following us the whole time. My hand tightens around the knife in my boot. If it is Army, they're not getting to me or Finn without a fight, not this time.

The two horses draw closer, and my fear turns to puzzlement since they appear riderless. And one isn't even a horse. It's a mule looks like. Pulling a tow cart with a solitary, shadowy figure sitting in the driver's seat. Since when does the Army travel solo?

"Good evening, gentlemen," the driver calls out as he approaches, his hand raised in a gesture of friendliness. "So nice to finally catch up with you. Would you perchance have a little extra supper you'd be willing to share? Maybe even a bit of fine ale or whiskey hidden in that bountiful cargo you are transporting? It has been a very arduous and arid ride tracking you across this vast land, and I'm quite parched."

Even though I can't see the face, that annoying way of talk could only belong to one person and my unease melts away.

"Tara, is that …?" and I nod in relief at Finn's question. "Yup, it's Tater."

CHAPTER THREE

The Journey

❦

The next three days pass in relative boredom, although it's nice not having to travel in the crawlspace anymore cooped up next to Jax. It's so much better out in the sun with the wind on my face. Tater's arrival with the tow cart had made that possible. While Finn and Cat rode in the back, I preferred to ride up front with Tater. Well, not quite the truth. I preferred to ride ahead as lookout, but since I'm denied that job by all my jackass companions, it falls on Jax to be the lookout. I hate that they're all treating me like I should be wrapped in soft cotton and kept safe. But my arguing falls on deaf ears, so I'm designated to ride in the tow cart between the two big wagons and listen to Tater's jabbering for hours at a time. To be truthful, it isn't all bad. At least Tater's non-ending gibberish keeps my mind off of Lily's words about my ma and how she'd died saving me. No, I push that thought away during the day. It only comes out to haunt me at night while I'm trying to sleep.

I'd been taken aback at first by the half man's ability to track us. Sometimes, he truly does surprise me. But I'm glad he did because he'd provided answers for me.

He'd arrived at Sanctuary mere hours after we all left to find that it had indeed been searched by the Army. As much as Lily hated to admit it, her people had talked if they'd been able to track down Sanctuary that easily. But Tater eased my worries for Lily and Zoe's safety. They didn't find anything, no trace that we'd even been there. With not finding us and not linking us to Lily, the Army had no reason to arrest her. And since she was an important person, personal healer to the high-ranking army officials, they had let her be. I was relieved to hear that. Although she and her rebellion would have to lay low for a while, the Army may not have been able to link her to the New Blood, but I'm sure as hell they were going to be watching her now.

Tater had been no fool. After hearing from Flip what was going down, he hightailed it out of Littlepass as soon as he could. I'm grateful that he had taken the time to at least get some supplies for us. We'd left in such a hurry that we never had a chance to take anything, and Tater had thought to provide me and Finn with hooded cloaks, useful for the cold nights out here in the outerlands. Finn's is way too big, and mine looks and smells like it had come from one of the ladies of the ill house. Probably did, but I'm not asking. I don't want to know what the person before me had been doing while wearing this cloak. It's decorated way too fancy for my liking too, beads and sparkly things surrounding the hood and all down the front, but Mack says it's a good thing. If he's to pass me and Finn off as his visiting kin from the South to get into Skytown, we have to look the part. Cat has to be snuck in through the wagon's crawlspace though. There's no way we'll be able to explain her presence with us. And I'm sure there's no way in hell she or Finn will ever let us leave her outside the city again, so bad idea or not, she's going in with us.

———•———

"… so as my dear mother would have said—oh look, Jax is back." I look up in relief at Tater's words, never so happy to see Jax as his arrival interrupts the half man's long-winded story. Jax raises his left hand and extends his two fingers as he rides into view, a signal that all's clear up ahead and it's safe to camp for the evening. Mack and Riven made the decision not to travel after dark. The raiders and thieves in the area leave the caravans of Riven's Runners mostly alone since its well-known affiliation with the Prezedant is only asking for trouble. But after dark with no campfire to identify who we are, it's easy for them to mistake the caravan for any other traveler and attack. And we're told the Prezedant's tanks are a common sight the closer you get to Skytown, and we certainly don't want to stumble upon them in the dark. No, better safe than sorry.

They maneuver the wagons into the same triangle

formation like the past few evenings, leaving enough room in the center for us to make camp. I watch as Beanie and Talbert tether the horses to the wagons with enough slack so they can wander over to the grasses and feed. The tall grass spooks me some since I'm not used to seeing grass grow to such a height, and it just don't seem right. Add to that the amount of ruins we'd passed these past few days, it's enough to give anyone night terrors.

Unlike the barren and empty sandlands, the lands between Littlepass and Skytown are filled with the ruins of settlers' junk and buildings. I asked Tater about the pockets of stuff that littered the landscape, and he said it's because after the Shift, the survivors had flocked to this side of the mountains. They thought it would be safer. The poisons in the air and water; however, had still done their damage. The people had all got sickly and died. But the stuff, well, that just stayed where it was left and rotted away.

It's fascinating to see. Yesterday, we passed a huge pileup of twisted metal and rust, skeletons of moving "veacals." Things I'd only heard about in folklore, yet here it was in front of me. Must have been a good fifty or more of them. Oh, the brush and sands had tried to reclaim it over time, but the rusted husks were still recognizable. I had so badly wanted to stop and look at them, but except for me and Finn, the rest of my companions weren't the least bit interested. We passed on by with not even a scant sideways look. I could hear Finn's disappointed "Awwww, man" from the back of the cart, and I kind of wanted to whine along with him.

Tater said the travelers and traders called this metal mountain the graveyard marker, the halfway point between

Littlepass and Skytown. A final resting place for all the settlers that had just up and died in their "veacals" trying to escape from their ravaged cities. The others who had passed through after them had simply just pushed them out of the way over time, and they had sat there ever since, rusting away slowly in the dry heat. Kind of sad when you think about it. All of them just pushed aside and forgotten. Now no more than a marker on the road to Skytown. Hope whoever they'd been in their lifetime, they were now all reunited with their kin in the afterlife. Grada always said every soul, whether good or bad, at least deserved that much.

Shading my eyes against the low sun, I look around at where they've chosen to camp tonight. Looks the same as the last three nights: flat open grasslands with nothing to break the monotony other than a few rolling hills and slabs of gray rock broken off from the "highway" we're traveling on. Mack's word for these gray rocks had made me chuckle when I first heard it. "Ass fault" he called it. I'm pretty sure that can't be the right word for it, but I'm not about to tell him that.

Finn and Cat shoot by me all of a sudden, nearly knocking me off my feet. Their pent-up energy from riding in the cart all day has them heading straight for the tall grasses, needing to let off some steam. My grin follows them, knowing their little game of grass hide-and-seek would soon start, and my warning of not to go too far would be ignored.

Jax's whistling reaches my ears, drawing my attention away from the two in the grass. His movements as he dismounts are graceful and unhurried, and he makes sure to reward the nag with a soft nose rub after he tethers her for the night. She snorts a little and nudges his shoulder in affection. He did seem to kind of grow on you, even the nag thought so. I watch as he takes off his hat and runs his hand through his hair, causing it to stick up at odd angles like usual. We haven't spoken much these past three days, not since our ride together in the crawlspace, but I'm still full of questions. I still don't understand why he insisted on coming with me to Skytown. I know why he thinks he should go. For some reason, he seems to think helping me would make up for standing by and allowing the Army to destroy his little sister—a New Blood like me. But I already told him once before he doesn't owe me a thing, and it certainly isn't gonna help Jenna by getting himself killed standing by me. But here he still is. I don't get it. As if he can feel my gaze on him, he looks up with those eyes and gives me that stupid little smile that makes my heart beat out of my chest. Instantly my cheeks heat up, and I drop my eyes and glance away. Shizen. What is wrong with me lately? Why did that jackass have such an effect on me? Thankfully, some yelling from the campsite seems to be more interesting at the moment than my flaming face, and I can feel his eyes move away.

"I told ya, the Mistress needs to be closer to the fire. Ya cain't put 'er 'ere; it's too far away from the warmth."

"But Talbert, it's the best spot it is."

"It's no good, I tell ya. Ya cain't put 'er there. Wot? No not there either, ya daft ass. It's too close to the 'orses. Wot if one of 'em takes a shite?" And a tug-of-war ensues between Beanie and Talbert with what looks to be my bedroll. Oh, for the love of gods. What are those two morons up to now?

"Give me that." I march over and yank my bedroll from

their hands, glaring at them both something fierce.

"How many times I gotta tell you I don't need you lookin' out for my every move. And I especially don't need your help placin' my bedroll."

They both look back at me with such wounded expressions that I can't help but feel bad for yelling at them.

"We's only tryin' to look out fer ya well-bein', Mistress," Talbert says, his eyes dropping to the ground and his shoulders all hunched.

"Look," I say, rubbing the back of my neck in exasperation and trying hard not to roll my eyes. "I know you're just tryin' to help, but maybe … maybe you shouldn't try so much?"

I can tell by their faces they don't get it. I sigh and try again.

"I don't need help with my bedroll; I can do that for myself. We do, however, need help findin' firewood for the campfire. That could be your job this evenin' if you like. I mean, I would appreciate if you could help me with that?"

Beanie's head starts bobbing up and down, and Talbert smiles his black-tooth grimace at me. It takes all my willpower not to shudder in revulsion. Instead, I stretch my own lips in what I hope is some resemblance of a smile and watch in relief as they head off.

"This way, Beanie."

"But I think this way is better, Talbert—"

"Mistress needs firewood. Ya ain't gonna find no firewood that way, ya mule's arse."

May the gods have mercy, I think as I pinch the bridge of my nose between my fingers, fighting against the approaching headache. We can't get to Skytown fast enough. It doesn't help matters none when Jax ambles by with that crooked grin on his face and whispers loudly, "Missus Talbert, sure does have a nice ring to it."

I hurl the new cuss word I learned from Mack just yesterday at his back, but it only results in a ruckus of laughter from the others.

"Glad y'all find it so funny," I growl, hands on my hips and staring them down. "Since I've already provided such amusement for y'all, then I think I'm just gonna take first watch tonight and someone else can cook this evenin's meal." I try to stomp off in an indignant huff, but I stop short when I swear I hear one of them say, "Thank the gods for small miracles." I can't quite pinpoint which one says it though, since all of a sudden they get real interested in setting up their own bedrolls and getting the fire pit ready, anything but look my way. Jackasses.

I climb on top of one of the wagons and sit cross-legged, gazing out over the horizon, my borrowed shooter lying by my side. The sun is setting now, bathing the grass and hills and "ass fault" in beautiful ribbons of reds and oranges. I like this part of the day best: evening watch. It allows me peace and quiet away from everybody else. Away from the strange looks of Riven's men as they watch me without thinking I notice. Away from the suffocating adoration of the two idiots. Away from Tater's incessant ramblings about his ma. Away from the confusion that just being around Jax causes in me. Up here, it's just me and my own thoughts. It's real nice.

I watch Finn skipping through the tall grass, arms stretched out on both sides, his hands skimming the tips of the blades and his face tipped up to the warm rays of the setting sun. Not quite sure what he's doing, but it brings a little smile to my lips. Even after all he's seen and been through, he can still be the little boy that he truly is and romp through the grasses like a fool. It makes my insides soften up a little and allows some of my earlier frustrations to melt away.

Cat must've had enough of playtime though because I can see her now stretched out on her back by the other wagon in a warm patch of fading sunlight, four paws in the air and sound asleep. I hear the laughter and murmuring of the men around the campfire. Now that they're settled for the evening, Tater's tin flask seems to be making its rounds. The half man's voice floats on the wind as the whiskey tin reaches him, and he raises it in a toast.

"May your beds soon be swimmin' with big-breasted women!" I snort in disgust at his words and ignore the rowdy braying of the men. I don't want them intruding on my quiet thoughts right now.

Turning my own face to the last remnants of the day, I bask in the sun's lingering warmth. Only a few more days and we'll be in Skytown. Closer to Ben. Closer to the Prezedant. It thrills me and terrifies me all at the same time. Will we be able to find him? Will we be able to free him? I pull my flower outta my tunic and hold it in my hand, my only connection to my old life. So much has happened, so much has changed. I've changed. What will it mean if I do find him? Where will we go? What will we do? Will he even still want to be around me once he finds out what I am? The questions swirl in my head, and I close my eyes for a bit, the weight of it all threatening to overwhelm me. *One step at a time, Tara,* I tell myself just like Grada used to say. Free Ben first, then worry about everything else after.

Sighing, I open my eyes to the quickly encroaching dusk. Time for Finn to come in from the grass.

I sweep the field until my gaze finds him. I open my mouth to yell, but his name falls short on my lips as I notice the slight movement behind him in the grass. It's swaying to the side, but there's no wind to be blowing it. What the hell? The boy stops to investigate something, and the movement stops too. Is it Cat slinking through the grass, playing a game? No, I check and Cat is still where she was last time I looked. My eyes go back to Finn. He changes direction now, heads for the horses, and the waving grass starts heading that way, too. I squint a bit more into the waning sunlight. That's when I see it, and my gut drops with a sickening lurch. A long, black object rising up from the grasses and aiming straight for Finn. I'm not sure what it is, but I do know one thing; it's targeting the boy.

"Finn," I yell as I jump to my feet and raise my shooter. "Get outta the grass *now!*"

I aim my shooter at the still unknown predator, but instead of heeding my words, Finn looks up at me with this stupefied expression. *Shizen, boy, get outta the way*, I think frantically as I try to target the threat. I watch in horror as the swaying in the grass gets closer to him and then…. Finn is gone. Disappeared into the sea of brown.

"Finn!" I yell again. I don't recall jumping from the top of the wagon, but I hit the ground running, the others milling around me in confusion and blocking my way. I barrel through them, screaming at the top of my lungs, "Cat!" but like she can read my mind, she knows what I want. She's already leaping into the grasses, and I rush to keep up. I follow her through the tangled brush, knowing she'll lead me straight to the boy and whatever it is that took him down.

I almost trip over her as I stumble out of the grass into a clearing on the other side, and my heart leaps into my throat at what I find. Cat don't make a sound, not even so much as a growl. I figure like me, she can't quite make sense outta what we're looking at.

Two squat creatures hover over Finn's motionless body. They are a dull, gray-black with three legs sticking out on either side and two deadly-looking pinchers snapping in the front. Their long, shelled bodies seem to be in two parts and curl up at the end into a raised, bulbous tail that has a fierce-looking barb on the tip. In my own confused head, they kinda remind me somewhat of sand biters from back home, but these are so big, at least a full armspan long. I've never seen a sand biter grow this big.

They stop moving at our stumbling onto them, but almost like they dismiss us as no threat, they go back to what they were doing. One of them has hooked Finn's tunic with its claw, and it starts dragging him away again, bringing me out of my stupor. I raise my shooter and aim, but my fear has me shaking like a leaf in the wind, and I'm afraid to shoot least I hit the boy. Cat is circling them now, growling like a she-devil and frantic to get at Finn, but every time she tries to get close, they hold her off with their razor-sharp snaps.

Shizen. I have to do something because I know what their intent is. I can see a hole in a mound of dirt about four armspans from us, obviously a nest or den or whatever else these hell creatures live in, and I bet my life that's where they're aiming to take the boy.

Thunk! I catch movement outta the corner of my eye as a knife whizzes through the air and sticks into the side of the creature dragging the boy. The thing makes no sound of pain, but it releases Finn, and its claws snap in spiteful anger as it scurries towards its attacker. Jax. It moves real quick, but now that it's away from the boy, I don't hesitate. I raise my shooter and fire before it gets too close, causing the creature to explode in a torrential rain of shell and guts and black goo, splattering the grass and Jax with its innards.

Immediately I aim for the second creature, but Jax's shout of "Behind you!" gives me just enough warning to turn and raise my arms protectively over my face as another one of the beasts leaps at me from the long grass. Its momentum knocks my shooter from my grip and sends us both crashing to the ground. I hold it at arm's length, its claws reaching for me and the tail rattling furiously above my head. I can almost feel its intense rage. I twist my head away from the serrated claw as it snaps terrifyingly close to my cheek and try to push it off me, but my arms are starting to weaken and shake from holding its weight. In slow motion, the pinchers move closer, and I ready myself to feel the pain of having my face ripped apart.

Suddenly, the crushing weight is shoved off me with enough force to flip me over face-first into the dirt. Choking on the grit now in my mouth and nose, I push myself to my knees to find Talbert grappling with the creature, his piercing knife sending spurts of black goo into the air.

"There's more of 'em comin', Mistress. Move!" he yells

over his shoulder at me, his face dripping with the slick blood of the creature he'd just killed. He's right. They're swarming from the tall grasses: a horde of angry, pincher-snapping, killing machines.

Spotting my shooter on the ground, I dive for it at the same time another of those things takes a flying leap at me. With no time to think, I snatch the shooter as I fall hard on my shoulder and fire into the air at the menacing shadow just inches from my head. I don't miss. Its hot innards splatter my face and my arms, and my stomach heaves at the putrid smell that fills my senses. But there's no time to void my gut like the desperate urging wants to do. Bolting to my feet, I fire at the next creature and the next, each shot finding its target true. All around me are the echoing shouts and shots of the others as they defend themselves from the drove, but I don't dare take time to check on them. It takes all my concentration to keep myself from being gutted. I shoot until the clicking of the empty chamber lets me know there's no more slugs. Throwing the now useless weapon aside, I grab the knife from my boot.

"Come on!" I scream at the beasts, my fear stripped away now, leaving nothing but the primal instinct to survive.

A loud wailing pierces my anger-clouded brain. It draws my attention away from the creatures and to Cat. She's standing protectively over Finn, one of the creatures slicing her good with every swipe it takes at her, but she doesn't move. She won't leave the boy unprotected.

Finn. Seeing him lying there, not knowing if he's even still alive, I act without thinking of consequences. I run and leap onto the hard, shelled back of the beast threatening him, burying my knife deep into its head before it can get me with its barbed tail. It bucks and twists under my weight, but I hold on tight, stabbing again and again. My hand is so covered in its slick blood I almost lose my grip on the knife. I don't even realize I'm screaming like a madwoman until someone grabs my shoulder, shaking me and yelling over my shrieks.

"Tara. Tara, it's over."

"No," I snarl as I shake Mack's hand off. I give another stab for good measure, but the creature doesn't move any more. It's dead.

The silence hits me along with the realization that Mack is right. The shouting, shooting, and screams had stopped. The silence is almost painful. I look around in stunned confusion at the carcasses of the creatures littering the ground. Black shelled corpses are everywhere, but at least there's no human bodies other than—I locate the small figure on the ground.

"Finn!" I cry, stumbling to him, but Mack beats me to it and rolls him over gently with his big hands. The boy's not moving, his face pale and ashen, showing no signs of life. I pull up short.

"Is he—" I can't bring myself to say the rest of the words; they stick in my throat.

Mack just shakes his head at me, his face strained with worry. "He's alive, but they pierced him."

I can see the raised, red welt on Finn's side as soon as Mack lifts the tunic up over the skinny little frame. The raw lesion already has angry veins of red radiating from the puncture wound, and my breath catches in my throat. Mack draws his knife and runs its edge sideways over the welt, and

I immediately start screaming at him and grabbing his arm.

"What the hell you doin'? You're gonna cut him."

He shoves me away roughly. "I have to get the barb out."

Jax grabs my arm, preventing me from interfering anymore. "Mack knows what he's doing, Tara. Leave him be."

I yank my arm away. "Why ain't he wakin' up then? If Mack knows what he's doin', why ain't Finn wakin' up?"

Mack, done with the knife, jumps to his feet and scoops Finn up, ignoring my caterwauling. He runs in the direction of our camp through the tall grass, yelling over at Riven, who has joined him in his desperate dash.

"Get the medicinals from the wagon. We have to draw out the venom before it spreads any further."

Riven nods and sprints ahead to the campsite. I watch, dumbfounded, as they all rush off, Cat on their heels, not willing to let Finn out of her sight. They leave me standing there with Jax and Tater, Talbert and Beanie. We all just stand there looking at each other, covered in guts and goo, too shocked for words I reckon.

"What are those things?" I say finally to no one in particular. I just need answers; I don't care who gives them. I stumble over to the half man. "Tater, what are those things? Did they poison Finn? Their poison ain't deadly if it's caught in time, right?"

He looks up at me, and the tears in his eyes jolt me through to my core. I don't like what they imply, and I sure as hell don't want to hear it.

"Tara, Finn is so tiny and—"

"No," I say, cutting him off. I refuse to hear it. "Just tell me what they are."

He rubs his cheek, inadvertently causing the gob of black goo sitting there to spread a little more. "They are called Scorpi-ants, I believe, though I have never had the misfortune to come across one before. Wasn't even aware they lived in the wilds anymore. Last I heard, they had almost become extinct. That is why the Prezedant started farming them. As black as their blood runs, cooked properly, their meat is as tender as the meat of the gods. But I have never seen one in the wild before. They are far too dangerous to mankind to be allowed to spread into our cities. For as much as we enjoy their meat, they have acquired a taste for ours in return, perhaps even more so."

I shudder at what Tater's telling me. They took Finn to eat him? I swallow the bile in the back of my throat. "So if people know about 'em, then they know how to treat the poison, right? Mack can save him?"

"Mack is an educated man, Tara. If anything can be done for the boy, he will know. But I must warn you, girl. The toxins the Scorpi-ants deliver have a very paralyzing effect. Once delivered into the bloodstream of any other living creature, odds are—"

"Tara, maybe we should go see if Mack needs our help," Jax interrupts, glaring at Tater, who shuts up immediately. "Besides, when Finn wakes up, he's going to want you to be there."

I nod, not trusting myself to speak right now. Jax is right. *When* Finn woke up I should be there, since I know he's going to be so scared. Probably just as scared as I am right now.

The campsite is a scene of organized confusion. Finn is laid out on a bedroll, Cat at his head with her own head resting on her big paws as close to him as she can get without being in the way. Mack kneels at his side, cleaning the wound as Riven hovers over him, mixing a paste in a bowl. One of Riven's crew is tearing strips from a blanket and handing them to Mack. I watch in silence as Mack lathers the strips of cloth with the black paste and places it squarely over Finn's wound. It must hurt like hell, but the boy doesn't even flinch. He looks so tiny lying there, so helpless. My throat is tight with my tears, and I just want to bawl at the sight of him.

"What is that, Mack?" My voice sounds horse, and I give a small cough and swallow hard.

Mack don't look up at me, but he answers quietly, "Charcoal poultice. It helps draw out poison. Well, it does with smaller bites and stings. This is something totally unfamiliar."

"But it will work, right?" I reckon he can hear the desperation in my voice for he studies me for a bit before giving me a slight nod.

"It is a very effective method, yes. But we shall see. Only time will tell."

I guess his answer was better than nothing, but it doesn't make me feel any better. I want to go to Finn, hold him, but I know that won't help anything. I'm so full of anger and worry I can't stand still. I run my hands through my hair, trying desperately not to scream at the top of my lungs. I need to do something, anything, or I'm gonna lose it. A light touch on my arm jolts me like a bolt of lightning, and I turn to find Jax watching me with worried eyes.

"Come with me," he says quietly, but I shake my head no.

"I ain't leavin' here," I say.

"Tara, there's nothing you can do for Finn at the moment. Now come."

Taking my hand in his, I don't resist as he leads me to Tater's tow cart and sits me down on the back of the wagon.

"Stay," he says, and I surprisingly obey. He leaves me for a bit but is soon back with a bowl of water and one of the cloths Mack was using to bandage Finn. I watch as he dips the cloth in the bowl and gently starts to wipe my face. It shocks me at first when the cloth comes away covered in black pulp before I remember the Scorpi-ants. We're still wearing the remnants of our battle. Too weary to argue, I just close my eyes and tolerate his ministrations as he wipes my face and hair. It's somewhat soothing, his touch lulling me into a sense of calm, and I have to stop myself from leaning into his solid chest and breaking down like a young'un.

How did I let this happen? I was supposed to be on watch. Why did I wait so long to warn Finn to get out of the grass? He's hurt, probably dying, and it's my fault.

"Hey, it's okay. Finn will be just fine," he says gently, breaking my reverie, and my eyes pop open in surprise. I haven't said anything out loud. Why would he feel the need to console me? But then his two thumbs brush against my cheeks, and I'm surprised to feel wetness there. I'm crying. And in front of Jax, how humiliating.

I want to push him away, hide my weakness. But instead, I let him continue to wipe my tears and don't even try to move away when he leans in and brushes my forehead with his lips. It's the slightest of contact, a comforting gesture, nothing more, but the touch sends a current jolting through my body. I let my traitorous body do what it wants and lean into his warmth, a sob catching in my throat as the tears flow freely. His arms pull me against his chest, and I bury my face in his tunic, not caring anymore that I'm bawling like a baby. I hear the steady thrumming of his heart echoing in my head, the beat calm and comforting.

His hand rubs my back, the heat from it burning through to my skin, scorching me where it touches.

"He'll be okay," he murmurs over and over again, reassuring me so that I almost believe him. Almost.

"Mack!"

Riven's yell makes my blood run cold, and I push Jax away. I'm on my feet and running. I pull up short at the sight before my eyes, swallowing the scream in my throat. Finn is thrashing wildly, his body bucking so violently I'm afraid he'll break his neck. White froth is leaking from his blue lips, and his eyes are opened wide, rolled back, nothing but the whites showing.

"He's dyin'!" I scream helplessly, unable to hold it in any longer. Cat is pacing back and forth, wailing so loud it hurts my ears. Riven and Mack try to hold Finn in place to keep him from hurting himself, but even with four hands, they can barely contain him.

"He's burning up," I hear Riven yell and then Tater's mournful, "No, no, no."

I can't move. Finn is dying right in front of me, and I can't move.

"Tara, don't watch," Jax shouts in my ear as he tries to pull me away, but I shrug him off. Finn can't die. We have to do something. I have to do something.

All of a sudden, an image of a wilted stem pops into my frantic brain, and I remember Lily's demonstration.

She told me that I could use my Chi and apply it to objects and others.

Apply it to others.

I need my Chi, but it failed me last time in the alley with the thieves. It hadn't come. I can't have that happen again. Finn doesn't have much time.

Ignoring Jax and the chaos around me, I close the distance between me and Finn, knowing what I have to do. I kneel at his side between Riven and Mack and clear my mind of the world around me. I picture my Chi as a slight flame growing brighter, flowing in me, emanating from every part of my being. I imagine it bursting from me, covering Finn in healing waves. The frantic noise around me stops as I feel the welcoming calm enveloping me, though whether there's actual silence or if it's just all in my head, I can't tell. I rip the poultice off, place my hands on the inflamed wound, and Finn thrashes under my touch. I imagine the poison flowing through his body reversing, pulled back by my hands, and sucked out by my aura. I picture the wound in my head healing and the swelling disappearing from existence. A fierce heat suddenly encases my hands and I watch them exude, well, a flash of light I guess is the only way to describe it. This bright light seems to hover for a bit around the wound; not sure for how long. In my own head, time stands still as I picture the wound healing, over and over and over again. Then slowly, the aura fades away, leaving me woozy and nauseous.

A cold sweat covers me, and I fall back on my heels, the exhaustion instantaneous. I look down at my hands. They look normal. No light, no aura. Had I just imagined all of what happened? I look at Finn.

He's still now, and his eyes closed. Oh gods, he's dead. I couldn't save him. The panic threatens to destroy me until I notice his chest. It moves up and down. The movement is very shallow but definitely happening. He's still breathing. I look down at his wound, and I'm shocked to see that the ugly, red veins have disappeared. Hope swells in my chest as I scrape off the charcoal paste to find the skin around the puncture wound returning to its normal color, the wound itself just a pale shade of pink. Did I cause this?

I glance up at the others; I need them to confirm what I think to be real. They're all staring down at me with wide-eyed shock. I don't even remember Riven leaving Finn's side, but he's now standing with his two men, gawking at me like I'm some sort of freak. Their look tells me it's real all right. It's not all in my head. Everyone just witnessed what happened. I wait for the accusations of freak or mutie to leave their lips, but there's just this deafening silence.

"What?" I question, unable to stand their silence any longer.

Talbert and Beanie step tentatively towards me then, and I watch in horror as they drop to their knees, heads bowed in reverence. Then Tater follows suit. Wait, no. What are they doing? Don't bow down to me. Jax and Mack smile at me like they just witnessed a god appear in front of them. No, don't look at me like that. I want to scream it at the top of my lungs. Stop looking at me like that. My eyes find

Riven, hoping that he'll be the one sane person in this sea of madness right now, but he just gives me this smile of pure wonder and covers his heart with his hand, his two men following his example.

"Well, boys, seems like we've just witnessed our first true miracle. All hail the New Blood."

I think I would've rather been called freak or mutie, anything but that.

CHAPTER FOUR

The City

———◆———

Skytown could not have been more aptly named. The dead city ruins we passed through, even Littlepass, nothing could compare to the sheer scope of this entity that is Skytown. Even after all I've already seen, this place still leaves me speechless in wonder.

At first sight of it, I'd reckoned it to be another mountain range—a dark, hulking figure on the horizon. But as we ride closer, the blurred, hazy image takes on definition, and Finn, who's riding at my side, gasps out loud. I know exactly how he feels. My own heart beats something fierce at the sight of the metal structures that seem to grow from the ground straight up into the sky itself. These aren't just iron bones either. These are honest to goodness buildings still intact. Rows upon rows of them stretching far into the horizon. Shizen. How is it possible for buildings to be built so high? And how do they stand and not topple over in the fierce winds? The old folk had spoke of this, but I don't think I truly believed it to be real, let alone that I would ever see it.

The towering structures are surrounded at their base by a thick, stone wall that must be at least five armspans high. On top of the wall, there are what appear to be layers of spiked wire, giving more height to the enormous palisade and adding to the belief that this is a place you enter by invitation only. Through the coils of wire, I can see people moving about on the wall: spotters, I reckon. I can feel every one of them watching us, and I truly hope they're not the sort of sentries to shoot first and ask questions later.

But that's not all. Outside of the great wall stand four gigantic columns—two to a side—that reach straight up into the blue sky. Enormous, standalone pillars of gray, each of the columns contain three long, spindly blades at their tips. The sun glints off the blades as they spin lazily in the slight winds like the pinwheels Grada used to make me when I was a young'un. I wonder if it's the same basic principle for these. Are they being moved by the winds? And what exactly is their purpose? Tater's tale of Finn and the giant suddenly pops into my head, and I can't help the slight shiver that runs over me, even though I know I'm being foolish.

Enthralled by the incredible sight in front of me, I don't even notice where we're headed until the wagon takes a sudden dip as the road drops and disappears into a wide, yawning tunnel of black. I can feel the day's heat fade instantly as we enter the cold, damp darkness.

"Tater?" I question anxiously from the back of the cart.

His answer is subdued. "This is normal; don't worry. This is an underground tunnel, and it's the only way to enter and exit the city since it is totally surrounded by that wall and guarded by the Army day and night. Though whether they are trying to keep people out or keep people in, I have yet to ascertain. Now remember what Mack has told you both. Keep your hoods up, do not speak, and do not draw attention to yourselves."

I nod, but I'm well aware of the cold knot of fear growing in my belly. What if the guards didn't fall for our ruse? I asked Mack why we couldn't ride in the crawlspace again, just like Cat, and sneak into the city. To me it made perfect sense, and it had worked well before in getting us outta Littlepass. But he said our presence here had to be made known to the guards. The reason he'd given for leaving Skytown was visiting his kin in the south, so to bring us back with him as those same kin made perfect sense. If we're to stay with him, we have to be accounted for. Although he trusted his own people immensely, Mack was an important man in Skytown and had soldiers coming and going at all times. He couldn't keep us hidden indefinitely, he said, so announcing us as his visiting kin would not raise any suspicion if we should be spotted at his home. Made sense, he said. Well, maybe to him but to me it meant a much better chance of us getting caught. I don't like the plan.

Jax rides by me in the ascending gloom, and all I can see are his eyes as the rest of his face is covered by his wrapper. He winks at me and then takes his position alongside Beanie and Talbert, riding behind my cart like house servants would normally do. If Finn and I are to be Mack's kin, then those three are to be our servants. That's part of the plan. I wonder to myself how wealthy Mack is if riding with servants is expected of him, but I don't ask.

We enter the inky blackness and I can feel Finn move closer to me in the dark, but he doesn't pepper me with a hundred questions like he normally would have done. Ever since he'd awoken from his unconscious state, he'd been subdued, though whether it's because of the poisons still in his system or by the fright of what happened being too much for him to handle, I can't rightly say. He says he don't remember much of what happened, but over the past couple of days, I've caught him watching the grasses with a wariness that wasn't there before. Cat hasn't left his side either, making it difficult to clean her wounds properly, but from what I can see nothing's infected, so I'm not too worried. She doesn't want to take her eyes off the boy. I kind of know where she's coming from, so when I feel him touching my arm, I just put it around him and pull him closer. He relaxes into my side.

He may be a little quiet, but at least he's still acting normal around me. Jax and Tater, too. I reckon since they've already seen me raise a dust devil, healing a venomous sting isn't all that impressive. But things have changed with the others. I haven't told Finn what I did, and as far as I know none of the others have either, but I'm sure he's gotta notice the way they act towards me now. Gone is the ribbing and good-natured teasing. Instead, they're reserved and standoffish like they now fear me. Even Mack has changed his attitude towards me somewhat, though I know he's trying to hide it. I don't understand. They should be used to New Bloods. Nothing about me should surprise any of them. Why are they treating me this way? I tried to question Tater about it, but all he keeps saying is I don't realize how unique I am. What the hell is that supposed to mean? I'm still just Tara. I don't get why *they* can't see that.

We don't get far in the dank, stagnant hole, when suddenly lights appear on either side of us on the tunnel walls. The same kind of strange lights I'd seen in Sanctuary, like torches without the flame. "Electric lights" Tater had informed me. Settler technology. He tried to explain to me how they worked, but even after all his explaining they're still a mystery to me. I don't care how they work; they're a welcome relief against the suffocating darkness. Strangely enough, they seem to only light up as we approach, like our very presence is causing them to come to life. Their low hum follows us through the wide-spaced tunnel, the only sound other than the horses and the creaking wagons. Tater's warning echoes in my head, and I truly hope my pounding heart doesn't give us away.

After what seems like an eternity in this underground entry, the ground start to rise again, and I reckon we must be approaching the end. Two tall metal doors emerge through the gloom, and we slow to a stop. More lights come on so bright that I have to squint to see. Mack alights from the front wagon and walks straight up to the doors, though I have no idea how he's to open them. There's no handle or knocker that I can see. He walks off to the side to a little black box mounted on the left door, and unbelievably, it starts to talk to him.

"Identification," it says in a tinny voice, and Mack doesn't seem the least bit surprised by it.

"Captain MacKenzie and the Prezedant's caravan," he says, and I start at his words. Captain? As in Army captain? Lily had told me that Mack was a Prezedant elite, but I didn't expect him to be so high-ranking. Thoughts of Tater and his fake betrayal cross my mind, and I can't help but feel unease at the predicament we're in right now. Is this going to turn out the same? What the hell am I doing walking straight into the Prezedant's reach? I fight the urge to jump from the cart and run away. Instead, I squeeze Finn a little tighter, causing him to squirm and mutter, "Ow," at me.

Mack's words are followed by a moment of silence before the metal doors start moving with a gut-deep, grinding noise, like the old gears are protesting any sort of movement. They open just wide enough for a couple of soldiers to squeeze through, and Mack faces them calmly, giving no indication to the unease that's swirling inside all of us right now. They speak briefly, and I strain to hear. What are they talking about? Is he ratting me out? Then more soldiers file out of the opening and start circling the wagons. I reckon even with a man as important as Mack, they don't want to be taking any chances. They start looking through the wagons, and I hold my breath, praying for Cat to remain silent. The soldier Mack had been talking to approaches the tow cart and studies me and Finn so intently I'm sure he must hear my pounding heart. Unsure to what Mack has told him, I resist the urge to pull my hood down further to hide my face. Instead, I look up at him with the most innocent expression I can muster. He's young, fresh-faced and kind of nice looking in a way. I find it hard to understand that the young man standing in front of me and my enemy are one and the same. He gives me an unexpected smile.

"The captain informs me that this is your first visit to Skytown. Welcome. Any family of the captain is a friend of the Army. Enjoy your visit," he says cordially.

"Thank you," I reply. It comes out as a squeak.

He nods at me and then yells out over his shoulder, "Open the doors!"

One minute we're being studied by the guards and the next, we're past the gates and into Skytown. It happens so quickly I can't quite process the fact that we'd actually done it. We've made our way inside and not been caught. Shizen, is it really this easy?

The towering buildings are just as intimidating up close as seen from the outside. It's like riding through some huge, metal forest. They loom above us, blocking out any trace of the sun. But now I can see they aren't the iron perfection I'd thought them to be. These buildings are nothing more than ruins themselves, crumbling away with walls half gone and patched together with planks and tarps and sheets of tin. Gigantic shanties really. Gaping holes where glass once sat stare out at us like empty eye sockets. Burnt out husks of "veacals" litter the broken roads painted with bizarre symbols and lettering. Old signs hang off the side of another building, one somehow still intact, and its message flashes red at us with some unknown light source, "Girls! Girls! Girls!"

I don't need Jax to tell me what that means. It has ill house written all over it. Although from overhearing the excited conversations of Riven's men these past few days, I think brothel is the more common word.

But it isn't the buildings or relics that scare me as much as the inhabitants of Skytown. Whereas the people of Littlepass had paid us no heed and had gone on with their everyday trade, the people here watch our arrival closely with hate-filled eyes. I feel their malevolence as they stare at our progression. They're everywhere: lining the roads, hanging from broken windows, and gazing at us through the crumbling walls. There's no trading or bartering or falsely cheerful atmosphere like we'd seen in Littlepass. These souls aren't doing anything but taking up space. Just existing. Desperate, hopeless dregs of humanity. Their angry eyes condemn us and covet the wagons for I'm sure they know what cargo we carry and where it's headed. Their gaunt frames and faces tell me that the bounty we transport will in no way find its way to them, and their desperation shows. It scares me something fierce and I hate to admit it, but I'm actually grateful for the soldiers' presence I see, scattered about in the otherwise sea of filth clustered under the flashing Girls sign.

An old woman stands almost in the middle of the road, watching us approach. She is dressed in nothing but rags, and her dirty face and hair tell me that bathing isn't high on her list of priorities. She's munching on something, can't quite tell what it used to be, but now it's just a black, rotten thing in her hand. I catch her eye, and she stares at me with a dark, piercing look. I smile at her. I don't know why. Maybe I'm trying to tell her I'm not associated with the Prezedant like she's obviously thinking. Maybe to say that I understand her suffering. She doesn't get it. Before I can duck, the rotten food comes flying at me and splatters my fancy cloak and the side of my face with a nauseating stench. She grins at me then, this satisfied, half-mad grin. She's still smiling even as two soldiers rush her and knock her to the ground with the butts of their iron shooters. They smash her again and again with way more force than necessary, and I start to jump to my feet to scream at them to stop.

"Don't," Jax growls at me as he quickly pulls abreast of the cart, and I pause midway.

"But they're beatin' her," I hiss quietly, my anger controlling me.

"Think, girl," he answers back.

He's right. I can't draw attention to us. Any kin of Captain MacKenzie certainly wouldn't protest the beating of their attacker. I sit back down slowly, avert my eyes, and listen to the sounds of the beating fade away, anger simmering in my blood.

I don't know how long we ride through the squalor, how many empty, hopeless faces we pass. I don't even want to look anymore. I don't want to see the hungry, desperate eyes.

"Who are these people? How can they be like this in a land that has so much?" I question Tater.

"Not everyone lives the life of the privileged, Tara. These are the underlings, the workers, the slaves, and the flesh traders. The elite few could not have so much if it wasn't for the many that pay for it with their very souls."

So as much as I don't want to, I force myself to look. I see their suffering and their pain, knowing what they do not. That I'm one of them. I note every aspect of their miserable lives, and it burns and churns deep in my gut, but I say no more.

The squalor starts to melt away the further in we go. The buildings start to look fresher, newer. The dirty streets become wider and less strewn with filth. While I sit with my back to the front of the wagon and watch the city pass, Finn sits so that he can see what's approaching, and all of a sudden his eyes go wide. He kneels up and grabs my arm, shaking it in excitement.

"Tara, look!"

I do as he says.

If the sky towers had surprised me, then this … this astounds me. In the middle of this city—this place of squalor, decay, and filth—sits a place of indescribable beauty. An island of greenery speckled with oranges and reds so vivid it hurts my eyes just to look at it. It's cut off from the rest of the city by a wide span of blue waters so calm it almost looks like glass. It has a smaller version of the wall found outside the city in front of it, creating a barrier. But the top of this wall is curved out like a bowl so that even if you were to swim to the island, there would be no way you could climb out from under that lip to scale the wall. The only way to reach the island is a wide, stone bridge crossing the span of water and patrolled by no less than ten guards at the moment and those black metal monsters of my nightmares. Trucks, that's what the raider leader had called them. There are four of them, two flanking each side of the bridge and just sitting there, a menacing reminder of who holds the power. Even in the presence of such wonder, I can't help the shiver of revulsion that passes over me at the sight of them.

Vibrant, healthy trees, a total contrast to the sickly gray things I'm used to seeing, grow tall above the wall. The red and orange splashes—their blooming leaves. Compared to the iron grayness of the Skytown we'd just passed through, they seem almost garish in comparison. Buildings loom up out of the trees: ornate, immaculate, stone structures. Nothing like the towering shanties that make up the rest of the city. These are well-kept and in perfect condition and so opposite to the way the others of Skytown lived, it's no wonder they had grown such a hatred.

"Tater, what is that place?" I say, standing on my feet to get a better look. Finn joins me at my side.

"That is Royal Island, home to the great man himself. Magnificent, is it not? Wait until you get inside the perimeter; it is absolutely breathtaking. No matter how many times I see it, I still fawn over its beauty."

"You've been in there?" I ask.

"Oh, yes, but never as a guest. Oh, dear me, no … I'm in no way so privileged as to be a guest in this garden of ethereal delights. But I have sometimes gained admittance as entertainment for many of the parties thrown at those fine homes. There are advantages to being included in the Prezedant's elite. They truly know how to throw a party. Our friend Mack, here, can attest to that," he says with a trace of bitterness.

His words bother me in more ways than one."You mean Mack lives in there, too? With him?" The thought of that doesn't sit well. If I'd known we'd be so close to danger, I probably never would have come.

"Fear not, girl; it's a large island. Everyone who's anyone in this world calls this island home. There are thousands of inhabitants; you will not be found out. As my dear mother would say, 'The best way to stay hidden is to hide in plain sight.' Right as always."

Unlike the first gate, we're not stopped or questioned here. The guards stand at attention as Mack passes by, and he calls them all by name. His familiarity with them just adds to my unease, and I still can't shake that sinking feeling, like we're about to make some terrible mistake.

———•———

Entering this gated paradise is like entering a whole new world. A world of color and beauty and life. I know I must look like some fish out of water with my mouth gaping, but I can't help myself. How is this possible? How can the rest of the world be so barren and dead but then there is this? How has the Prezedant created such a world of beauty in the wake of so much desolation? And why here? In the middle of this gods' forsaken city? It doesn't make a lick of sense.

We roll through roads with homes so grand it's like being in one of Lily's picture books. The houses are surrounded by lavish grounds and rolling carpets of greenery and colorful flowers. The flowers amaze me. How do they stay alive? The only real flowers I've ever seen are the straggly weeds that poke from the ground after a rare rain, only to die hours later in the intense heat. But these are big and healthy. The old folks' tales of the settlers and their wasteful ways of life run through my head, but here I can see it's no folktale. It still truly exists. And Mack is a part of this. Why would he want to upset his picture-perfect life here? Why would he want to oust the Prezedant from power when he obviously lived a life of ease and luxury and plenty in a world where the rest of us had so little? It makes me question his motives again.

I catch Jax's eye, and like he knows what I'm thinking, he turns his head to stare at Mack with a furrowed brow. I'd be willing to bet the same questions are running through his mind. Is this one huge mistake? Will we end up in the Prezedant's hands through Mack's betrayal? I hate that those thoughts are even bouncing around in my head, but after all we've been through, I'm no longer that stupid, ignorant child from Rivercross. Besides Finn and Jax, I still don't trust anyone around me.

There are no dirt and mud roads to be found in here. Oh, no. Tightly woven stone forms this road and the wagon wheels clack noisily as they move over it. The sides of the roads are decorated with numerous flowers and colorful brush—signs of life everywhere—serving as a constant reminder of the contrast between here and the outside. Painted torch posts holding more of those electric lights are scattered about, creating a bright glow through the rapidly approaching dusk. It's a scene of undeniable beauty and wonder, meant to cause appreciation and gratitude for the man who'd made this all possible, no doubt. All it does for me is sour my gut with intense hate and dislike for the people who live here and turn a blind eye to the suffering of the rest.

A distant roar reaches my ears over the clacking wheels, echoing louder and louder in the approaching dusk, like hundreds of voices raised as one. I tear my eyes away from the unfamiliar sights, searching the evening's violet shadows for signs of what surely must be an approaching mob. Jax and Beanie and Talbert reach for their shooters, their heads swiveling like mine trying to find the source of this fevered cry, but I don't see anything.

"Tater?" I cry. "What is that? Are we under attack?"

Tater glances back, not in the least perturbed by this bloodthirsty roar that seems to be almost on top of us now.

"What?" Then as if finally noticing the noise, he nods his head towards a huge, white blob that has risen up from the shadows. "Oh no, no attack. No worries. That's just the bellowing of the people in the arena. That structure over there."

Is he saying that blob is a building? If this is true, then it's the most peculiar looking building I've ever seen. It looks like a giant, mountain-sized broth bowl that has been turned upside down. And there are screaming people inside of it. Is it some sort of torture place?

"Sadly, there must be mutant games happening this evening."

Mutant games. Where have I heard that before? Suddenly, Lily's tale of the Prezedant's "games" enters my head. What had she said? That they are fights to the death between captured muties. The winner of the fight is then forced to take the loser's life or else die anyways by having a wild wolfling let loose to rip them both apart. All done in the name of entertainment for the Prezedant and his elite.

I look at Jax in dawning horror, and his wide-eyed look of revulsion tells me that he, too, remembers Lily's tale all too well. The roar becomes one distinct word now, and the chanting raises the hackles on the back of my neck.

"KILL! KILL! KILL!"

This chanting is followed by a haunting scream that

echoes in my ears and vibrates in my bones. A scream filled with so much emotion: pain, fear, disbelief. It seems to stretch out forever, and I want to raise my hands to cover my ears, but Finn huddling against my arm prevents me from doing so. Finally, when I think I can't take it anymore, the scream stops, and the resounding silence is quickly filled again by cheers and shouts of glee. They're cheering. Someone, some poor mutie has just met their agonizing end, and these people are cheering? What the hell is this? I find myself shaking at what we'd just overheard, yet so thankful that I hadn't witnessed it with my own eyes.

"It's okay," I say to Finn, comforting him as he cries, his soft heart scarred by this new horror. "It's over now."

My attempt to comfort the boy belies the unease in my heart. Not for the first time, an understanding of what the rebels are trying to do bounces around my head. My earlier words of "Ain't my fight" don't seem to have as much truth to them anymore. It scares me something fierce. All I know is the faster I find Ben and Jane and Thomas and get away from all of this, the better.

CHAPTER FIVE

The Invitation

❦

"Miss ... miss, wake up." The voice is soft and delicate, but at this moment sounds like an annoying maskeeto buzzing in my ear. I don't want to wake up. I was having a glorious dream, one where Ben and Grada and everybody else who was ever taken from me were all still alive and well, and we were all together.

"Go away," I say crossly and turn over on my divinely soft pillow. I love this pillow. I love this bed. It's so comfy and cozy, and I snuggle in deeper ready to fall back into my slumber.

"Miss, the Master is asking for you. The morning is almost done," the voice says.

I roll onto my back and stare at the startling white ceiling. The master? Oh yeah, she means Mack. It's so weird hearing him referred to as "the master." But here in Skytown, in this grand house that he called his home, it's how he's known.

I sigh in resignation and look up into the kind face of Coral, my "handmaiden." Her word, not mine. I sure as hell don't reckon I need any handmaiden. Her job, she says, is to help me with my morning "ceremonials." I'm not quite sure what that normally consisted of, but my first morning here when she'd tried to get me out of my dirty tunic, I'd almost laid her out flat on her back. For the life of me, I couldn't figure out why this strange woman was in my room and trying to undress me. But in between my struggling to keep my tunic on and her trying to yank it off, I'd come to the understanding that she was actually here to help me wash and dress. *Help me wash and dress.* Apparently, that's what they did here in Skytown. Who the hell needs help washing and dressing unless you're ill? And help with using the inside privy. Who needs help with that? What a strange custom. She'd finally conceded to let me relieve myself and bathe in private, but then she had still tried to dress me and in a frilly frock no less. Refusing to do anything of the sort, I had gotten back into my filthy tunic and trousers much to Coral's dismay. That argument had ended with Mack's intervening and quickly bringing in a seamstress to dress me appropriately.

It's a strange sort of style, I must say. The torso of what she'd produced is very similar to a jacket with a high collar and long sleeves and fitted with so many shiny buttons that don't do anything it doesn't make sense. The bottom half of the jacket is split so that the material hangs over my arse and hips like a long cloak but cuts off at the front of my waist so you can see the matching trousers underneath. The new leather boots are good quality I can tell, but they're in no way as comfortable as my own worn pair, and they pinch my feet something fierce. But according to Coral, what I'm wearing is "all the rage" and that if I'm to be believable as any kin of Mack's, I had to play the part. I guess it isn't all bad. Finn looks a hell of a lot more uncomfortable in the stiff new trousers and shirt they'd forced him into.

"Is everyone already finished breakfast?" I ask, as I sit up, giving in to her demand. If Mack is asking for me, Coral isn't gonna go away until I do so. She nods, her graying head bobbing up and down.

"Ages ago. The boy and the beast are now outside in the covered gardens."

I don't panic anymore at the thought of Finn and Cat being outside without me for I know they're well under the watchful eyes of Beanie and Talbert. Ever since the run-in with the scorpi-ants, they watch over the boy like two mamas with a cub. Well, at least while he's outside. They'd set up camp in Mack's gated back garden, refusing to even think about staying inside. They said it reminded them of their confinement here in Skytown years ago. I'm not about to argue it with them. It's nice not having them inside watching my every move.

"And the Master is in the training room," Coral continues, wringing her hands nervously. "He says you are to forgo breakfast since you've been too idle to join them earlier and go to the training room immediately."

She has the decency to look a little chagrined at relaying that message to me, and I almost argue the point until I see her pull a couple of bread rolls outta her apron pocket.

"So I brought you these."

May the gods grant her three wishes. Maybe she isn't so annoying after all. I eagerly grab the rolls and take a bite, muttering a thank you around the hunk of bread in my mouth.

"Jax and Tater?" I mumble, but she understands.

"Ah, yes, the handsome devil," she says with an arched brow, and I stare at her in confusion. Why is she looking at me like that? Put that furry brow down, woman, before I rip it off your forehead.

"He is to be found in the shooting gallery," she says.

Typical. Ever since Jax had found out Mack had an underground shooting area, it's where he spent most of his waking hours.

"The imp? He was sent out very early this morning by the Master after a visit from one of the Prezedant's aides."

Now that captures my attention. Abandoning the bread, I bound out of bed and quickly pull on my old tunic and trousers, thankful they'd been returned to me after being cleaned. If I'm meeting Mack in the training room, then I can't be dressing all fancy-like. Don't bother me none, but I'm eager to know who his visitor was this morning. Since we had arrived in Skytown, Mack has had his feelers out, looking for any sign of Ben. There was no sign of him at the prisoners' compound or at the iron mines outside of the city limits. Wherever the Prezedant was holding him, it wasn't the typical places. Maybe the visitor this morning had been one of Mack's spies with some news on his whereabouts.

I ignore Coral's frantic fussing and bolt from the room with her shouts of, "Please, Miss, let me do your hair at least," falling on deaf ears. I run through the gigantic hallway, down the winding, perfectly polished stairwell, down another hall, and practically fall through the door of what we're using as our training room. Mack looks up in surprise at my noisy entrance, the long, skinny blade he's using to attack the stuffed dummy, stilling. I don't bother with any pleasantries.

"Coral said … you had … a visitor," I gasp out, trying to catch my breath.

He then turns his attention back to the dummy and starts attacking it again with precise strokes of the blade.

"Do you know how to tell time?" he asks, totally ignoring my earlier remark. I stare at him in confusion.

"Huh?"

"It's a simple enough question. Do you know how to tell time? Like when I say breakfast is at eight hours and training starts at nine hours, do you understand what that implies?" he says like he's talking to an idiot.

"Yeah, I know what that means. I ain't a simpleton," I answer curtly.

"So explain to me then why it is now ten hours and you are just showing up for your training? Do you not care to learn how to defeat the Prezedant? Or does saving Ben not matter as much as your beauty sleep? Because if you do not care for our cause, then don't waste any more of my time."

I'm not prepared for the attack, and I blink at the harshness of his tone.

"Of course I care," I sputter finally. "Why would you say

such a thing to me?"

He stops his assault on the dummy and turns to glare at me, and for a moment I feel like I should run because I fear that blade is going to come straight for my own heart.

"We don't have any more time to waste, girl. Now, I need to know if you're in this game plan of ours wholeheartedly or not. If this training is to continue, are you with us to the end? Can we depend on you to help us finish this? Or are you just in this for your own selfish reasons?"

I have no idea why Mack is acting this way, but it awakens my anger.

"I'm here until the end. I said so, didn't I?" I snap, but my answer doesn't seem to please him any. He just narrows his good eye at me some more.

"Prove it," he says quietly.

"Huh?" I say again.

"Prove it. Bring forth your Chi. Attack me."

"Mack, what—?"

"Do it!" he roars and lunges at me, slamming me into the wall, his blade against my throat. My hands move instinctively trying to get the steel off my neck, but he has the strength of ten men. I can't budge him.

"Mack!" I croak, unable to breathe and shocked at his attack, but he doesn't heed me.

"Summon your Chi, Tara," he growls again.

"Please ... stop ..."

"Summon it," he yells, his voice almost pleading, and I close my eyes and picture the now familiar flame like I'd done with Finn. I picture it growing brighter, the aura of it flowing through me and wait for the fire to catch. But it doesn't happen. Nothing happens no matter how hard I try. After a couple of minutes, I open my eyes to Mack's almost frantic face.

"Summon your Chi, gods dammit," he demands again, and I cringe from the fierceness in his glare.

"I cain't," I whisper, afraid for what he'll now do. He doesn't react like I'm fearing though. Almost in slow motion, his arm and blade drop away from me, and his shoulders slump in defeat. Watching him deflate like that, seeing his disappointment, well, it feels far worse than facing his anger.

"You are nowhere near ready," he whispers, not to me I don't think, but to himself. "I had so hoped … after seeing you awaken your Chi to heal the boy …"

His crestfallen face crushes me. Why is he acting this way? Why is my ability to summon my Chi so important today of all days? But he doesn't give me a chance to ask any questions.

"Leave me," he demands.

I don't want to leave. Not without answers. Who was his visitor this morning? Was there information about Ben? Why was he acting like some giant mule turd?

"Mack," I say, but he cuts me off.

"I said leave!" he roars at me, and I nearly jump from my skin.

Shizen, he's pricklier than spiked wire this morning. I back out of the room and close the door quietly behind me and look around in confusion. What the hell just happened? Where had all that anger come from, just because I was late? I take a mental note never to be late again.

I can't think of a single reason for him to act the way he

just did. I didn't do anything to him to be treated like that. The more I stand there thinking about it, the more it starts to piss me off. I turn to go back in and demand an apology, but Mack's angry whacks start on the practice dummy again and I hesitate. The enraged roar coming from the other side of the door makes me drop my hand from the door handle. Maybe this isn't such a good time. Another roar reaches my ears. Yeah, I'll wait. I turn on my heels and head for the lower levels of the house where the shooting area is. Maybe Jax had been around this morning, and he has some idea on who this visitor was. And maybe a little shooting of my own would help me let off some of my steam.

I hear the iron shooter long before I get there. Jax is in fine form this morning. But as I slowly enter the room so as not to startle him, I spot Jax off to the side. His back is to me as he lounges in a chair, his feet propped up on some crates, and his chair tipped precariously back on two legs. What the—? If Jax is sitting down, then who's doing the shooting? I slip in as quiet as a mouse and stop suddenly as I recognize the shooter. Finn. Jax is letting Finn use an iron shooter? The boy can barely walk and talk at the same time.

Has he gone completely mad? Furious at Jax for letting the boy do such a stupid thing, I storm up to his unsuspecting back and kick at one of the weight-bearing chair legs, and he scrambles to catch his balance before he topples over.

"Shizen, Tara. What the hell was that for? I could have broken my neck," he sputters as he leaps to his feet. Finn stops shooting, now aware of my angry entrance. I can see the excitement mixed with guilt written all over his face at being caught red handed, and it prickles at my anger. I stride over to him, yank the warm piece of metal outta his hand, and ignore his indignant "Hey!" as I march back to Jax.

"Have you lost your mind?" I hiss at Jax, even though I want to scream at him instead. "Why the hell is Finn usin' this shooter?" I shake the butt in his face. "Do you want him to lose a finger or a foot or even worse, his life? He ain't got no reason to be usin' an iron shooter. He's never been trained to do so. Why would you be as daft as to let him have one? Woulda served you right if he'd shot you by mistake."

"Calm down, you little spitfire," he says, laughing as he pulls the shooter out of my hand. "And give me that. I think it's more dangerous in your hands at this moment than the boy's."

His laughter at my expense just serves to irritate me even more.

"I told ya she'd be mad, Jax." Finn says matter-of-factly and Jax nods.

"Right you are, my boy. But she doesn't know how good you are, does she? She's never seen you shoot. Why don't you show her?"

Finn nods at this suggestion and runs over, raring to go at Jax's words. He takes the shooter against my protests, and readily positions himself in this exaggerated shooting stance while Jax replaces the old target piece with a new one. Peering all squint-eyed at the target's red circle, he takes aim. Cat, who'd been lounging in the furthest corner of the stone room, hunches back down and tries to make herself as small as possible. I kind of want to do the same. *Why ain't I stopping this?* I think just as Finn lets go at the target in rapid-fire succession. Six deafening shots, but the following silence almost hurts my ears even more. I have to stop myself from running my hands over my body to make sure I'm not hit. Finn don't seem to notice though; he's looking at the smoking shooter in his hand with smug satisfaction. It reminds me of Jax. Scary.

I study the target. Did Finn really do that? I tilt my head in question at the boy, and he nods at me that he's done shooting. I head for the target thinking my eyes must deceive me, but nope, the little stink turd had done it. He'd hit the target all six times, and four of them are even within the inner circle. What the hell? Not that long ago, he didn't even know what an iron shooter was. How did he get so good?

"Jax's been teachin' me," he says, beaming that goofy grin and answering my unspoken question. "All the while you been trainin' with Mack, Jax's been teachin' me how to shoot. He says he's gonna try and get me a shooter of my own, one my own size. It's good, right? It's good because the next time I get attacked by scorpi-ants or any other creature, I can protect myself."

I don't quite know what to say. A boy Finn's age should be more concerned about swimming and fishing and playing than learning to protect himself. So no, as far as I'm concerned, it's not a good thing at all. But this is the first time since he was attacked that I've seen him so happy. He's almost back to the old Finn again, so I just nod at him, and it seems to please him.

"Finn, why don't you and Cat go play in the back gardens

for a bit? I think that's enough training for today. We don't want to overdo it. Just make sure Cat doesn't go around to the front of the house; we don't want her being seen," Jax says.

The boy answers with a simple "Sure," at Jax's command and lays the shooter on the crate with the utmost of respect before scampering off, Cat on his heels.

Jax starts speaking as soon as Finn disappears from sight. "Now, before you say anything—"

"No, it's alright. I understand what you're tryin' to do," I say, and he just stares at me, mouth agape. "And for gods' sake, shut your trap. You look like your tryin' to catch maskeetos."

He ignores my biting remark.

"Wait ... what? You're not gonna rip my head off for training Finn how to shoot?" He narrows his eyes at me suspiciously. "Who are you, and what have you done with the real Tara?"

I don't take the bait. "No, truly, it's okay. I haven't seen Finn this content in a while. It's good to see him smile again. You did a good thing, Jax."

He studies me a bit more in silence.

"Okay, see, it's kinda hard to believe you're fine with it when you still look like you're gonna spit fire at any moment and roast me alive. So if it's not Finn, what is it?"

I shrug at him. "Nuthin' truly—"

"Don't lie to me, Tara. I'm an expert when it comes to your moods. You only have two: pissed and more pissed. And right now, you're the latter. What's going on?"

"It's—I don't know," I say, running a hand over my face. "Something ain't right with Mack. I went to our trainin' session as normal, but he was so angry at me. He was demandin' that I summon my Chi, and when I couldn't, he got so frustrated with me. Like I disappointed him to no end. And I got no idea why it's so important to him because when I tried to ask, he yelled at me to leave him be. Coral said he had a visitor this mornin'. You know anything about that?"

He gives a slight nod. "I saw someone leaving earlier. He was dressed in soldier garb. Mack seemed upset, too, after he had left, but he didn't stay long enough for me to ask, and I figured it wasn't none of my business anyway. I figured he would have told me if it was any concern of mine. He went straight to the training room after that. I thought you were waiting for him there," he says.

"No, I was late. By the time I got there, he was fumin'. He was questionin' my loyalty to the rebellion. Askin' if I was only in it for my own selfish reasons or if I truly wanted to help. I don't get it."

Mack's behavior had really upset me, and I expect Jax to share in my indignation, but he just gives a hollow laugh at my words.

"And that surprises you? You haven't made any secret, Tara, that you're in this for one reason and one reason only: Ben. Everything else is secondary to you."

I stare at him, shocked.

"That's not true!" I say. "I care about other stuff too. Findin' Jane and Thomas … helpin' the rebels … tryin' to make the world a better place for everybody."

"That's a crock of shite, and you know it." The venom in Jax's words startles me. "Not once have I heard you mention defeating the Prezedant or making the world a better place. All you ever say is, 'When I find Ben,' or, 'When we rescue Ben.' And you know what? I don't get it. I don't get your obsession with rescuing the golden boy. Is his rescue the end all for all of our problems? Is the world going to be all sunshine and roses once you have him back? News flash, Tara, the world is still going to have the same problems. The Prezedant is still going to be around bringing his misery and fear and oppression. The children and mutants and less fortunate are still going to be in danger from him and his kind, and that includes Finn and me and my whole village. Maybe for once, you should look beyond the length of Ben's shadow and consider helping others than just yourself. Mack has every right to question your commitment because, come to think of it, I do too."

My shock changes to a slow-burning anger. First Mack, now Jax? What the hell had I done to either one of them to have them talk to me this way? I'd done everything they asked of me so far, including bringing forth this stupid New Bloods' curse that I'm still not sure I want to possess, and still they question my loyalty? And how dare he question the importance of my freeing Ben.

"Rescuin' Ben is extremely important to me," I growl. "He's all that I have left of my entire kin. I guess I cain't expect you to understand that since you still have your ma and Sky and the rest of your village, but me, I have no one. I have no kin, no family to call my own, and that scares me something fierce. He is, and always will be, a huge part of my life. Without him, there ain't no me."

My words stun him into silence before it's broken by a

harsh snort.

"Shite, Tara is that what you actually think? That he's all the family you have? That he's the only person left for you to care about?" He runs a hand through his dark hair. "I can't believe you even feel that way. That is so unbelievably selfish and stupid and narrow-minded that I don't even know what to say."

Why is everyone attacking me today? I kind of wish Coral had just left me asleep in my bed.

"Oh, I think you've said enough already," I snap. "I've had just enough of you lot today, you and Mack. I don't need to stick around here to hear any more of what you both think of me."

I ignore his insistent yelling of my name as I hurry from the room. I don't want to hear any more of what he has to say. All I know is Ben would never treat me like that or say any of those hurtful things. Ben would know how I felt. He wouldn't have to question any of my motives. And he would never have called me stupid or selfish.

Damn Jax for pissing me off. Just when I think he's starting to turn around from being a complete jackass, he proves me wrong again. How can he in one moment be the kind, caring Jax who comforted me when Finn was sick and then be the arrogant, know-it-all shite head in the next? I just don't get it or him. And why do I always let him push me this far into anger? I should be used to his self-righteous ways by now. It shouldn't get under my skin so much.

I'm not sure where I'm headed. I just know that I need to get away from this place and Jax and Mack at the moment. There's too much in my head right now. Where do I go, though? Is there any place I could go that would make me feel normal anymore? Any place where I could just be Tara and not a New Blood or a mutie or a freak? Somewhere where nobody wanted anything from me or didn't want me dead. My predicament hits me with alarming clarity, and I suddenly feel like I can't breathe. Like if I don't get some fresh air soon, I'm gonna suffocate, so I make a beeline for the front door. I don't make it out before I hear my name.

"Tara, stop."

I think about ignoring Mack. I mean, he already yelled at me enough today. Why should I stick around to hear more? I take another step towards the door, desperately wanting to get outside.

"Please, I need to talk to you. I need to explain."

Sighing, I stop and turn around. He's standing at the door to his book room, but he doesn't call it a library like Lily did. What was the name he used? Study. That was it. They can't even decide on the same name for a book room. No wonder this new world messes me up so much. I stare at him with wary eyes and raise a brow.

"You gonna yell at me some more? Because if so, I don't need to hear it," I say.

"Just get in here," he says in irritation, and I give in, following him into the richly decorated room. I'd been in this room before, but the feel of it never ceases to amaze me. The numerous books that lined his walls are worn from use and overflow from every nook and cranny. Weapons, knives, and shooters are stacked haphazardly in corners, and messy piles of papers and charts litter his desk. It's the only room in this massive place that none of his help is allowed to touch and it shows. But for some reason, the messy room calms me. Maybe on some deep level, I connect with the room. Like no matter how messed up I am, I still serve a purpose like this room does.

He sweeps aside the mountain of papers as he sits and motions for me to take the other chair. I do as he suggests and sink into the soft, fragrant leather. He watches my every move with that one eye, and even though I want to fidget under his stare, I meet his look without flinching.

"Sooo, we kind of got off on the wrong foot earlier," he says. I stay quiet. He clears his throat and continues. "Yes, well, forgive me. I did not mean to question your commitment or your abilities. I know you're trying your best. I received some unsettling news, and I took my anger out on you. For that, I am sorry."

"What news?" I ask, my curiosity piqued.

"It doesn't matter," he says, trying to brush it aside, but I argue the point.

"It does matter. If you want me to be a part of this whole thing, Mack, then you cain't just tell me certain things and keep other stuff from me. I need to know everythin' that's happenin'. If I need to be totally committed, then you need to be the same."

Forming a steeple with his hands at the tip of his nose, he thinks for a moment, staring at me over his fingers before nodding.

"Very well. You're right." Sighing, he drops his hands to his desk, and drums his fingers in a nervous pattern. "The visitor this morning was a soldier. A Prezedant aide. A spy for the rebels. He brought me news of one of our people.

Someone very close to our cause. She has been detained."

I can tell by the pained look on his face that there's more, and I feel that familiar clench of worry in my gut.

"Mack …"

He looks at me with eyes filled with sadness, and I know before he even says it.

"It's Lily."

"No," I yell as I jump to my feet. "No. She said she was gonna be fine. Tater said they let her be."

"Tara, calm down. She has been taken to the Prezedant's estate, yes, but she is not harmed in any way. She's alive; do not fear."

"Alive? For how long?" I cry. "How long before he kills her tryin' to make her talk? You have to get her outta there, Mack."

"I am aware. She's not in any immediate danger for the moment. She's not a prisoner in relative terms. She has not been charged with anything. Apparently, the Prezedant has his suspicions, so he 'invited' her to his estate to keep an eye on her. Thank the gods she is such a well-known healer. That's the only thing keeping her alive right now. He's just keeping her close to watch her, to see if she will slip up and lead him to others. Lily's smart; she knows what his game plan is."

My fear lessens some at his words but doesn't go away entirely. First Ben, now Lily. We have to do something. Enough of sitting on our arses. I settle back down in the leather chair and take a deep breath.

"Why didn't you tell me this earlier? Why didn't you wake me this mornin' when your spy was here with the news?" I say, my fear escalating to anger.

"Your training is integral to our plan succeeding, Tara. I didn't want to distract you from that. I guess I didn't want to upset you," he says.

I snort at him."Well, guess what? Big time fail. I'm upset. Question is, what are we gonna do about it? What's the plan?"

"This," he says simply.

One finger stabs a white square of paper on his desk and pushes it towards me with such a look of disgust that I hesitate to pick it up. It looks harmless enough, but Mack's face scares me. Fighting my hesitation, I pick up what I believe to be paper, but I'm surprised at the stiffness. Is paper supposed to be solid? It's neatly folded, a beautiful bird in a rainbow of feathers adorning the top of it. I run my finger over the raised drawing, marveling at the workmanship. Inside of the fold, there are words written with such a flourish of loops and swirls that I find myself struggling to pick out the letters as I read it aloud.

"The Prezedant requests your presence at his annual masq … masqa…"

I struggle with the word, and Mack says it for me.

"Masquerade."

"Masquerade party at his home on the evening of the three and one… s…t."

"Thirty-first." Mack corrects my pronunciation of the numbers, and I shoot him an irritated glance.

"Thirty-first," I repeat it as one word like he'd done. "Festivities begin at 1600 on the eve hour. Please join him for an unforgettable night of delight and entertainment.

Re…re-pond-ez… sil… voose…."

I give up on trying to say the last few words, but I get the gist of it all. It's an invitation to a party. It doesn't make sense.

"A celebration? We have to save Lily and Ben, and you're goin' to a party?"

"Actually, we're going to a party. As in me and you. Invited into the beast's lair itself," he says and gazes at me as I sit up straighter in my chair, letting his words sink in.

"You're actually thinkin' about goin'? About me goin'? Why would you want me to get near him? You said yourself I'm nowhere ready to face him yet. I don't understand."

He nods at me, his one eye sparkling brightly.

"Just think about it, Tara. I didn't consider this damned event of his as a possibility at first either. I had forgotten all about this party and how announcing you as my kin would automatically put you on the list for an invitation. An error on my part to be sure. When this was handed to me this morning along with the alarming news of Lily's capture, I panicked a little." He grins at me. "I guess you got the brunt of that panic. You are correct; my first thought was that you could not be anywhere near him yet. You're in no way ready, but then I realized there is a silver lining. It gives us access to that fortress of his without question. And no doubt that is where he's keeping the boy as well as Lily now. There has been no sign of the boy anywhere in Skytown, but it's said the Prezedant keeps his own little house of horrors in the bowels of his estate that not even I have been privy to. If the boy is being held anywhere, then that's where he would be. A masquerade ball is a costume party, an event where your face is expected to be covered. We walk straight in; we won't have to sneak by or fight our way in. It's a great opportunity for us to freely roam about to search for Lily and Ben."

Ah, so that's the plan. To get his own little band of rebels inside to search for our people. Sounds like that's the easy part. I reckon the hard part is getting them back out.

"Who will be going in?" I say eagerly now, realizing the impact of what he's telling me.

"Well, my 'servants' will have to accompany us of course. That will give me the excuse to bring at least three men. The invite stands for me, you, Finn, who will not attend of course—he's way too young, and this will be far too dangerous. And Jax. That gives us a total of six—"

"Wait, what? Jax?" That catches me off guard. "Thought the plan was to pass Jax off as one of your servants. Why would he be included on the invitation?"

"Yes, well, sometimes the best laid plans go awry. Jax simply does not have the humbleness and obscurity to pass himself off as a servant, so I improvised. When I introduced you all at the gate, Jax's identity was changed to your betrothed."

Funny. I could have sworn Mack just said Jax is supposed to be my betrothed, my promised. But that can't be right. Surely, I misunderstood.

"Can you say that again?" I say, sticking a finger in my ear and jiggling it to help my hearing. "I think I heard you wrong."

"You did not," Mack says, and as the horror of his words sink in, he at least has the decency to look embarrassed.

"Shizen. Are you pullin' my leg, Mack? Jax is supposed to be my promised?"

"In name only. Don't get yourself worked up over this. I had to give some sort of explanation to his presence here," he counters.

"And that was the best you could come up with? Servant, stable boy, hell, shite shoveler woulda been better than my … promised." The word sticks in my throat.

He rolls his good eye at me.

"Stop overreacting, girl. It's not as if I am asking you to truly wed the boy. It's just a cover story. One that we will all have to pull off with perfection if we are to attend this event. The thirty-first is but three weeks away. We will have to do an incredible amount of training in that time, and you must work on your social skills. In preparing for that, I sent Tater to fetch someone to help you in that area. Someone knowledgeable but who we can trust to stay tight-lipped on everything they will see here. It's necessary to help Ben and Lily."

I can't believe we're to go through with this. And what the hell does he mean help me with my social skills? I'm social enough, I reckon. But just like the dumbest fish, I fall for the dangley bait and ignore the little alarm bells going off in my head. If it meant helping Lily and possibly finding Ben, then so be it. I will do whatever it takes.

"You really think that's where he's bein' kept? In the Prezedant's estate?" I ask.

"Makes sense, really." Mack taps himself lightly on the forehead. "Don't know why I didn't think of that before. Ben has to be there. He is a very valuable asset; the Prezedant would want to keep him close."

My mindset changes in an instant. The slight panic I felt

earlier at attending this celebration turns to excitement. This may be the opportunity we've been looking for to find Ben, finally. And all I have to do is attend a party. Mind you, I still gotta pretend that I fit in with elite society and treat Jax like my promised, but how hard can it be?

CHAPTER SIX

The Training

————◆————

"I told you I cain't do it," I snarl and stumble for about the twentieth time, falling painfully to the floor as my ankles twist yet again in these torturous devices called "dress shoes." What the hell is the Duchess thinking putting me in these and expecting me to walk normal. They have to be at least three times higher than my boots with a pointy, spiked heel that could probably take out an eye. No possible way I can walk in these death traps.

Duchess tuts at me in a way that has come to grate on my nerves these past few days and in her high pitched, nasally tone says, "Again. Pull her up, boys."

At her command, both my arms are grabbed and

I'm hoisted to my feet by Beanie and Talbert, who quite mysteriously have overcome their fear at being inside Mack's home to be at her every beck and call. I'm sure it's got nothing to do with Duchess's tight dresses, or the way her chest seems to threaten to fall out of her dress at any given moment, or the fact that she ran the ill house, the brothel in Littlepass that Tater had tried to hide us in. I'm sure they're not swayed by any of that, not those two. I'm not gonna lie. At first, it had been kinda nice having them not focus on me, but now? Now, their devotion to her just irritates me to no end.

I reach for them as they plop me back on my feet and step away, leaving me tottering on the ridiculous shoes and the fear of falling over again very real. Duchess steps in front of me. She wears the exact same shoes and makes it look so easy that I actually hate her at this moment.

"Try it again, girl. Lean slightly back and walk heel to toe like I said. Don't rush … walk fluidly. Like so."

She takes a couple of steps and then twirls gracefully on her heels, looking like she was born with those damn shoes on her feet. I try to follow her example. I lean back and take a couple of steps, my feet hitting the floor with exaggerated thuds as I try to walk across the room. I concentrate hard, each step deliberate and measured. Finally, I reach the other side of the room without falling over, and I look up with a self-satisfied grin. I did it. But then I notice Duchess and Tater's looks of horror, and Beanie and Talbert, well, they're trying hard to keep it in, but I can see the idiotic grins behind their hands. They're laughing at me.

"What?" I say, miffed at their reactions. I'd done it. What's the problem now?

"Er, maybe, Duchess, we should get her some lower shoes. Yes, that's it. Smaller heels would be more suitable for the girl, don't you agree?" Tater finally breaks the heavy silence. "Because to be quite honest, I've seen elephants walk with more elegance and grace."

The insult doesn't go unnoticed by the two morons, and it seems to be more than they can handle. They crack up, flooding the room with their obnoxious laughter, and I feel the angry heat rushing to my cheeks.

"Shut up!" I snarl, my emotions getting the better of me. "Don't know what you two find so funny. You probably have no idea what an elephant even is."

"No, yer right, Mistress, we don't. But we reckon it can prolly walk better than you in dem shoes," Talbert drawls, causing Beanie's laughter to turn to outright snorting. He snorts so hard he chokes on his own spit. Ignoring the choking man and the other one now furiously pounding his back, I focus instead on Tater. As much as I hate these damn shoes, there's no way I'm giving up now—just to prove a point.

"I can do this," I hiss at him through gritted teeth, and taking a few more test steps, I start to make my way back across the room.

"This is useless, Tater. I have never seen any girl take so long to learn—"

I dismiss the comment, as well as the murmuring and sniggering still coming from the other side of the room, and focus on staying upright. My ankles twist again, but I catch myself from falling.

"Really? Any fool should have been able to master this by now," Duchess snips as I pass by her. "Slow your steps. Don't walk so quickly. And straighten your back."

Okay. Enough is enough.

"Lean slightly or straighten my back. Which one is it? Make up your mind. What the hell you tryin' to say to me?" I'm in her face, and she steps back, startled.

"Tara, dear, maybe we should take a little break," Tater interjects smoothly as he steps between me and my torturer, attempting to placate me. "A little breather, shall we say? As my dear mother would say, 'Elegance is found in the mind; the rest can be learned.' You need to step away for a bit, but you will learn."

"Aye, she'll learn, but it prolly be easier if ya trained the eleefent," Talbert says outta the corner of his mouth, his words meant for Beanie's ears alone, but I hear him. I also hear Beanie's maniacal laughter in response, and my control finally snaps. Bending over, I yank a shoe from my foot and throw it across the room with the force of my red-hot fury. The laughter cuts short as Beanie ducks, barely avoiding the shoe from smacking him in the head. Instead, it smashes into the wall, breaking off the heel, and I hear Duchess yell in horror, "My shoe!" I feel a certain vengeful smugness as I stare at the mutilated footwear.

"You little brat," Duchess yells at me in disbelief. "Those were a pair of my best. Do you know how much they cost me?"

"Tara! What the—oh, I am so sorry, Duchess," Tater blusters, his hands flapping in the air.

I don't pay no mind to his antics. I'm too busy reaching

for the other shoe, intending to throw that as well at the still-laughing Beanie, who's now howling at Talbert, "She tried to kill me wif a shoe!"

"Tara, don't you dare," Tater yells as he catches my arm. "What are you doing?"

"She's ruining my best shoes is what she's doing!" Duchess screeches as she tries to yank the other shoe from my hand, but I hang on to it for dear life.

"Give me that," she grunts as she tries to ply it out of my hands, and I swat at her with the shoe like she's some pesky maskeeto.

"No. Get offa me."

"She threw a shoe at me," Beanie moans.

"Tara, stop it," Tater orders.

The little man dances around the both of us, trying to separate us, and I can still hear Beanie and Talbert laughing, fueling my wrath. Duchess is yelling cuss words at me that I've never heard before, and I swear Tater even threatens to put me over his knee at one point. The clamor is almost deafening.

"What the hell is going on here?" Jax's face staring at us through the now open doorway reflects a mixture of shock and disbelief. Finn's head pokes through underneath his arm; his wide eyes filled with curiosity.

"We could hear you from all the way down the hall," Jax says.

"The girl has gone mad is what's happening here," Duchess squeals as she tries yanking the shoe from my grasp again, but I let it go, and she stumbles, falling back on her arse with a sharp cry.

Tater clucks his tongue in worry as he swiftly pulls her back on her feet. Glaring daggers at my smirking face, she pulls the liberated shoe close to her chest with one hand while trying to smooth her dress with the other.

"I am done here," she says to no one in particular as she tries to fix her disheveled hair that has fallen from its perfectly coiffed bun.

"Duchess, wait," Tater begs as he tries to stop her dramatic exit.

"Let her go," I say, shrugging my shoulders. "Ain't no big loss. She's not much of a teacher anyways."

She whirls on her pointy shoes and comes to stare down her nose at me. "I am a perfectly capable teacher. You, on the other hand, are an idiot."

Did she just call me an idiot? Oh, hell no. Without thinking, I pounce on her and knock her off those damn heels as we both go crashing to the floor. I can hear Tater shouting in dismay and the two in the corner laughing out of control as they yell, "Cat fight!" I ignore them all, my only thought to pull that insulting tongue from her head. I try to get my hands around her neck as I feel her jerk painfully on my hair.

"Ow," I yell as she tugs so hard I expect to see a handful of my hair come away, "You bitch." I raise my fist, intent on giving her the shiner of a lifetime, but I barely graze her chin as I am pulled away and lifted into the air.

"Let me go," I scream, my legs kicking at empty air.

"Calm down, you little spitfire," Jax hisses in my ear as he holds me tight to his chest and pulls me outta reach of the Duchess.

I watch, simmering mad, as Tater helps her to her feet, but Jax still doesn't let me go no matter how much I struggle. She no longer resembles the perfect image she was when we first started out. Her hair hangs in clumps about her shoulders, the sleeve of her dress is ripped a little, and she has lost one of her own shoes so that she is leaning to one side. She looks befuddled, like she's not quite sure what just happened. To be quite honest, I kind of feel the same way. Did I really just attack her?

"If I let you go, will you behave?" Jax murmurs in my ear, and I struggle a bit more, but finally I give in and nod in agreement. He slowly loosens his grip, still not trusting me, but once he sees I'm as good as my word, he puts me down. I move quickly to the side, embarrassed at my overreaction.

"Duchess, are you okay?" Tater is hovering about the woman like a worried hen as she stares at me with wide eyes.

"She attacked me," she says in wonder, and Tater gives a sympathetic nod. "She is truly mad."

I bare my teeth and growl like some devil cat, and she backs away, expecting another attack most likely.

"I am not getting paid enough for this," she sputters, and turning on her good heel, she starts limping from the room. Tater follows behind her, trying to appease her with his words.

"I am so sorry. I cannot possibly understand what the girl was thinking. You must stay; I'm sure Mack will compensate you for the shoes—"

"Boys," she snaps at Beanie and Talbert as she walks by, ignoring Tater's pleading. "Come carry my bags. I am leaving here today."

Even though they come to attention at her command, they both shoot me lopsided grins like I'd somehow made their day. Talbert even sends a sneaky salute my way before he disappears out the door, and it makes me snigger.

"Glad you find it so funny," Jax says. He stands with his arms crossed, legs spread, and looks at me with such stern disapproval that I have to turn my head so he doesn't see my sudden smile. "Mack is going to be furious."

My grin disappears, and my stomach drops. He's right. Mack is gonna be pissed.

"She started it," I whine in my own defense. "She kept insultin' me. She called me an idiot."

"And that gave you the right to attack her? I'm starting to think she is right; quite possibly, you are mad. What the hell was that? We don't have time for this foolishness, Tara. The party is only two weeks away. We have to be ready, and you have just driven away your trainer."

"Trainer for what?" I snap. "I don't need to learn how to walk in stupid shoes for this plan to work. This whole idea, this whole trainin' is stupid if you ask me. We get in, we rescue Lily and Ben, we get out. Why are we even wastin' our time on this?"

"Mack don't think it's a stupid idea, Tara. And ain't you willin' to try anythin' to help get Ben and Lily back?" Finn asks.

I had forgotten Finn was even there. His words, well, they make me feel real stupid for what I'd just done and more than a little guilty for him having seen me do it.

"You're right, Finn. I *will* do anythin' to get them back. I'm sorry I lost my temper. You shouldn't of had to see that,"

I say.

He shrugs. "She shouldn't have called you an idiot. That wasn't nice either."

Ah, to see things always through the eyes of a child.

"Be that as it may, what are we going to do about our training? If we're going to pull off being Mack's kin at this party, we have to know what we're doing, how to act. This may be our only chance at getting them out. We can't risk getting found out before we even have had a chance to find them," Jax says.

"I know, I know. It just seems like … like we're takin' so long. Who knows what they may be goin' through? What he may be doin' to 'em. I hate waitin'."

"Really? I hadn't noticed," Jax drawls, and I narrow my eyes at his sarcasm. "Well, the first thing you're going to have to do is apologize to Duchess. Mack paid good coin to bring her here, and for you to drive her away … he's not going to be happy."

I shake my head. "I ain't sayin' nuthin' to her. She brought it on herself. I'm not apologizin' for anything." I fold my arms stubbornly.

Jax nods at my words and strokes his chin as he studies me. "Okay, then you need to go tell Mack what you did and why she's leaving. He's in the training room by the way, practicing with his white sword. You know the one that looks like a meat cleaver? Looks like it could chop a man in two with one stroke? Let me know how that goes."

I stare back in defiance but finally drop my shoulders in resignation. "Fine," I say, choosing the lesser of the two evils. "I'll go apologize … but it ain't because I mean it."

Don't know if it was the apology or Mack doubling her payment, but Duchess agrees to stay, much to my chagrin. I think she really does believe me to be mad, though, since she doesn't insult me anymore and keeps eyeballing me like I might jump her at any moment. She has even given up on the idea of the heels, though I think that may have been more of Tater's doing. The torture devices are replaced by a pair of white, flat shoes, so soft to the touch it's almost like wearing nothing. I love the feel of them. "Silk slippers" Tater had called them. I call them relief. They hug my feet perfectly and slide across the floor like I'm floating on clouds. Like my word learning though, I reckon they would be just as useless out in the sand lands, so I didn't want to put too much stock in them. Just another silly thing the city folk had come up with far as I'm concerned.

As impractical as they are, I can't help but run my hands in admiration over the soft material as I wait for Duchess to join me to start our training today. Dancing, she'd said. Like I need to learn how to dance? You just had to move your body to music. It wasn't that hard, really. But I'd promised Mack I would behave and do whatever she asked of me no matter how stupid I thought it to be. Lily and Ben deserve that much of me at least.

She soon arrives with her typical party in tow: Tater, Beanie, and Talbert, but I'm surprised to see Jax with them as well. Is he supposed to be Mack's spy now, making sure I behave and do as I'm told? I'm about to protest his presence when I notice the two idiots are carrying something very strange looking indeed. It's a fair-sized, boxy object with a rounded top and what appears to be a golden horn growing out of it. Very odd.

"Do I even wanna know?" I mutter as they place it with care on a tabletop, Tater hovering anxiously and watching their every move. Impatient, he shoos them away as soon as they finish and starts running his hands lovingly over the box.

"Is this not magnificent? I have not seen one in over twenty years. Not since my dear mother passed on. She owned one of course, back in the day. Her clientele loved the music she had playing all the time. I think some of them came for that purpose alone. She—"

"No way! That thing plays music?" I ask, cutting short Tater's ramblings. Don't need to hear any more stories about his ma that much I do know.

"Oh, yes, and quite beautifully, I might add. It's called a gramophone. Quite the invention, I must say."

"You're pullin' my leg," I say, very much the skeptic. There's no way this thing made music. Where are the flutes or pickstrings or squeeze boxes? This don't look anything like a musical instrument.

"Oh, I assure you, this is quite genuine; no leg pulling on my part," Tater says, and I study their faces to see if anyone is laughing at my expense. Tater's face just spouts excitement while Jax and the two others look as puzzled as I am. Duchess, well, she's just looking impatient as always.

"Come," she says, clapping her hands. "Enough already; let's begin."

From the smaller box that she carries, she pulls out a round, flat object and places it on the gramophone. She then cranks a handle on the side of the box with such fervor that it causes her chest to bounce up and down. So much so that maybe, I'm thinking, she's gonna give herself that shiner after all. Talbert and Beanie nearly fall over each other in their attempt to move closer, so as they can get a better view, and I roll my eyes in disgust. Done cranking, she moves a smaller stick thingy over the now spinning round object and places it carefully. You probably could have knocked me over with a feather as the sounds coming from the horn reach my ears. By the gods, it is music. Tater's not lying.

The beautiful melody washes over me with sounds I've never heard before. What kind of instrument made such a tinkling noise? It reminds me somewhat of a summer rain sprinkling on a tin roof. The music is so soothing, and I soon find myself lost in its peacefulness. But then Duchess starts talking again, breaking the beauty of the moment with her cat screechin' tone.

"So today, we will be learning the basic waltz called the box step. Very easy, very simple, and should suffice to get you through the evening without making you look like complete and utter idiots."

I narrow my eyes at her. Is she insulting me again?

"Jax, if you will be kind enough to join me."

Ah, so that's why Jax is here, he has to train too. Finally. She glides to the center of the room, and Jax joins her, standing in front of her, arms hanging like two dead tree branches at his side, and I snicker at how uncomfortable he looks.

"The waltz is a very smooth dance that travels around the room in a counter-clockwise direction." She points in the direction like we're morons again, making me wish that she was indeed sporting that shiner I'd so desperately wanted to give her.

"It basically consists of three steps. Left foot going forward, step to the side with your right, step back with your left." She demonstrates as she speaks, arms out to an invisible partner.

"There is a rise and fall with this waltz, so when stepping forward, you go down a little, the next two steps, up, up. Like so … one-two-three, one-two-three. Left-right-left, left-right-left. Down-up-up. Down-up-up." She makes it look so easy, but I feel my gut clenching. Why does city dancing have to be so technical?

She stops in front of Jax, and he looks up from studying her feet.

"Arm position as so. Palm to palm," she takes Jax's hand. "Ladies, left hand just below the shoulder, gentlemen, right hand on the shoulder blade. Jax, move slightly to my right, so we can move in harmony. Now, left foot forward … step to the side … back with your left. One, two, three … excellent."

She's right. He is doing amazingly well. How did he learn that so quickly? Guess Sky wasn't wrong when she had called him the best dancer. I start to panic. I can't dance like that. I could barely dance without tripping over my own two feet let alone something like that.

"Tara."

"Huh?" I look up at my name being bellowed.

"I said it's your turn. Come here." Duchess moves aside from Jax's grasp and motions me in with a wave of her hand.

I don't want to. I don't want a repeat of yesterday with everybody laughing at me again. But Finn's words echo in my brain. Ain't I willing to do anything to help Lily and Ben, he'd said. So swallowing my pride, I step into Jax's arms like Duchess had done. Palm to palm, she had said. Left hand on the shoulder. Stand a little to the side so we could move together. So far, so good. Jax smiles down at me.

"You ready?" he asks, and I nod as the music starts playing again.

Left foot forward, well, I try at least, but Jax does the same, and we smack into each other, my forehead banging into his chin.

"Ow," I cry at the same time as he mutters, "Hell, Tara."

I drop my hand from his and rub my forehead. What had I done wrong?

"No, no, no, you both can't lead," Duchess puts her hands on her ample hips and heaves a dramatic sigh.

"You must let Jax lead, girl. If he is stepping left foot forward, then you must start with right foot back."

"Well, why didn't you tell me that?" I snap as I hear the familiar sniggering coming from the two idiots. *Why are they even in here?* I wonder for the umpteenth time as I send a threatening glare their way.

"Because I thought you would know… never mind. Begin again," she says impatiently. "Jax starts with left foot forward, and you counter with right foot back. Remember, one-two-three, one-two-three."

"She didn't tell me that," I whisper at Jax as he takes my hand again. "How was I supposed to know if she didn't say so?"

"I know," he agrees, but I think it's more just to shut me up. "Ready?" he asks once we are in position, and I nod.

The music begins again, and I make sure to step back, counting in my head, *One-two-three, one-two-three.*

"Tara, don't look down at your feet. Chin up; look at your partner. Stop counting and moving your lips. And for the gods' sake, smile. Dancing is supposed to be a pleasure, not a punishment." Duchess's voice scrapes over me like a dull blade, but I do as she says, smiling at Jax through a mouthful of gritted teeth.

"I'd love to dollop some punishment on her right now," I mutter through my fake smile, and he cracks up laughing. His laughter, it relaxes me somewhat. It says to me our dancing together isn't that bad. And it really isn't. Now that we're getting the rhythm down, it's surprisingly easy.

"That's it, that's it. You have it. Now, just follow the room. Whatever the others are doing, just go with the flow," she cries.

"What others?" I question, but Jax takes her words to heart and starts moving me across the floor. The tempo of the music picks up, and he does the same, forcing me to move faster and follow along. We're dancing so fast now we're almost hopping, and I start giggling at our jerky movements.

"Jax," I cry through my laughter. "Slow down."

But that just causes him to go even faster.

"Jax," I protest again, and his laughter joins with mine, throwing off my count. I can't keep the rhythm straight in my head anymore, and my feet miss a step, tangling with his and sending us both sprawling to the floor.

I land flat on my back, and he falls on top of me, his arms planted on each side of me stops his fall, his face hanging just a breath above mine. His laughter makes his eyes sparkle with a thousand pinpoints of light. Those damn eyes. I stare into them, my own laughter catching in my throat. I've never been this close to him before, so close that I realize his eyes are not the truest of blue like I believed them to be. Instead, I can see they're flecked with tiny bits of gray, like storm clouds moving in on a sunny day.

"You're an idiot," I say a little breathlessly, and his eyes crinkle up at the corners.

"Aye, I have called myself that more than once these past few weeks," he says, his voice soft.

I smile at him then and startle at how his face changes. All the laughter fades away, and his eyes darken with some new emotion. He reaches down and touches my parted lips with his fingertips, outlining their shape.

"Has anyone ever told you how pretty you are when you let your guard down and smile?" he says, and I suddenly feel like every breath of air is sucked from my lungs.

My gut starts doing those stupid flip flops again, and my heart starts beating like I'm on the run from some wild wolfling. The way his finger is tracing my lips, well, I'm not quite sure if it's pleasure or pain. Feels like every nerve ending is raw and exposed, and his touch is setting them on fire. I have no idea what's happening, but I do know I don't want it to end.

"Ahem … which one of ya messed up?"

I reluctantly tear my eyes away from Jax to find a pair of dirty, battered boots by my head. Talbert bends over us with inquisitive eyes, his black lips stretched tight in a wide grin.

"Which one of ya messed up? I bet Beanie a week's worth of cleanin' up the big cat's shite that the mistress would be the first to mess up. Was I right?" he asks Jax and then looks back down at me apologetically. "No offense, Mistress. Yer a woman of fine talents but dancin' ain't one of 'em."

"None taken, and yup it was me," I say and can't help but laugh at Talbert's victorious whoops and his little two-step jig.

"Wot I tell ya? Beanie, my boy, get used to bein' the shite shoveler fer a bit."

Normally, that would have pissed me off. But not this time. Not today. I'm still grinning like a fool as Jax pulls me to my feet, his hand holding mine a little longer than necessary before he lets go.

"Back to work?" he suggests, and I shrug, belying the excitement I feel at knowing I would be spending most of my day in his arms.

CHAPTER SEVEN

The Tea Party

❦

I'm truly sick of the word "practice." It just never seems to end. Between the dancing, the sparring, the weaponry, the walking, the table manners, and hell, Tater even had me practicing talking. What the hell is wrong with the way I talk? I know I don't want to end up speaking like him with his big, fancy words that nobody can understand. He'd even taken to calling me his "Eliza Doolittle" at times, whoever the hell that is. Thank gods it hadn't lasted long, though. After of couple of days of him instructing me, "Repeat after me. *Cain't* is not a word. Can't or cannot. *Ain't* is not a word. Isn't or is not," he'd finally given up and told me to play shy and let Jax do all the talking. Fine by me.

I guess it's not all bad though; the practice keeps me busy. Busy enough to keep my mind from driving me crazy with worry for Ben and Lily. Now Jax? That is a whole other story. I have no idea what's happening there. What he'd said to me that day of our fall, the way he'd touched me, well, there's been nothing remotely close to that happening again. Oh, he's still the same Jax, joking and teasing and irritating, but that softer side of him hasn't shown itself no matter how hard I looked for it. There's been no nice words or soft touches. Hell, even when we're dancing, it's almost like he's afraid to hold me too close. I don't know what has changed since our first dance lesson. Had he been playing a game with me, or is it the guilt of Sky that's making him keep his distance? Maybe it doesn't mean nothing at all, and I'm the only one putting any stock into what he'd done. Maybe to him, it was just a simple comment and nothing more. I've got no idea, and I sure as hell haven't found the nerve yet to ask.

The thought of Jax still runs rampant in my head as I lay on the soft, sweet-smelling grass of Mack's back garden, letting the sun's warmth almost lull me asleep. It was one of those rare moments when no one was demanding my attention. No sparring, no dancing, no nothing. Mack was off doing whatever he did. Tater and Duchess had gone into the city in search of some material for costumes for this stupid masquerade party. I wanted nothing to do with that. Beanie and Talbert, I didn't know and didn't care what they were up to as long as they weren't bothering me. It was just me and the boy and the cat. It was nice.

I watch Finn and Cat as they try in vain to catch the little fish jumping in the massive fishpond built in the middle of this "garden." Cat is immersed in the shallow pond up to her belly and waits patiently for her prey. I laugh out loud as one tiny fish seems to jump and brazenly slap Cat on the lips as she nips at it and misses, causing the big black beast's eyes to open wide in disbelief and growl in frustration. I swear sometimes that creature is more human than I am.

I'm unaware the object of my thoughts is anywhere near me until a shadow falls over my face as he blocks out the sun.

"Been looking all over for you," he says as he sprawls beside me on the grass. I turn my face from him and blame the flush rising in my cheeks on the fireball above our heads.

"Well, you found me," I say, pretending I could care less one way or the other. "So why you botherin' me?"

He chuckles softly.

"Is that any way to greet someone who comes bearing gifts?" he says, drawing my attention to him. I sit up. He is indeed carrying something wrapped in a piece of cloth, and I watch as he unwraps it to show me the three lumps of brown … well, I'm not quite sure what it is. But it sure as hell don't look like anything I would call a gift.

"Umm, yeah, I can see why you're eager to share that with me," I say, but he ignores my sarcasm.

"Here, eat it," he says as he tries to shove a dark glob at me.

 I shake my head. "Nuh uh. I ain't eatin' that shite. And that's exactly what it looks like."

He shrugs at me.

"Suit yourself," he says and pops a hunk into his mouth while I watch in disgusted disbelief. Finn has noticed Jax's arrival and comes trotting over to plop himself down between us.

"Oh, gods, is that what I think it is, Jax?" he says eagerly. "Can I have some?"

"Sure," says Jax and hands one hunk to Finn.

Wait, am I missing something here? How come Finn knows what it is but I don't?

"What is that then?" I ask in irritation, but Jax grins at me, showing me his now brown-stained teeth.

"Since you don't want any, you don't need to know. More for us, right, Finn?"

"It's called choc-a-let, least that's what I think Coral called it. She gave me some yesterday, and it's soooooooo good. You gotta try it, Tara."

I reach for the last remaining piece with hesitant fingers, but Jax hauls it out of my reach.

"Nope, too late. You said you didn't want any." He pretends he's gonna eat it himself, but I snatch it outta the cloth.

"Jackass," I say. I raise it to my mouth but stop with it halfway there. "You sure you two ain't lyin' to me? This actually tastes good?"

"Yes, I swear." Jax grins at my distrust. "Now eat it already before it melts all over your fingers."

Too late for that, I notice, so I toss the whole thing into my mouth before I can change my mind. My eyes scrunch up, waiting for some cruel joke to kick in, but as soon the taste touches my tongue, they pop back open in amazement.

"Oh, my gods," I try to say around the melting slice of

heaven in my mouth. "This is ... this is so ... oh my gods."

Why have I never known about this choc-a-let before? The rich, sweet creaminess feels so indulgent and sinful as it melts in my mouth. My pleasure leaves me speechless as I savor every bite, trying to make the taste last longer. Finally, I swallow the delicacy and then lick the remaining traces off my fingers.

"Do you have more?" I ask Jax hopefully, but he shakes his head, grinning as he reaches over and wipes the corner of my mouth with the cloth in his hand.

"See what happens if you trust me a little? I'm full of surprises."

"Aye, well, you're full of something all right," I drawl as I knock the cloth away, and Finn snorts into his hand. Jax scowls at him and then pulls him into a loose headlock, making the boy howl in protest. The ruckus catches Cat's attention. She runs over, fishpond forgotten, and leaps on top of them, trying to get in on the fun. Her waterlogged fur covers them both like some wet blanket, making them yell at her, "Get off!" She does as they say but then does what every wet animal tends to do: she shakes herself dry. Sitting behind the two boys, I'm pretty much protected from the onslaught of water, spittle, and mud that otherwise coats the two in front of me.

Oh, my gods. I start laughing. I can't help it. The look of disgust on their faces, it cracks me up something fierce. I laugh so hard tears roll down my cheeks, and I gotta hold my stomach it's hurting so bad.

"Oh, you think this is funny, do you?" Jax drawls dangerously low as he peers at me through narrowed eyes.

Since I truly can't talk right now, I only nod.

"Yeah? I'll show you funny," he says.

I should have known what he was up to from the dangerous look on his face. Before I can run, he scoops me up in his arms and starts heading for the pond.

"Jax! Don't you dare," I shriek, knowing what's coming.

He keeps going, ignoring my frantic kicking and screaming.

"Put me down. Stop!"

He dangles me over the pond.

"Put me down or else, jackass," I say.

"Or else what? What you gonna do to me, Tara?"

His question is innocent enough, but it makes my body quiver as he stares at me. My laughter dies away as I realize my arms are twined tightly around his neck, and I can feel his heart bumping frantically against mine, making it feel like one single beat. My fingers itch to run through his wet hair and wipe the glistening water droplets from his skin.

"Well? What you gonna do to me?" he says a little lower this time, and his eyes stare into mine, full of suggestion.

I feel my breath catch in my throat. "Jax," I protest softly.

"Tara," he mocks.

"Argh!" The scream leaves my lips as we both hit the water, and I swallow some of the foul stuff before I manage to sit up, sputtering.

"What the—?" Jax is taken as much by surprise as I am by the cold dunk. Finn is bent over at the edge of the pond, slapping his knee and laughing his fool head off. The little stink turd had pushed us both in.

"Now that," he says in between hysterical bouts of

laughter and pointing at us, "that's funny."

"You little shite head!" Jax bellows, and before Finn can run, he's grabbed by the ankle and yanked into the pond with us, his startled gasp at the cold water quickly followed by squeals of laughter.

"Take that,' Jax teases, slamming his palm down flat on the water, causing it to splash Finn in the face. The boy retaliates by grabbing a handful of mud from the pond's murky bottom and splatters us both, starting an all-around water fight. It's not long before Cat jumps in, and our shrieks at almost being squished by the massive beast echo all over the back gardens.

"What the hell?" Mack roars as he comes barreling through the garden, concern written all over his face and his hand hovering above his shooter. He stops short at what he sees, shaking his head in shock. For some reason, he doesn't look as amused as the rest of us.

"Really? And to think the future of our rebellion may lie in the hands of you three idiots. Get your damned arses outta my fish pond and inside to freshen up. Have you all forgotten that we have to attend high tea this afternoon? You better learn to take this seriously, or we will fail with this plan of ours. Do you understand what I'm saying?"

Shite, I did forget about the tea we had to go to. Tea of all things. Apparently, our living at Mack's was becoming public knowledge now amongst the island's elite, and people were getting curious. They were asking to meet the captain's kin. As much as none of us wanted to do this, Mack included, we knew we couldn't keep turning down the invites. It would only arouse more suspicion, and we can't have anyone asking questions.

Mack stomps off without waiting for an answer as we all look around at each other with sheepish expressions. He was right; as much as this idea of afternoon tea is stupid, it was also a test of what we had learned so far. Being able to fool these people into thinking we belonged may make all the difference in our plan succeeding, so I try to stay serious and hold it in, but I can't help but laugh when Jax crosses his eyes and sticks out his tongue at Mack's back.

"I heard that," Mack bellows over his shoulder. "And I said *move!*"

We don't dare disobey. We move.

———•———

I … can't … even. This is how these people spend their days? Sitting in overstuffed, over-perfumed, sweltering rooms pretending like they're all so interested in each other and the city's problems but really are there just to criticize what the other is wearing. If I have to hear one more story about how some missus was dressed for tea last week, I'm gonna scream.

I cover my yawn with a hand and pull at the neck of my new outfit Coral had dressed me in this afternoon. Ugh. I want to get this over with so I can get out of these suffocating clothes. Why is it so damned hot in here? And why can't I be sitting with the men? At least they looked like they're talking about interesting stuff. I can even hear Jax chuckling ever so often. But noooooo, I'm stuck here with … what are these women's names again? The old gramma, her name is Missus Camon, and the other one—the one who has been eyeballing

Jax all afternoon like he's a slab of meat—is Missus Bots. No, Bodes. That's it. Apparently, she's a new widow, according to the gramma, but from the way she's staring and flirting with Jax, I reckon she's trying to remedy that real quick. And I'm pretty sure Jax was introduced earlier as my betrothed, but it doesn't seem to make any difference to the slag.

"Would you care for some more tea, Miss Sara?" I don't even realize the old gramma is talking to me at first. I must have blocked out their irritating droning about this one's terrible dress and that one's awful hair. Finn bumps my knee with his, bringing me back to the present and making me remember that by saying Sara, she's referring to me. Mack had insisted on us not using our real names in public just to be on the safe side. Sara, Jackson, and Quinn had been the names recorded at the wall to Skytown, so that's who we are now.

"Yes, please. That would be lovely," I say to the gramma, remembering Tater's "correct response" training. She bends over, her blue-veined hands reaching for the most delicate glass teapot I've ever seen. It's a pale yellow with flowers etched all around the base and up the spout. I woulda been afraid to touch it. I was used to tea being made in a tin pot over a campfire. I somehow doubt these women have ever seen a campfire, let alone a tin pot, in their lives.

"Another sweet cake, boy?"

Finn's eyes light up with delight as he mutters, "Yes please, ma'am," and then proceeds to stuff his mouth while I watch on, annoyed.

I would like to have another one too, but since I'm not offered, I figured it would be impolite just to take it. Stupid city people and their society rules.

"So, my dear, I assume you have all received your invite to this year's social event?" gramma says to me, but I just stare back at her, puzzled.

"Huh?" I say, but another nudge from Finn has me stammering to cover it. "Uh, s-sorry, ma'am?"

"The Prezedant's masquerade ball of course. Surely any kin of the captain has received an invitation?"

"Oh, aye. I mean, yes, we did," I say, taking a huge sip of the still hot tea so as I don't have to talk no more. It causes me to burn the roof of my mouth all the way down to my gut. I start coughing, and Finn pounds my back. I hope my choking will somehow stop the questions but no such luck. She simply waits for me to catch my breath and then goes right on talking like I didn't almost just die.

"Oh, isn't it exciting? We all look forward to this every year. He throws such marvelous parties, doesn't he, Clara dear?" Gramma addresses the slag who can't take her eyes off Jax.

What is wrong with that woman? She's worse than a cat in heat. True, Jax did clean up real nice. With his hair all slicked back, and the whiskers on his face cut down to just stubble, and wearing that new shirt and trousers, he looks like he fits in here. *More so than me,* I think as I pull at my neckline again, coughing some more. But still, doesn't that woman have any sense of decency? I want to yank her ogling eyes right out of her head.

"Wonderful indeed," the slag answers, the corner of her mouth turning up in a weird sorta grin. "Especially the extracurricular activities."

Both women laugh at this. I have no idea what they're talking about, but I got a strange feeling if I did, I wouldn't find it as funny.

"True, Clara dear; they are quite enjoyable for you young ones at least. I'm afraid I'm a bit too long in the tooth now for that sort of thing. I'm reduced to having to live vicariously through you now, my dear." The old woman says it with a smile, but I swear I can see an evil glint in her eye. Like somehow she resents that fact and if she could suck the younger woman's life force out of her, she would do it in an instant. It makes me shiver.

"That one will be my first conquest," the slag murmurs, still eyeing Jax.

Gramma nudges her and ever so slightly nods her head my way, reminding her of my presence. The dark eyes finally flick my way, staring me over before dismissing me. She doesn't elaborate on her earlier statement, but her look pisses me off something fierce. It says to me that she doesn't consider me threat enough to stand in her way. I'm not that daft. I can tell she has a hankering for Jax, and she's not about to let me stop her. My hand tightens on my teacup, and I have to stop myself from throwing the hot liquid right into her slag face. *We'll see about that,* I think.

Almost like the old woman can sense what I'm thinking, she changes the subject.

"Tell me, my dear, who is your dressmaker?"

"My dressmaker?" I repeat stupidly and then clear my throat again. I don't have a clue how to answer that.

"Surely, you have started on your dress by now? Who's making it? Is it Gormichi or Donneto? Oh, I do hope it's

Donneto. I do so prefer her workmanship over that atrocious beast Gormichi."

How the hell do I answer that? Is it a trick question? Sweat beads my upper lip as I rack my brain. *Just pick one, you idiot*, I think.

"Neither," I find myself saying. "I had my dress brought from Southpoint." I smile smugly to myself at my clever answer.

"Ohhhhh Southpoint! They have beautiful designers as well. Who was it? Do tell," the gramma demands.

Shite. I'm saved by none other than the slag who, bored with our conversation, jumps to her feet and glides effortlessly across the room in her heels. Makes me hate her even more.

"My dear, Jackson, please let me show you the gardens." The smile that lights up her face actually makes her annoyingly pretty in a way. "The gardens of House Camon are a legend here in Skytown, almost rivaled to the Prezedant's himself."

I glare at Jax across the room. *Don't you even dare!* I yell at him in my head, but he seems to be charmed by the woman and oblivious to her intentions.

"I would enjoy that, ma'am, thank you," he says, and my anger at his stupidity boils over.

"So would I," I pipe up, setting my teacup down with a loud clank. "And Fin… Quinn too, wouldn't you Quinn? As a matter of fact, I think we all could do with a bit of fresh air. And I'm sure no one is more suitable to show us around the gardens than Missus Camon herself. After all, she would know 'em the best."

I smile sweetly at the old gramma, and to my surprise, she agrees with me.

"That's a wonderful idea. Shall we?" she says and gets to her feet.

I'm pretty pleased with myself and the crimp I put in the she-devil's plans with Jax, but if looks could kill, let's just say they would be digging a hole in that garden for me right about now.

———————

Well, Missus Bodes didn't lie about the garden's legend. As soon as we enter, we're greeted by a wave of smells and colors. The air is perfumed with lavender and grass and other stuff I can't quite make out, but it has to be coming from the sea of flowers. The garden floor is ablaze with shades of red and white and purple. Unfamiliar pale pink trees surround us on either side, creating pathways through the garden. Occasional orange trees dot the landscape, the fruit hanging heavy on the branches and some of it already lying rotting on the ground underneath. The beauty of it all is beyond compare, yet I can't help but be angered by the wastefulness of it all.

Missus Bodes laid claim to Jax as soon as we entered the grounds, and they now amble ahead of us, arm in arm. She leans in every now and again to explain or point out an area of interest to Jax, her chest lying heavy on his arm. Seriously, does he not feel that? Why don't he at least try to pull away? Peeved at her forwardness and Jax's stupidity, I send Finn ahead to pepper them with questions and the parting words of "Don't hold nuthin' back." I can hear her exasperation in her answers as Finn starts questioning her about everything and anything he sees, and I grin to myself. Good boy.

Mack and the gramma totter slowly behind us, which leaves me stuck with the tour guide of the gramma's better half. Mister Camon is a nice enough old coot, and with his neatly trimmed gray whiskers and watery blue eyes, he kinda reminds me of Grada. Even though I know he's a member of the Prezedant's Army, I can't help but find myself liking him against my better judgment. He doesn't say much to me, content to let all the others do the talking, but answers me politely every time I do speak.

"What is this flower?" I say as I point to the beautiful, blood-red blossoms growing on a row of bushes to our right. I touch it lightly and am amazed at the soft, satiny texture of its petals.

"A rose," he answers with his old man voice voice. "A beautiful flower indeed, but be careful. Its beauty hides many sharp thorns."

I kinda draw my hand back at his warning as I can now see the hidden thorns underneath. He approaches the bush, snaps one of the blossoms off, and tucks it behind my ear. I'm immensely glad for Coral's trick of darkening the white stripes in my hair with tea. Old man or not, I sure don't want him seeing those.

"You are from Southpoint, yet you do not know what a rose is? It has been numerous years since I've been there, but if memory serves me correctly, I'm sure they have just as many beautiful gardens as we do here in Skytown."

The eyes I had considered weak and watery earlier now contain a shrewdness that I hadn't noticed before, and it chills me. I choose my words carefully.

"Yes, they do have beautiful gardens, but I'm afraid I'm not one much for flowers. Learnin' names don't interest me much. I would rather be spendin' my time in the barns or with the animals. Thank you for the gift." I touch the rose in my hair and smile at him. He inclines his head at me slightly, and we continue walking.

"Captain MacKenzie informs me you are his niece and the little one his nephew. His sister's children?" he says.

"That's correct," I say. A story we had already agreed upon.

"Hmmmm, you do not carry much family resemblance."

My laugh is light. "No, we do not. I look like our ma while Quinn looks like our pa."

"And neither of you bear any resemblance whatsoever to our good Captain," he says.

I swallow nervously and plaster a smile on my face. "Not true. Put an eye patch on me, and you wouldn't be able to tell us apart." I laugh at my own joke, but old man Camon don't even crack a smile. I try to distract him from his line of questioning. "Your gardens are very beautiful. And are those cages I see down there below us? Do you keep animals, too?"

I don't give him time to answer. I yell out to the boy, eager to get away from the questions.

"Quinn, they have animals! Let's go see." And the boy rushes ahead of me down the 'crete steps to the lower garden. He beats me there, of course, but draws up short at the first cage in front of him. I can see it has to be a larger animal, a brown ball of fur huddled in the corner of the cage. Can't quite tell what it is, though, but as I get closer, I can see Finn backing slowly away. What kind of animal is it to scare the boy?

"Tara," he whispers as I touch his shoulder, and I look around to make sure no one noticed his slip with my name, but the others aren't close enough yet.

"Careful, Quinn, you—" My words catch in my throat. The brown ball of fur has turned in its cage, and a pair of tortured eyes stare out at us from the barred prison. Only it's not the eyes of some wild animal. These eyes are very much human.

I stare back, not understanding if I'm seeing correctly. What the hell is this? The mutie, maybe recognizing our wide-eyed shock, starts up a keening that soon has Finn covering his ears with his hands. I'm too dumbfounded to do the same, even though the sound is like a knife piercing through to my brain. I can only keep staring back as it makes its miserable sounds.

"Shut up!" Mister Camon smacks the bars of the cage with his walking stick as he approaches, and the mutie immediately goes silent as it cowers back into his corner. I feel like I should say or do something, but my shock is far outweighing my indignation at the moment.

"This is Horax. One of the best arena fighters you will ever get to see. We were very lucky to have been able to buy him and quite cheaply too, I might add. Though now I can see why his old owners sold him at such a bargain price. His noise can be very distracting to say the least."

They keep muties locked in a cage in their garden? What kinda madness is this? The creature doesn't make any more noise, but the look he's giving me starts a small flicker of flame burning in the pit of my stomach.

My eyes search the other cages. There are at least five

or six more, and they're all filled with the same pathetic-looking occupants.

"You have mutants in cages," I say, like hearing it out loud is the only way to get my brain to accept it as reality.

"Not just any mutants; these are all top-notch arena champions."

He says it with such pride, and I can feel the slight flame starting to burn a little stronger. This is not the time to show my Chi, but I can't seem to stop the boil in my stomach from happening.

"You have mutants in cages," I say it louder this time, and the old man regards me with a look that says he thinks I may just be a little bit crazy. Maybe I *am* giving off the crazy vibe because Mack arrives at that moment, takes one look at me, and starts saying his goodbyes. Jax suddenly shakes Missus Bodes off like some damned sand biter, grabs my arm, and starts ushering me outta the gardens.

"Jax, they have people in cages," I whisper loudly, but he shushes me.

"Not now, Tara. Hold it in. Your hair is starting to glow. The white is showing through. You need to hold it in. Quinn!" he barks over his shoulder, and Finn comes scampering to my other side.

I don't know what excuse Mack gives them for our abrupt departure, and I truly don't care. I cannot stand to be in this garden or around these cruel people for one more moment. The look in that mutie's eyes, the suffering and misery. How could they? The memory of the cold-blooded yelling and the screams we'd heard coming from the arena on our first night here, it all comes flooding back to me.

"Jax, we have to help 'em," I say suddenly, trying to pull away, but he doesn't let go.

"We can't do anything right now, Tara," he hisses in my ear. "Other than get you out of here."

"But—"

"Not now. We'll do something, I promise. Just don't argue with me right now, okay?" And I nod at his words. He promised, so I believe him.

With the gods as my witness, we will do something.

CHAPTER EIGHT

The Masquerade

———•◆•———

I t's finally here: the Thirty-First. Everything we'd done this past few weeks, the plan to rescue Lily and Ben, it all hinges on today. We'd gone over the plan a hundred times. Over and over, discussing and analyzing everyone's part.

There are seven of us going. Me, Mack, and Jax, we're the inside people getting a layout of the estate—every room and corner. Our goal is to find the underground cells in the lower levels of the estate. Mack's inside man had already given us a basic layout of where the cells are located. With a little luck, we could get to them no problem. If Ben and Lily are being held there in the estate at all, then it makes sense that's where we will find them.

Talbert, Beanie, and Riven—Mack's "servants"—are to patrol the outside under the guise of taking care of the carriage and horses. Their job is to scope out every nook and cranny of the grounds, trying to formulate the best escape route in case our plan went awry. They will mark all the guard posts and take care of the guards if necessary.

Tater had gotten himself a spot on the entertainment staff with Mack's help. The original storyteller hired for the task had found himself suddenly and violently ill-disposed, so Mack had thrown Tater's name as a fill-in. His job is to deliver some nightweed and two costumes to Mack's inside man. He, in turn, would make sure the nightweed found its way into the cell guards' supper. Each evening watch consisted of two guards, and they are fed from the kitchens at exactly the same time every day. Nightweed works quickly and is long-lasting. Once the guards are out, we will have a two to three-hour window of time to search the lower levels.

We are to wait for Tater's signal that it's a go. If everything has fallen into place and the spy has successfully delivered the nightweed and costumes we need, then Tater's story will be Sinbad and the Seven Lands. Any other story means the plan has failed. At the signal, me, Jax, and Mack will sneak out of the party. I'm to remain on watch outside of the cells while the other two are to steal the cell keys and go in to find Ben and Lily. My job is to distract any stray guard that wanders our way with my "feminine wiles." Well, that was the original idea, but after seeing me practice those said wiles, Mack had finally decided I should just pretend to see a mouse, scream really loud to alert them, and fake faint. Sounds good to me.

Once we have Ben and Lily dressed in the extra costumes and masks, we'll just casually walk them out of there along with the rest of the party guests and drive them away in the carriage. Simple enough. Now, we just need all the pieces to fall exactly into place liked planned. And for the gods to be truly on our side. A lot can go wrong. I'm not gonna lie; it worries me something fierce.

———✦———

My innards clench in knots, but not sure if it's to do with our plan or the image staring back at me from the gilded mirror Coral had pushed me in front of. Who is this strange-looking creature staring back at me? The image moves when I do, but surely, it can't be me. The long, black hair looked like mine, but the white stripes are gone, hidden again by the tea, and the curls hanging over my shoulders are a result of her tying my wet hair in strips of cloth and leaving them for hours to dry. The rest of my hair she has tied up into a loose knot on the top of my head. The colors that adorn my face are the Duchess's doing. I'd fought tooth and nail to not let her paint me. I'll be wearing a half mask. What's the point? But Coral insisted I wouldn't fit into the elite crowd otherwise, so against my wishes, I let her have her way. I have to admit, the results are … startling to say the least. What I'd always thought to be my drab, colorless gray eyes now actually seem to sparkle from the colors she'd placed on my lids and lashes. My normally sun-darkened skin is made a shade lighter from the gunk she'd dusted on, and my cheeks shone with the palest of pink, like a constant blush.

My lips still sting from whatever she'd rubbed them with, but they look plump and red. Duchess's warning of not to lick them is hammered into my head. I look like a totally different person, and I'm itching to rub every last drop of this shite off my face.

But that isn't the worst of it. I've been squeezed once again into a form-fitting dress so tight that the color in my cheeks isn't from the powder alone. Does she seriously want me to wear this? It isn't the shockingly bright blue color or the fact that it clung to me so tight I can barely breathe that's the problem. It's more of the fact that there's so little of it. I think the ladies of the ill house wear more clothing than this.

Oh, the bottom of it is fine. In fact, the bottom has enough material I could probably make another dress. The silky layers swirl around my legs with a soft swishing sound every time I move. And it's roomy enough to hide the knives that I'd strapped to my thighs, much to Coral's horror. She'd almost fainted when she caught me doing that earlier. But there's no way I'm not taking some sort of protection with me. No, the problem isn't with the bottom of the dress; it's the top half that's bothering me. The top half, well, I use the term "half" loosely. There are no sleeves to begin with. The dress is held up with these two tiny straps that tie around my neck and leave my shoulders totally bare. And without my flower necklace hanging there, my chest feels naked. The impossibly tiny waist of this torture device called a corset squeezes my own waist so tight that it has no other choice but to move up and push my normally small chest out, so it looks almost doubled in size. No wonder Duchess always looks like she's gonna fall outta her dress at any moment.

Now, I know how she felt. And I've come to understand why she's always so irritable. Wearing a corset all the time would be enough to piss anybody off.

I try in vain to push my overflowing chest back inside the scant material but to no avail. I feel like I'm about to smother myself. Do they seriously expect me to go like this? As if in answer to my unspoken question, Duchess approaches me from behind and covers my shoulders with a gauzy, light wrap, her arms encircling my neck to clip it at the front. Thank the gods. The wrap may be almost see-through, but it's better than nothing.

"Now remember, any refined lady in the Prezedant's circle will be elegant and poised. No shows of temper or sharp-tongued remarks no matter what you see. Do not engage in prolonged conversation. Your accent is a dead giveaway you do not belong. Stay by Jax's side; let him do the talking."

The way she says accent almost sounds like an insult but I don't let it bother me. I'm too thrown off by her tone. She is giving me advice, and she sounds concerned. Is she actually worried about us? About me? We'd gotten along a little better these past two weeks, but I've had no indication she was invested in what we're doing. I reckoned all she was interested in was her payment. But as I study her preoccupied face, I realize I may have been wrong. She steps around me and studies me, her head tilted to the side.

"You do look the part. Your dancing will pass. Anything strange you may do they'll probably just pass it off as you being from away. I've done all I can do. Just don't do anything … strenuous. Mack has promised me that dress as part of my payment, and I intend to take him up on the offer. I want it back in one piece."

She's concerned over the dress? I should have known. I'm about to put my sharp tongue to good use when she speaks again.

"And please, promise me you'll watch out for Tater? He is indeed an old friend. I owe him much, and I do not wish any harm to befall him."

If I didn't know any better, I'd swear there were tears in her eyes. Before I can tell for sure, she turns away from me, busying herself with packing up her pots of colors and powders. My biting retort dies on my lips. She truly did care for the half man. I hadn't realized they were so close. I find myself wondering what their connection is. They must have a hell of a history if it has the ability to change her from the unfeeling, coin-hungry witch she normally is into an actual human being. Maybe after this is over, I'll find out.

Coral is a bit more forthcoming in her praise. She looks at me with a beaming smile, her hands clasped to her chest as she studies her handiwork.

"Oh, my gods. You look beautiful, Miss. A true queen fit for any ball. Oh, don't forget this. You are so going to enjoy your evening."

She rushes at me with the sparkling blue half mask, the most important part of this stupid costume.

Enjoy my evening? Not exactly the words I would use. She seems to be forgetting that this is a rescue quest, not a true ball. I almost wish it was just some stupid party to worry about. Maybe then my heart wouldn't be beating out of my chest, and I wouldn't feel like I'm gonna retch up my supper. And the evening is only beginning.

Mack and Jax and Finn wait for me at the bottom of the stairs, and I almost bolt at the sight of them standing there. I feel like such an impostor in this costume. *I cain't do this,* I think frantically. I can't pull this off. I halfway turn, about to run when Jax looks up at me, and I'm immobilized by his mere presence. He's dressed in black trousers and long-tailed coat. The startling white, high-collared shirt is stretched across his broad chest and offsets his sun-kissed skin, making it appear even darker. His unruly hair has been closely cut and shaped, every hair in place. The prickly stubble I'm used to seeing is now gone, replaced by a clean-shaven face, enhancing his square jaw and the little dent in his chin. Shizen, he looks damn good. I feel my jaw drop and quickly snap it shut, the embarrassing heat rolling over me in waves.

Stop starin', I chide myself, but I can't help it. He looks so damn good. I try to tear my eyes away, but I can't. They lock with his as we simply stare at each another.

Oh, gods, what is he thinkin'? I wonder. *I look stupid; I know it. This whole getup is stupid. What was I thinkin'? I ain't got the right amount of chest to pull off this dress.*

A thousand self-doubts rush through my head, but I still don't take my eyes off his face. If only he would say something.

"Tara! Tara!" Finn's voice cuts through my frantic thoughts, and my eyes finally leave Jax.

"What?" I yell down the stairs to Finn.

"I said you look pretty and be careful. Didn't you hear me? I said it like three times. You gone deaf or something?"

"I heard you," I say, cutting off his rambling. I don't need Jax knowing how much he's rattled me.

"Well, why didn't you answer me then? Geez, last time I tell you that you look nice," he says, glowering at me.

"Sorry," I mutter, slowly descending down the steps to keep from tripping over the dress and silently thanking the gods that I'm not wearing heels. Finn is still glaring at me as I finally reach the bottom, but then his face cracks and he flies at me, his scrawny arms going tight around my waist.

"Please promise me you'll be careful, Tara. I don't want anything bad to happen to you or Jax or Mack…"

His words break off, and I can feel his skinny little body trembling with emotion.

"Hey, it's okay. We'll be fine. You ain't gotta be worryin' about us. It's just a party. Nuthin' dangerous about that, right?" I say as I pry his arms from my waist. I bend down to his level, so I can look him in the eye. "Besides, you know I'm super strong. You've seen it. Between my New Blood powers and Mack's training, the Prezedant or his stupid soldiers don't stand a chance. It's them you should be worried about," I tease, and he lets loose a shaky laugh.

"Now, you and Cat behave yourselves. Coral said she would make you some sweet biscuits if you're real good. Just make sure you save some for me and Ben, all right?"

He nods at me as he wipes his sleeve across his nose, and I ruffle his hair. Cat sticks her big head in between us and nuzzles Finn's arm, trying to comfort him, and I give her a quick scratch behind the ears.

"Take care of him, girl," I whisper at her, and the blue tongue gives my hand a quick lick of agreement.

"We should go," Mack says, and I stand back up.

Jax meets my eyes again, but his soft look from earlier

is gone, making me think that I'd imagined the naked admiration I thought I saw.

"You have your mask?" he asks, all business now, and I nod at him as I hold it up. His is nowhere as fancy as mine. It's just plain white, and he jams it into the inside pocket of his jacket.

"Okay," he says, looking from Mack to me. "Let's do this."

And my rolling gut threatens to spill my supper out over the fancy dress once again.

—◆—

I take one look at the massive house upon our arrival and feel the bottom drop outta my stomach. Shizen. It looks like the medieval castles I'd read about in Lily's picture books. How in the gods' names will we ever be able to find Ben and Lily in a place this size? It made Sanctuary look like a shanty in comparison. And the lights. The oversized palace is lit up like a thousand stars in the night sky. Lights in different shades of blues and greens and reds sparkle, and I'm unable able to tear my eyes away. Even the pathway and stairs under our feet from the carriage to the house is lit with the wondrous colors. Going to be real hard to get away under the cover of darkness when it's lit up like the middle of the day.

But that's only the beginning of the curious oddities this place has to offer. At every point you looked, your senses are assaulted with images. People are spread out everywhere over the lit-up grounds, watching the festivities being carried out under tents of all colors and sizes, almost like the marketplace stalls in Littlepass. There are jugglers tossing and catching knives of all things. I'd seen that sorta thing done with stones before but never with knives. Grown men dressed as fools riding in circles on one-wheeled, metal contraptions, kind of like what I'd seen in the underground iron city. Then there are others who appear to be swallowing long, metal swords and some breathing fire. What the hell kinda night terror place is this? Are they people or monsters? People don't breathe fire. I reckon Mack feels my panic since he places one hand under my arm to calm me and whispers in my ear, "It's all tricks, Tara. Gimmicks used to amuse and entertain. It's all harmless."

Harmless? I have a feeling here, in the Prezedant's territory, there's no such thing.

I lose count of the number of guards we pass by, but at seeing there's so many of them, my gut burns with fear. Having to walk Lily and Ben back past them all, whether in costume or not, is a risk. I can only hope there are way too many people here for them to even notice two extra guests. As much as I don't want to think about it, all the doubts about our plan come bubbling back up.

I'm grateful Mack does all the talking. I simply paste on a wooden smile and nod as they welcome me. We show our invitation with every bunch of guards we walk past until finally we're ushered into a large, cavernous room.

This room is the epitome of luxury. White marble floors are spread out before us. They are shined to perfection, making them look more like glass, and with so many lights sparkling off them, it kinda hurts my eyes. It must have taken hours for his people to make them shine that way. Statues line the room in all different sizes and poses, but all of the same man. The Prezedant sure does think highly of himself, seems like. Two grand stairways flank both sides of the room, and right smack in the middle of them is the biggest hearth and fire I've ever seen. A number of people lounge in the comfy looking chairs in front of the fire, and their laughter echoes around the large room. The stone hearth is built to reach the upper floors, and the walls on either side of it are lined with so many paintings there's barely any wall to see. The paintings are a strange collection. There's one that consists of a bunch of long-haired, bearded men in robes sitting around a long table, having supper looks like. Next to that is one of an old gramma and grada standing in fronta their cabin holding a giant pitch fork. What an odd thing to paint. Maybe they were the Prezedant's ma and pa?

My eyes are pulled up even higher, and I crane my neck to get a better view. The ceiling above us isn't really a ceiling at all but a glass dome so as you can see straight through to the night sky. A glass roof. Out in the sand lands, that roof wouldn't have lasted a week. It's as pretty as it is impractical. A thousand stars sparkle back at us through the amazing structure, and I find myself fervently hoping one of the sparkling bodies is Grada, watching over us and keeping us safe. Thinking this somehow makes me feel better.

A young man dressed in white approaches me and touches my shoulders ever so slightly.

"Your wrap, Miss?"

My wrap? What about it? He looks at me expectantly. Does he want me to take it off? I glance at Mack, and he nods at me. Gritting my teeth, I undo the ties, and the young man takes my covering. A cold shiver passes over me, but whether it's caused by the night air on my shoulders or the look of appreciation in Jax's eyes as they roam over me before he quickly looks away, I'm not sure. A slight smile touches my lips. *Take that, slag,* I think.

I reckon the Prezedant has a weakness for shiny gold baubles just as much as statues of himself since the grand ballroom we are ushered into next is awash with them. Everything is gold, from the doors to the statues to the fancy electric lights hanging from the ceiling, bathing the room in a yellow glow. The room is also full of men and women, decorated in an array of colors, feathers, beads, and bangles. Each one is dressed in the finest of materials, though some of the dresses make mine look modest in comparison to their skimpiness. One woman walks by, and her dress is so sheer I swear I can see most of her lady parts. Her mask covers more than her dress. Talk about no sense of decency.

The sight of them all, shizen, even the smell of them all is overpowering. Their fancy body oils and perfumes hang so heavy in the air I find it hard to breathe. Everyone seems to be wearing the same kinda masks we are; the disguises do nothing to hide the undercurrent of excitement buzzing throughout the room. You can almost feel the frenzied energy like a pulse.

To my surprise, a young girl no more than thirteen or so born years approaches us immediately. She, too, is dressed in pristine white just like the boy out front, right down to the boots on her feet. Not a scuff on her. She doesn't look at me at all as she offers a silver platter to me, her head bowed in obedience and maybe fear. I can't decide what. I study the tray offered in my direction. It's filled with a bunch of pale vials of silvery liquid. Curious. Figuring the thing to do is take the offering, I reach out only to have my hand grabbed away by Mack. I reckon he doesn't want me taking it, but to cover his panic from everyone else, he affectionately pats the back of my hand and draws me closer to his side.

"Trust me, Tara, that is something you do not want to indulge in," he whispers in my ear, but he is still smiling, belying the urgent warning he's sending my way.

I give a slight nod to let him know the warning is noted. No taking the silvery drink. Got it.

"Thank you, but not now, little one," I say to the girl, and she starts as if not used to being spoken to with kindness.

She glances up, her expression hesitant, and I'm gut-punched at how her little heart-shaped face reminds me so much of my kin, Jane.

"What's your name?" I ask, and panic spreads across her pale face and she darts off like a little mouse suddenly confronted by a starving cat. What did I say?

I watch her hurry past others dressed the same as her, and I realize they are young'uns too. All of them. In fact, every person in the room that isn't wearing a mask is a young'un. They are all dressed in the same identical white outfits and carrying platters filled with those pink vials or tall glasses containing a golden liquid. As I watch them serving the brightly dressed patrons, I understand the role they fill. They're servants, captured or bought through flesh trading, no doubt. Innocents, here to tend to the needs of the elite. The thought of that bothers me something fierce, and I can feel that familiar spark shoot through my blood, but as if Jax can sense everything going through my head, he grabs my other hand.

"Let it go," he says through the fake smile plastered on his face, and I can see why.

A gaggle of half-dressed women treat us to intense scrutiny. The dress the woman in the front wears barely contains her body, and her bulgy parts fall out wherever they can over the tight confines. She flips up her mask, and I feel the familiar, coal-black eyes rake me over dismissively and then move on to Jax with interest. Missus Bodes. She heads towards us, and I can feel Mack and Jax stiffen beside me.

"Captain Mackenzie," she drawls in a silky voice. "I'd recognize that one beady eye anywhere. And I would definitely recognize you, my dear Jackson."

"Good evening, Mistress Bodes, a pleasure as always." Mack's tone suggests anything but, and I find myself prickling at her rudely overlooking me.

"Good *evening*," I say loudly, taking care to pronounce it like Tater had taught me with the "ing" on the end. Didn't matter. I could have told her to go suck a rotten egg; she's not the least bit interested in what I'm saying. She flicks her eyes my way for a brief moment, gives a stiff nod, and then turns her attention back to the men.

"I'm surprised we didn't see you last week, Captain Mackenzie, what with the investigation and all at the Camon House."

Mack's surprise is genuine as he stares at her.

"I'm sorry, I have been occupied elsewhere. What investigation is that?"

"Why, the attack on their gardens of course. Apparently, someone broke into their gardens and let loose all their caged muties. It was quite the uproar; the Camons are quite distraught. That garden cost them a small fortune I heard," she says, like it's the news of the century. Mack's eyes glance my way as I fiddle with an imaginary hangnail, and Jax suddenly finds his shoes very interesting.

"Did they find the ones responsible for that horrendous crime?" Mack says, and Missus Bodes shrugs her shoulders, her eyes now fixated on Jax.

"Who cares? Keeping trolls in your garden is so last year." She waves her hand at Mack, the conversation obviously done.

Good, I think. *Don't wanna be talking about that right now anyways.* Although from the look on Mack's face, the conversation between us is far from over. I'm gonna have to fess up to him about what me and Jax had done sooner or later. As much as I don't regret what we did, later sounds better to me.

"I was waiting very impatiently for you tonight, my dear." Her strange, over-bright eyes travel over Jax as if she truly wanted to gobble him up. Her gloved hands grip his arms and move up and down in a way much too familiar for my liking.

"Oh, I had forgotten those muscles you hide under your clothing. You are so strong! And that little dent in your chin, I did not notice that before. It is very alluring. Do you dance, darling?"

Darling? I have to bite my tongue to stay quiet when all I want to do is snarl at her to back the hell off. I want to take his hand in mine to let her know she has no claim on him. He is, after all, my betrothed. But I can't cause a scene, and to his credit, Jax answers much more politely than I would have.

"I cannot say no to a beautiful woman. Shall we?" He leads her away, her delighted laughter echoing in my ears like a braying donkey. I fight back the unexplainable urge to lay her out flat with a knuckle sandwich. Instead, I give in to my burning curiosity.

"What's wrong with her, Mack? Her eyes are so strange," I say, my own eyes watching every move of the couple on the floor. Jax is trying hard to keep his distance, but I swear the woman Bodes is trying to fit him inside her dress along with the rest of her.

"Silver spack," Mack says.

I glance over at him in puzzlement. He nods at the young'uns still circling the room with their fancy platters.

"The vials they are offering. A mood-altering medicinal known as silver spack. Very common among this crowd and provided in abundance to his elite by the Prezedant himself."

I still don't understand. "Mood alterin'? What do you mean?"

"It is known to have different effects on different people, from intense euphoria and elation to hallucinations to violence sometimes. A very volatile substance, one never knows what effect it will have," he says.

"Then why drink it?" I say, baffled.

"Because they can," he answers simply, and I suddenly understand why the room has such an undercurrent of frenzy and mania.

It's the silver spack. They're all drinking it. Oh, gods, as if tonight isn't dangerous enough, now we have a room full of crazed maniacs to deal with. Great.

To my annoyance, the music seems to go on forever, but finally it ends, and I watch Jax bow politely to the she-devil and walk away. She watches him with those over-bright eyes, and I swear I see her lick her lips like some wolfling about to eat its prey. Like Jax is gonna be her next meal. I almost expect her to leap and take a bite at his unsuspecting back, and I feel my muscles bunch, ready to come to his defense and take her down. But instead, she returns to her pack with obvious reluctance.

"I'm expected to mingle with my men," Mack says as soon as Jax joins us again. "It would draw too much attention if I stuck by your side all night. Just … try to fit in. Dance, eat, check out the room, but remember, do not take any of the silver spack. I will rejoin you as soon as I am able."

As I watch Mack walk away, I feel exposed to the curious looks of the people in the room. Mack had acted as a barrier and without him it's almost as if they can tell we are fakes. That we don't belong here.

Jax feels the same since he whispers in my ear as soon as the music starts up again, "I don't know about you, but I wouldn't be able to keep a bit of food in my stomach right now. Maybe we should dance before anyone tries to engage us in conversation."

I nod my agreement.

Duchess's training kicks in, and I start the counting in my head, letting Jax lead me. I don't even stumble as we start gliding around the room with the flow of the other dancers.

"Are you okay?" Jax whispers to me as I glance nervously over my shoulder.

I can't help it. I feel like at any minute some guard is

gonna grab my shoulder and out me for the fraud that I am. I take a deep breath, trying to control my fear as I offer him a halfhearted grin.

"Aye, it's just that this is a little … overwhelmin'. Don't you think? I'm findin' it a little hard to wrap my head around all this."

"I know what you mean. That food display over there could feed Gray Valley for a year! Not to mention those poor starving souls we saw outside in Skytown," he says.

"I don't understand. They have so much—more than enough to share. Why are only the select few allowed to live this way while the others starve? It makes me so angry."

"Don't think about that right now," Jax says gently as he tips my chin up so that I'm looking into the blue eyes glittering at me through his mask. "We can't afford for your Chi to show. Now, smile at me like you're enjoying yourself because we are on the receiving end of a few curious looks."

I don't look around, but I can feel the eyes on my back. I smile at Jax the best I can, but he quietly laughs at my effort, and I can feel it rumbling in his chest.

"That's a terrible attempt. You have such a beautiful real smile; I don't understand why you don't show it more often. Your whole face just lights up when you're happy."

I know he's just trying to distract me, but it works, and I flash a real smile at him.

"You are so fulla shite," I drawl, and he shrugs.

"Hey, whatever works." He glances over my shoulder. "I see the double doors over there that Mack's guy told us about. I'm gonna turn you so you can see," he says as we twirl slowly to the music.

He's right. Those doors, according to our source, are where we need to go to find the entrance to the lower cells. There are no guards standing there at the moment, but we have no idea what's on the other side. Just knowing it's our doorway to finding Ben and Lily; however, sends a shiver of excitement over me.

"Do you think—"

I'm interrupted as a loud ringing reverberates throughout the room. As if one, the crowd comes to attention, and the dancing and music stops instantly. The excitement rippling through them is catching, and I feel my own heart beating faster in response to their fervor. Without command, they start to filter to either side of the large room, creating an opening through the mass of bodies. We follow their lead and shuffle off to a side as Mack finds us in the crowd and joins us once again.

The loud bell clangs again, and the two double doors we'd just marked slowly open. A number of Army soldiers filter in, and even though I'm an invited guest and in disguise, the fear I feel at seeing them is intense. They walk in formation, two by two, followed by a tall woman dressed in the finest of robes. I can't help but notice the chains encircling her neck and hanging down her back. Her hair instantly catches my attention. It is as white as the puffiest clouds but intertwined with crow-black streaks—the opposite of mine. Curious. I'm so interested in her hair that I don't notice anything else until I hear Mack swear under his breath, and Jax grabs my arm in shock.

Holy mother of gods. My breath catches in my throat as the woman's face comes into view.

Lily.

What happened to her? What have they done?

I want to run to her, to yank that chain from her neck. She's here, in front of us, so close, yet she may as well be be locked behind a dozen iron doors because the end of that chain is held by no other than *him*. I know it is him right away. I don't need to see the crazed idiots bowing as he enters the room or hear their awed murmuring or watch as the other guards in the room come to attention. I just know. I can feel it. I can feel him. I can feel his pulsing essence enter into my own blood like some slick, cold *thing* worming its way through to the pit of my stomach, making it boil in protest. Mack had warned me being near him may have some effect on me, but I sure as hell wasn't expecting *this*. I feel nauseated, like I'm gonna retch any time now. I stagger a little, and Jax catches me and keeps me upright.

"Easy girl," Mack mutters outta the corner of his mouth. "Don't let him feel you. Fight it like I showed you."

I suck in my breath and concentrate on blocking out the invading waves. As if he senses some disruption in his power, the Prezedant pauses in his grand entrance, and the eyes hidden behind the gold, sparkly mask start scanning the room.

I do what Mack had made me practice: I imagine an invisible wall around me, blocking his probing, unseen feelers. I reckon it does the trick since the queasiness leaves my stomach, and I feel back in control again. He doesn't seem to find anything else amiss since he passes over me and continues on with his entrance.

Now that I have gotten over the initial shock of seeing

Lily, I study her captor a little more closely. I had imagined, I don't know, a much bigger man for sure, more imposing. But this? This is the man that has haunted my dreams and caused my night terrors? He's of average build, not even as tall as Lily herself. He looks normal. I almost feel let down.

He walks with a regal, self-important bearing, his dark head held high. The gold jacket and trousers he wears fit him like a glove and are crafted from the finest materials. He passes through his adoring subjects like nobility, like he truly is their king. The only thing missing from the picture is a jeweled, gold crown on the top of his head. And they are his subjects, no doubt. They admire him like he's one of the gods just descended from the heavens. I feel my gut drop at their reverence, and I realize it isn't just the guards we will have to get past but them as well.

"Mack, it's Lily," I whisper, and I catch his slight nod.

"This does, indeed, throw a wrinkle into our plans."

"What have they done—"

"That's not for us to worry about right now. Change in plans. After we receive word from Tater that our man has taken care of the guards, it will be up to you and Jax to search for the cells. I will try and figure out a way to get to Lily."

I don't like changing the plan. Not at all. Getting close to Lily meant getting close to *him,* and that meant capture or worse. I don't get to argue my point before the Prezedant reaches the platform erected in the middle of this gold room, and the cheering crowd goes mad. We get jostled and tossed about as they try to get closer to their idol. The man at the center of attention holds his hands up, palms out, and just like that, the shouting crowd falls silent. He stares at his subjects for so long and with such intensity, that I find myself holding my own breath in anticipation along with everyone else. Finally, he speaks.

"My friends, loyal allies, and fellow countrymen, thank you for joining me on this special occasion. You have all honored me greatly with your presence." His voice is pleasant sounding, friendly even, but it fills me with disgust.

I look around at the eager faces, the overly bright eyes. I don't think it would have mattered what he had to say. Either they're so enamored with this supposed immortal or so hyped up on silver spack, they would have been excited about anything.

"Tonight, we celebrate another fruitful year. A year of great success in our harvesting. A year of great success in our mining. A year of great success in our manufacturing. And a year of great success in eradicating that scum of a rebellion from the face of our beautiful lands. Tonight will be a grand event. Bigger than anything you have ever seen before. A plethora of surprises await you all this evening." Another round of cheering explodes. "But all in good time. So please, eat, drink, dance, indulge to your heart's content, and let the festivities begin!"

The roar is deafening now as the entertainers we'd seen upon arrival start filtering into the room, still breathing fire and performing all the other strange, weird talents they possess. I can see Tater in among the jugglers, but he passes on with no acknowledgment that he's seen us in the crowd. We will have to wait for his signal like planned.

Mack takes advantage of the crowd's ruckus to pull us both close.

"As soon as we get word from Tater, you two know what you have to do."

Apparently, along with the dancing and celebrations this evening, romantic "interludes" would also be quite common among the partygoers. It was expected to see people leaving the great room looking for a spot of privacy for some sort of dalliance without arousing suspicion from the guards. As a matter of fact, we'd been told "special rooms" were put aside for just that sort of thing, whether it be two, three, or a dozen people looking to be "intimate." That was Mack's way of describing it to me. Tater had just plain out called it flesh binges, but it sounded wrong no matter what way they described it. I now know what the slag had meant when she'd said extracurricular activities. There's no way in hell she's getting her hands on Jax for that, over my dead body. It would; however, be our opportunity to sneak out.

"I will not be accompanying you as earlier planned, so it's up to you two to search for the cells. Lily will be my concern right now. If you find the boy, you know what to do. Get him to the carriage. If I'm not there, do not wait for me. Stick to the plan."

"But—" I start to protest, but he cuts me off.

"You heard me. You won't have a lot of time. Get yourselves out."

I want to argue with him. To let him know there's no way we're going anywhere without him or Lily, but the dancing has started up again. Out of the corner of my eye, I see the slag heading our way, her eyes devouring Jax in their greediness. She certainly is persistent. Jax sees her too and he suddenly grabs my hand and whirls me onto the dance floor, and we lose ourselves in among the throng of people.

I stumble, but quickly recover and get the counting down in my head. Jax leans close to me like he's about to whisper sweet nothings in my ear. I can feel his breath on my neck as he speaks.

"I am only going to say this once. You heard Mack. We find Ben; we get out. No arguing, no resisting, no coming back for Mack. Got it?"

I stiffen at his words.

"No, I ain't 'got it.' We're not goin' anywhere without Mack or Lily. How can you even think that?" I say.

"Because we have no other option. Mack can take care of himself. We have to get you out of here. If we get caught … if you get caught, then this has all been for nothing. Shizen. I can't believe we're even actually here risking our necks for someone I don't even know."

"Wha-what are you sayin'?" Is he having second thoughts about helping me rescue Ben? And what about Lily? Didn't he think she was worth saving? I start to ask that very thing but we're interrupted as some pot-bellied, masked man with a shiny, bald head approaches.

"May I cut in and dance with this lovely young lady? And please do not refuse me; I have been waiting patiently for my opportunity," he says with a strange little grin, and a shiver of repugnance races along my spine.

I take a deep breath, try to hide my panic. I can't dance with someone else. They will instantly know me to be a fraud, but Jax doesn't have a choice in the matter. The minute we stop dancing, the she-devil swoops in. I don't even know where she comes from, but she descends with the force of a dust storm and whirls Jax away, leaving me standing there with the little bald man. His grin widens as he yanks me close. His hand slides down my back and cups my butt cheek, and it takes all my willpower not to smack the leering grin from his face. Instead, I force a timid smile and move the offending hand up higher. He laughs. "Oh, a shy one. This is going to be fun."

We start moving to the music, but he holds me uncomfortably close. I try to move away.

"What is your name, young miss? I'm certain I have never met you before for I am sure I would have remembered someone with such lovely … assets as yourself." His eyes sparkle with the unnatural glow of the silver spack as they leave my chest and travel to my face. The revulsion makes my skin crawl.

"T-Sara," I sputter. "I'm Captain Mackenzie's kin from Southpoint." The words leave my lips automatically, but to my horror, his face lights up in recognition.

"Ah, Southpoint. A lovely city. I, too, have kin there. Do you know of the house of Purcell? I'm sure you do since they are one of the most prominent families in the city."

My brain goes into panic mode. Oh, gods, he knows of Southpoint. What do I say? What do I do? Change the subject. Feminine wiles, don't fail me now. I smile at him, hiding my disgust, and push my lower body into his, coming into contact with a part of his build that I would rather have not touched, not even with a flaming stick. His eyes widen with surprise.

"Everybody knows about the house of Purcell. It impresses me that you're kin with such an important family.

Are you wedded?"

My little trick works. He forgets his line of questioning. His lips grow wider, more predatory, and he grinds back, almost causing me to retch.

"It matters not. What does matter is how beneficial it would be to such a lovely young woman as yourself to become good … friends with a man in my social position. I can make your time in Skytown very memorable. Why don't we retire to one of the side rooms and get better acquainted?" His voice drips with insinuation, and it's all I can do not to knock him backwards on his disgusting arse.

"I'm not sure my betrothed would approve of that," I say, smiling coyly at him.

"The young man you were dancing with? Bring him along; he was quite the attractive fellow. I do not mind young flesh either way, you see. The more the merricr. I may even acquire the services of one of the white garbs if you so desire."

The white garbs? At first I'm not sure what he means, but then understanding hits me. He's talking about the servants, the young'uns. The thought of what he is suggesting makes me want to gag. I want to jam my knife right into his degenerate heart. But I keep the smile plastered to my face, all the while thinking desperately how to escape from his slimy grasp before I give in and slit his damn throat.

My salvation, unfortunately, comes in the form of the little one from earlier who'd been offering me the silver spack. As nimble as she is wading through the crowd of bodies, a sharp nudge sends her slight frame in our direction, and she falls on her knees, her tray of silver goodies hitting the floor with a crash and splattering all over my dancing partner's trousers and boots. Her head jerks up, her terror-stricken eyes looking at us.

"I'm sorry … I didn't mean—" Her tiny voice is lost in his angry roar.

"You idiot!" he screams and kicks at her like she's a dog.

The kick to her stomach sends her sprawling across the floor, and she lands hard on her hands and knees.

"Bastard!" I snarl at him under my breath as I push him away and go to the little one, trying to help her sit up.

"Are you okay? Are you hurt?" I say quietly, but she's still too winded to answer me.

Instead, silent tears run down her pale face as she holds her belly. Witnessing her pain and degradation, I can no longer resist the urge to snap the bastard's neck. I stand and lunge, but before I can reach him, a rough hand catches me and forcefully yanks me away.

"As kind-hearted as you are, my dear, this is none of your concern," Mack speaks indulgently and smiles at the now watching crowd as if he's speaking to a simpleton. A couple of them snigger at his comment, believing me to be a fool no doubt, but the startled fat man observes me with wary eyes.

"Be still," Mack hisses at me through his gritted smile and I heed him, but only because the crowd gives way to a couple of soldiers, who yank the girl to her feet. She apologizes again, sobbing, but one of the soldiers silences her with a sharp backhand, and she falls silent as they drag her away.

"As you were," the Prezedant's voice cheerfully resonates throughout the room, and the dancing picks back up without missing a beat. Like nothing had just happened. Like her fear and pain were nothing. My heart is beating out of my chest and my fists curl at my sides. I'm so damned angry. How can they be so unfeeling? How can they treat people this way? My eyes finally make their way to him, sitting on his gilded perch, Lily chained to his side. He's smiling at something one of his men is saying to him as he sips a glass of the golden liquid. All of this, the excess, the extravagance, the indifference, the callousness, it's almost too much. I can't wrap my head around what these people are, what they are capable of, and he was the one in charge of it all. He was the one who treated others' lives like they didn't make one little bit of difference. My hatred for him and everything around me fills me up, oozing from my body. I feel the familiar heat starting to flow through my blood. *I could probably do it,* I think as I stare at him. I could end this right now. The knives rest heavy at my thigh. I could get to him and drive one through his heart. I certainly wouldn't make it out of here alive; I know that much. But it wouldn't matter, not as long as he lay dead at my feet.

As if sensing my thoughts, he pauses in the middle of taking another sip and leaps from his chair. His excited eyes scan the room. But it isn't his eyes I make contact with, it's Lily's. She's staring at me, the recognition flipping from disbelief to sheer panic. She shakes her head at me, and I swear I can hear her voice in my head, just like the young boy at the flesh trading.

"Stop it, Tara, before he finds you. Stop your Chi!"

Knowing she's right I do as she says and try to put out the flame growing inside of me, but I can feel his essence again, probing the room, looking for me. The searching tentacles pass over me, and their touch is like ice-cold fingers grazing my neck, causing all the fine hairs on my body to stand on end. Frantic now, I try to concentrate on putting up my defense, but the invasive fingers are back, poking and prodding. I can feel them piercing through to my brain, and I have to bite my lip to keep my scream of agony from letting loose.

This is it, I think. *He's found me. All of this is for naught. I've failed!* But then the painful searching abruptly ends, and I gasp in relief at the sudden release from the torment.

Then I see the reason for my release.

Lily has somehow managed to get close enough to him to wrap the chain hanging from her own neck around his and is pulling on it with all of her might, distracting him from searching for me.

Lily, what are you doin'? I think, my fear for her outweighing any for myself. I watch in horror as the chain snaps offa her neck, and she flies across the room to crash into one of the massive golden statues, like an empty tater sack blowing in the wind. It happens so fast, like time has somehow been sped up. I hear the sickening crack as she hits and watch helplessly as she slides down and crumples at the base of the statue, leaving behind a trail of blood.

CHAPTER NINE

The Prisoner

———✦———

I don't scream. I don't cry. I don't react in any manner, even though my heart feels like it's being ripped apart by a thousand sharp claws. I know remaining calm is the right thing to do, but I wouldn't be able to do anything anyway. I'm numb. But while the rest of me is frozen, my brain is in overdrive. I can't react. I know that. To show any reaction would be to give myself away, and that's what he's waiting for. Jax comes up behind me and wraps his arms around me, and I'm thankful for his solid body against my back, keeping me upright and hiding my tremors.

I can't take my eyes offa Lily. I don't want to look at her crumpled body lying there, but I'm scared to look anyplace else. Someone may see the hatred and grief in my eyes right now. It would be a dead giveaway. I suck in air through my nose, trying to control my panicked breaths.

"Well, I did tell you it would be an unforgettable night, did I not?" the Prezedant sounds amused, but the humor is forced. He is trying to cover his exasperation. He couldn't find me. Lily had distracted him enough so that he couldn't find me. She had saved me yet again, and I'd done nothing to save her.

Jax and I force out our own laughter along with his silver-spack-hyped followers, but mine is just a hollow echo of grief and self-loathing. Why didn't I do something to save her? I'm useless.

The Prezedant waves a careless hand towards Lily's body, and three soldiers jump to attention and whisk her away. Her head lolls to the side as they lift her, and I swear her lifeless eyes stare at me with such accusation. "Another one dead because of you," she seems to say, and I can feel the grief and guilt welling up in my chest. I swallow hard to keep it from spilling out. There's no time for grieving now; it will have to wait for later.

"A little bit of excitement to add to the night, eh?" He smiles at his followers, and they continue to laugh along with him, but I can see that the little pink vials are being picked off the trays more quickly now, like they're all trying to subdue their fear with the medicinal.

"A little intro for the games coming up shortly. I couldn't have planned that any better if I had tried. But while we wait, let's hear a story, shall we? Imp!" he bellows and gives a single clap, causing Tater to step out of line from the group of entertainers in fronta his elevated stage. I can see his pale, blood-drained face, but his voice is as strong as always, belying his shock.

"Thank you, gracious Lord." He bows to the Prezedant. "And thank you all fine folk of Skytown. It is a great honor and privilege to be here." He bows to the congregation.

"Tonight's story is one for the ages. A tale of grand adventure, magic, and monsters. Tonight, I will chronicle for you the tale of Sinbad and the Seven Lands!"

That's it. That's our signal that everything is a go. Tater had accomplished his mission; now, it's up to us. Jax's hand finds mine in the folds of my dress and gives it a tight squeeze. I sense Mack approach me from behind.

"We are calling it off," he whispers in my ear, and I shake my head. "You are to leave now, Tara," he hisses, and I step away from him.

There's no way I'm backing out now. Lily deserved a lot more from me than that.

"Tara, Tara," he whispers urgently at my back but falls silent when a couple of soldiers move our way.

"Captain Mackenzie?" One says. "The Prezedant requests your presence immediately."

"May I ask why?" Mack says with bored indifference, but I hear the concern underlining his words.

"Don't know, sir, but he is requesting all top aides to join him in the morning room ASAP. Come with us please, sir."

He lets them lead him away, not daring to say another word to me, but his one eye burns fiercely into mine, practically shouting at me to leave. Sorry, Mack. There's no way in hell that's gonna happen.

We watch the procession as they leave. I take a little comfort in seeing it's not just Mack whose presence is required but many other guests as well. At least suspicion doesn't fall on just Mack alone. I can hear Tater's voice droning in the background, but the words are all jumbled and don't make any sense. The only thing I can focus on right now is the blood-spattered statue and my inner rage, taking up any space where grief should have been.

Time seems to have no meaning for me. I guess Tater tells his story, but nothing registers. I don't hear a word of it. I don't even realize Tater's story is at an end until Jax starts whispering in my ear.

"Tara, the sparring is about to begin. This is it, now or never. Are you up to it? Mack and the others, they're not back yet. The plan is going to hell. Maybe we should call it off."

"No," I whisper loudly, drawing the attention of a few people around us. I wait for their eyes turn elsewhere. "We're doin' this. Let's go."

Without waiting for Jax, I head for the huge double doors the Prezedant had come through earlier, picking a glass of golden liquid off a tray as I pass by a young'un. It's now or never.

There are a couple of guards standing watch on the other side of the massive doors, and they study us with suspicion, but Jax pulls me close, and I giggle loudly and pretend to stumble as I snuggle into his side.

"A little help here, boys. Couldn't tell me where I can find a quiet corner? A place with no interruptions if you know what I mean."

He winks at one of the guards, who smiles broadly as I stumble his way and push my chest up at him. The other stares back, stone-faced.

"You shouldn't be in here," he says and motions to the solid doors closing behind us. "Go back. There's plenty of rooms at the front of the estate. These are private quarters and off limits."

"Come on, friend," Jax cajoles the serious one as I totter into the grinning guard and tickle his chin playfully.

"You're cute," I slur, pointing my glass at him before I take a sip and then pretend to sway a little like I'm about to fall over. The guard laughs and catches me.

"I think you've had enough of this," he says as he pulls the glass from my hand, and I pout at him.

"Just asking for a little privacy. Maybe this will help." Jax pulls two coins from his pocket and tosses them at the scowling guard, who manages to catch them both in one swoop. "Besides, there's a little something back there I don't want to run into ... namely the lady's jealous husband. Just a little private time is all I'm asking for, friends. Trust me; I won't need long with her."

This finally manages to make flinty crack a smile. He throws a coin to his friend, pockets the other, and gives a quick nod with his head.

"Just around the corner, there is a curtained alcove— should give ya the privacy you're looking for to do what you want. But don't take all night. And if the missus tends to pass out during your ... ministrations, come get us. We don't mind taking turns. This one looks like she'd be worth it."

The guard reaches over and pinches my breast through

the thin material, and my fist comes up ready to smash that leer from his face before I can even consider how wise that would be. Jax catches it; however, and raises my hand to his lips, stopping my show of temper before it becomes a problem.

"I promise, mate," he grins and yanks me away before I can do anything to blow our little ruse.

We walk slowly through the hallway with me slouched all over Jax until we round the corner, out of their view. Immediately, I stand up straight and start looking around.

"There," I say, ignoring the numerous other doors lining the long corridor and point directly to the set of double doors at the farthest end. Just like our informant had said. The double doors were where we needed to go.

I'm about to head in their direction when Jax pulls me off-balance and into the curtained alcove the guards had mentioned earlier. He pushes me through the draped entrance of the little niche, and I fall onto the softly padded lounger that takes up most of the space.

"What the hell—" I begin, but he quiets my protest as his lips cover mine. "Jax," I try to say, but he kisses me even harder, silencing me.

I'm stupefied and non-responsive. What does he think he's doing? My outraged shock is quickly forgotten as his kiss softens, and his lips coax mine into surrender. The hands that were planted flat on his chest to push him away now curl into his jacket, trying to pull him closer. His lips probe and explore mine, pushing every other thought out of my head. I don't know what brought this on, but the kiss feels so damn good. Shizen, is that his *tongue*? The root of some unknown emotion blazes in the pit of my stomach and fans out like wildfire throughout my body. The heat is so intense I fear I may just melt into the lounger underneath me. Even my Chi has never felt like such lava flowing through my blood. After what seems like a lifetime, he finally pulls away, and I can hear the little sounds of protest in the back of my throat. My lips suddenly feel too bare. *Come back,* I think desperately.

"We have an audience," he whispers, and at first it doesn't make one lick of sense in my head.

Who the hell cares if the Prezedant himself is watching? *Do it again.*

"A little privacy please, friend, and there will be more coin involved for you after." He turns his head slightly, and I finally see the beady eyes peering through the curtain, watching our every move. Watching our kiss. I hear the low chuckle of the one or possibly two guards as they walk away. So that's what this is all about? He did this because he knew they would follow us? I feel mortified. Utterly and truly humiliated at the way I responded to the kiss that was just a ploy for Jax. An act to convince the guards we were only what we appeared to be: a lusty couple looking for a secret spot for our dalliance.

"I think they're gone," he whispers.

Along with my self-respect, I think, but I say nothing. I'm just real glad the alcove is barely lit, and I'm still wearing my mask so he can't see the heat flooding my cheeks.

"Do you still hear them?" he asks, and I shake my head no since all I can truly hear is the beating of my own frantic heart. He stands and peers through the curtain. "Yeah, they're gone. Let's move."

Gladly. Now if only I'm able to stand on my wobbly legs, then all will be fine.

—◆—

I hurry down the corridor ahead of Jax, not wanting to make eye contact with him right now. I'm still too shaken. I'm the first to reach the double doors. They open with a loud creak, and I suck in my breath, but no one appears. Stepping inside, we find ourselves on a small landing at the top of a flight of stairs. And not the fancy, lit-up kind that we'd walked up earlier to get into the palace. No, these are metal, rusted in places, and old looking. The whole stairwell looks abandoned, like it's a leftover relic from years ago. It doesn't fit in with the rest of the grand building. We look at each other in question, but since there's no other way to go but down, that's what we do.

At the bottom of the two flights of stairs, hidden in the back of the stairwell, we find the paper-wrapped costumes like expected. Mack's man had delivered. We also find another door, metal like the stairs, but with a little glass window in the corner of it. Jax peers through the window and then quickly jumps back.

"Army," he mouths at me, and we flatten ourselves on either side of the door. I reach under my numerous folds of material and pull the knives from my thighs, tossing one to Jax. He deftly catches it but raises an eyebrow at my method. I shrug and twirl the knife in my hand, holding it blade down. Breathlessly, we wait for the confrontation. And wait. What the hell? Maybe they didn't see Jax. Finally, I can't wait no more, and I peer through the door myself. I see the two guards sitting at a crude table with what appears to be food dishes in fronta them. As I watch, one guard falls from his chair and hits the floor face-first, surely causing his nose to break. But he doesn't move a muscle. They're out cold. Or dead. Either way, Tater's nightweed had done the trick.

Nodding at Jax, I open the door and carefully enter the room, watching for any sign of movement and listening for any telltale footsteps of other guards.

"Looks clear," Jax says into my ear, and I nearly jump outta my skin.

"Shizen, Jax, I can see that for myself," I snap, but he ignores me and heads for the guard stretched out on the floor. While he searches for the keys, I look around the room. It's just a square, windowless box. A gray, colorless room with the only pieces of furniture being the table and two chairs the guards had been sitting at. Quite a contrast to the luxury we had just witnessed two floors above us. Obviously, this isn't a place the gold-loving Prezedant spent a lot of his time.

There are two other doors in the room besides the one we'd entered through, so I choose the one with the big, glass window first. I peer through cautiously, but there are no guards inside that I can see. It's full of stuff though. No idea what it could all be used for. I see a couple of beds looks like, but they seem to be on wheels. Strange. Numerous steel poles line the sides of the beds, and they have see-through bags hanging off them. Some of the bags appear to be full of liquid while others look empty. In the middle of the room stands a long, metal table covered with needles and blades and other shite. Things I have no name for. Even though the room is empty of life, it gives me the heebie jeebies, and a cold finger of fear tickles down my spine. I eagerly turn away from the room since it's not what we're looking for.

I move my focus to the other door. It, like the rest of the room, is gray, but it has a metallic box sitting directly where the door handle should have been. I approach it and give it a hard shove, but like I'm expecting, it doesn't budge. Locked. I examine the box. It has a slot on the side of it and a couple of lights—one of them flashing red right now—but no keyhole. Where is the damned handle and keyhole?

"What's takin' so long with the keys?" I say impatiently, and Jax looks up at me, perplexed.

"They don't have keys on them. Not any that I can find anyways. All I found is this." He holds up a short piece of ribbon with a strange-looking, square card attached to it. "They both have one."

My mind instantly makes the connection to the slot on the side of the metallic box.

"Bring it here," I say, and he does as I ask.

I grab it from him and slide it through the slot on the door. There's a slight pause, then a loud click as the other light on the box turns green, and the door effortlessly glides open. Taking a deep breath, we go in.

As soon as we step through, my innards bunch in sickening knots. It isn't the bright lights or overload of undesirable smells that shock us; it's the sounds. From every angle, we are assaulted with the low moans and unmistakable sobs of agony and pain. They are everywhere, echoing down the long corridor of cells. My feet stick to the floor as the cloud of human despair envelops us. We'd no doubt found the Prezedant's dungeon of horrors that Mack had spoke of.

"Tara, we don't have time to stop." Jax nudges me from my stupor, and I force myself to walk through the wide aisle, strange, plastic-like walls the only thing separating us from the prisoners inside.

Some of them watch our progress with gaunt faces and hollow, vacant stares. Others are so caught up in their own misery they aren't even aware we're there. Hooked up to more of those bags on poles like I'd seen in the other room, they pay no heed to the two masked people staring in at them. I stop at one of those cells. The woman lying on the cot inside shows no sign of being aware of us. The face pointing our way doesn't appear to be that old, but it's gray and ashen, her eyes half closed to her surroundings. Her matted hair is the same washed-out gray as her face and hangs off her mattress like limp rags, puddling on the floor. If it weren't for the involuntary moans of pain escaping her pale, cracked lips, you would think she was already dead. Her lifeless arm hangs over the side of the bed; a tube snaking up from the equipment on the floor appears to go straight into her skin. As I watch, the tube seems to take on a heartbeat as it pumps little globs of something through the line. My eyes follow the line down to the fat, saturated bag of blood sitting on the cell floor below the poor creature's bed, and realization dawns with sickening clarity. She's being drained of her life force ... her blood. Just like my ma. Is she a New Blood? A wave of nausea and dizziness passes over me, and I have to prop myself against the wall to keep from falling over. Jax's hand falls on my shoulder, and I shrug it off.

"I'm all right," I say over my shoulder. "Keep lookin'."

Every cell we pass has someone or something in it. I can't quite tell if it's man or mutie sometimes, but the waves of suffering and hopelessness emanating from every prisoner is all the same. It makes my chest go tight, and it takes all my willpower not to break down at the cruelty of it all.

I stop suddenly in front of another cell, causing Jax to bump into my back. I stare at the young man inside. His long, yellow hair is matted to his head, and his face is as dirty as the bare mattress he's sitting on. His head is leaned back against the wall, eyes closed. But there's something about him, something familiar. Could it be?

I approach the see-through wall slowly and peer in, both my hands planted firmly on either side of my face. The filthy prisoner garb he wears does nothing to hide the gaunt frame underneath. Scraggly yellow whiskers compete with the grime for room on the thin face. He bears little resemblance to the strong, healthy boy of my memory, but I'm certain it's him.

"Ben," I whisper, the word barely able to pass through the tightness in my throat.

I know there's no possible way he could have heard me, but the brown eyes I remember so well pop open right away and stare at me with undisguised fear. Shizen. Why is he looking at me like that? Then I remember the stupid mask I'm wearing, and I push it up off my face as I bang on the plastic with my free hand.

"Ben! It's me. It's me!"

There's a moment of vague confusion before his eyes clear and alight with such joy I think my heart will burst.

"Tara?" I can barely hear him through the wall. He sits up,

brown eyes staring at me like I'm some sort of hallucination. Then he stands and limps to the wall, placing his palm against mine. His eyes stare at me, unbelieving, like he doesn't truly trust that I'm really standing here.

"It's me," I say again. Hot tears fill my eyes as a single sob of relief escapes him, and he lays his forehead wearily against the plastic.

"You came," is all he says.

I nod, unable to speak at the moment as my fingers itch to touch his beautiful face. Instead, I make do with laying my own forehead against his, the cold unforgiving plastic keeping us apart. I'd found him.

"Really hate to interrupt your reunion but we don't have time for waterworks." Jax's harsh words are like a splash of cold water on my overheated emotions. I'd forgot he was even there.

"Let's get golden boy and get the hell outta here."

He's right. Dashing away a stray tear before Jax can see it, I search the metal door to Ben's cell. It's very similar to the one we'd just passed through, and I'm relieved to see the same kinda metallic lock on it. I hope the card key worked on this one as well. I frantically jam it in, almost dropping it in my haste to get the damn door open.

"I told you there was something fishy about those two."

The voice echoes down the long corridor, and we freeze in place. Someone is outside in the room we'd just come from, which means they already found the unconscious guards. And it isn't going to take them long to figure out where we are. In desperation we search for somewhere, anywhere to hide, but there's nothing in the open corridor other than us.

I can see Ben's worried puzzlement at our panic-stricken faces. He can't hear what we are hearing, and I mouth the words 'guards' at him. His eyes open wide in fear.

Jax points silently to the door at the end of the corridor and whispers, "There."

I know right away what he's thinking. We have nowhere to hide, no option. Our only hope to wait by the door we had just come through and tackle them head on, hoping we catch them off guard. And hope that Mack's training was good enough.

Pulling my mask back into place and hiking up my cumbersome dress, I run. Both of us run on silent feet trying to get behind the door before it opens. Almost there. Just another few steps—

Bang! The door hits the wall with a deafening crash, and we come face to face with the two guards Jax had bribed earlier. I skid to a stop as their shooters rise chest level, but Jax don't stop. With a roar of anger, he lunges at them as they come through the door, barreling one right into the wall. The other spins slightly to avoid Jax's attack, and takes aim at Jax's head.

I don't think; I just move. I jump on the guard's back, wrapping one arm around his neck and jerk my whole body back as hard as I can so we both go down. We fall with me on my back and the guard on top of me like a sack of taters. It works. The shooter goes off wildly, missing Jax by a long shot and hitting the ceiling.

I wrap my legs around the guard to keep him from flipping us over, and I can feel my dress rip straight up to my thigh at my movement. *Duchess is gonna kill me*, I think, but I don't got time to worry about her wrath over the torn dress right now because the guard is fighting back like a madman. I tighten one arm around his neck, and use the other hand to complete the noose, choking off his air. He struggles in vain to escape, but I refuse to let go, not while he's still holding that shooter. After what seems like forever, I feel him weakening, and the shooter falls out of his hand as he tries to pull my arms away.

He may be weakening, but I can also feel my own arms throbbing with the effort of holding on so tight.

Come on already!

He bucks a couple more times and claws at my forearms, desperate to get me off his neck, but I can feel his energy fading and I don't let go.

His body goes slack, and his protesting hands fall away, but I hold on. I'm not taking any chance he may be faking. When he's still, I move my arm away and watch for any movement, but he's out cold. I shove him off me in disgust and search frantically for Jax and the other guard.

They are still struggling, but I can see that the guard has dropped his shooter too, and I snatch it off the floor, kicking the other one away out of arm's reach. The guard manages to land a blow to Jax's chin, and Jax falls back against the wall, momentarily stunned. The soldier doesn't hesitate; he moves in for the kill, but the sound of me cocking the shooter right next to his head seems to make him change his mind.

"Get up!" I snarl at him, but he just glares up at me sideways.

It's the flinty one from earlier, and I know he's not gonna be ordered about easily.

"I know how to use this, and I ain't squeamish about puttin' a slug right between your eyes. Now get up."

I guess something in my voice convinces him since he does as I say. Jax has shaken off the punch and is back on his own two feet. He stands there rubbing his jaw and staring at the guard out cold on the ground. He grins at me in thanks.

"Open up that cell." I point with my chin, and Jax yanks a card key from around the scowling guard's neck and opens the cell door nearest to us. The wizened, gray-haired old man sitting inside watches us quietly with beady little eyes, but as soon as the door opens, he scuttles out and spits on the guard as he passes by. The guard don't flinch, but the man cackles with laughter. Then, without us asking, the old man starts dragging the unconscious guard into the cell while Jax ushers in the other one.

"The other one might have a card key too," I say to Jax. "You should check him."

But the old one answers my question. "No need; the doors don't open from that side, key or no." His voice is raspy, I reckon from disuse, but it doesn't hide the tone of glee. "Thank ye, Mistress," he continues and smiles at me with toothless gums.

He is as dirty and covered in filth as the rest of them here, and the red sores that cover his arms and face look painfully familiar. The stench wafting off him brings tears to my eyes, but his stiff little bow is of utmost respect.

"For what?" I say. "Takin' ya outta the pan and into the fire? I let you outta your cell, but I don't know how you're gonna get outta here. Not unless you plan on walkin' through the Prezedant's ballroom lookin' like that."

I don't wait to hear his response because it would only add to my own doubts and fears. The plan is going no way near like it should be, and winging it like we are scares me something fierce. I push that out of my mind for the moment and rush back to Ben's cell. Grabbing the card I'd dropped earlier, I draw it through the lock with shaky hands. The door's opening click is the sweetest of sounds.

Ben doesn't even wait for the door to fully open. He squeezes through, and I fly into his arms. He smells just as bad as the old man, but I don't care. I bury my face into his thin chest, and his arms tighten around me; I don't even try to stop my tears this time. I'd found him. And he's alive. That's all that matters to me at this moment in time. We don't speak, both of us too overwhelmed with emotion. We just hold on tight, the touch enough for the moment. I'd found him.

Now getting him and us out of here is a whole other story.

CHAPTER TEN

The Escape

—◆—

"Tara, we can't take them all. We have a costume for Ben alone, and I don't even know if that's going to work considering the way he looks and smells. You better hope they're all too whacked outta their skulls up there to notice anything odd about him. But I sure as hell know they'll notice the rest of these prisoners walking through."

I know Jax is making sense, but we can't just leave them all. By now, most of the prisoners have noticed what is going on, and they are standing at their plastic walls, watching us expectantly. Most. Some are too far gone, lost in their own misery and damaged minds to even notice we're there. Those few I know are beyond help. But there's no way in hell I'm leaving the rest of them to suffer that same fate.

"There has to be a way," I say stubbornly. "We cain't just abandon 'em all."

"Tara is right," Ben says quietly as he stands, holding his injured side. The sight of his blood-stained tunic hurts me so bad, but I blink away the tears. "We cain't leave 'em here. What they do to 'em … it … it ain't right," his words trail off in a whisper, and they convey the horrors he has seen and endured. That settles it then.

"Easy for you to say," Jax says to Ben with such anger and force that it truly surprises me. "You wanna back up those words with some plan, genius? 'Cause I got nothing."

"Ease off, Jax," I warn through narrowed eyes. We don't need to be arguing amongst ourselves.

"Ease off?" Jax stares at me, flabbergasted. "In case you don't realize the seriousness of our situation, let me recap it for you. We're in a house full of Army that would rather see us all dead, besides you that is. Our plan has turned to shite, our leader is missing, and other guards are gonna get suspicious soon and come looking for that bunch," he motions to the cell holding all four guards now, "and you wanna stay around and play hero to a bunch of crazies. Let's stick to what's left of our plan and get out of here."

"Er, I may have a solution." The little, gray-haired man whose cell we had commandeered interrupts Jax with a raised hand.

I look at him in surprise. I forgot he was there. Why hasn't he made a run for it already? He was freed.

"There is another way out of here, back in the lab."

I blink at him, puzzled.

"Lab?" Jax says.

The oldie bobs his gray head up and down. "The other room out there." He jerks his thumb over his shoulder.

"The torture room," Ben says quietly, and a slight shudder runs over his body.

Were they talking about the room I saw with the beds and poles?

The old man nods in agreement. "There is a … a shaft, I guess one would call it, where they dump the bodies of the ones who don't make it."

"Dump the bodies?" I say.

"Aye. Once they've drained all the blood and they got no more use for the carcass, they need to get rid of it. Since they can't very well parade it through the upstairs, they dump it down that shaft."

He says it so matter-of-factly, but it makes me quiver in revulsion.

"Where does this shaft lead to?" Jax asks, but the man just shrugs.

"Not sure, but anywhere but here is fine by me," he says and shows us his toothless gums again, making me believe he truly is one of the crazies Jax was referring to earlier.

Jax shakes his head. "Too risky. Could lead to anything. Could be a ten-armspan drop, causing us to all break our necks. Could be an oven ready to burn us all to ashes. Could be a pen full of wolflings ready to rip us all to shreds. I mean, they have to get rid of the bodies somehow."

Or it could be our way outta here. Without a word, I grab one of the guards' iron shooters and use the card key to open the cell door. The other three guards are still out cold, but flinty eyes me furiously from the other side of the cell. I ignore Jax's stunned stare and throw flinty a hard look.

"I know you been listenin'," I say, pointing the shooter at him. "Now, you're gonna tell me what I need to know. Where does that shaft go?"

He sneers at me. "You don't have much time left. Someone had to have heard that shot or notice we're missing. They are going to be here soon, and you're all going to rot in these cells."

I nod at him in agreement. "You're right," I say and pull the trigger on the shooter. He screams in pain and falls to the floor as the slug slams into his thigh. "Like you said, we ain't got much time." I ignore Jax's, "Shizen, Tara!" and Ben's look of disbelief and keep right on talking. "I'm a pretty good shot, so if you don't want this next slug aimin' for that dangley bit between your legs, you'd best tell me what I need to know. Where does it go?"

"You crazy bitch," he snarls at me as he cradles his bleeding thigh, and I aim the shooter again.

"Wrong answer," I say coldly, but he holds his bloody hands up at me.

"Wait! Okay, okay. It leads to the cellars. The bodies get dumped there and picked up for disposal." I ignore his winces and moans of pain.

"How much of a drop is it?" I say.

"About a flight of stairs … not much," he gasps.

"Are we gonna run into any guards in the cellars?" I say.

"No, no guards. Don't need guards for the dead."

"You lyin'?" I narrow my eyes at him over the shooter, but

he shakes his head vehemently.

"No! It's the truth. I swear!"

I believe him and back outta the cell, closing the door behind me and blocking out his cries of, "Wait! You can't just leave me. I'm going to bleed out."

I toss the old man one of the card keys and nod at the cells.

"Get 'em outta here … the ones that can go."

Right away, he does as I say, yelling "Through the shaft!" as he releases each prisoner. Some of them barrel out and make a run for the shaft right away while others just look stunned, like they're not quite sure what's happening. I take the other card key and head for the back of the corridor, yelling at Jax as I go, "Get Ben outta here."

He answers, "Like hell," as he follows me.

Should have known better.

A loud pounding somewhere near the back captures my attention. Someone is banging on their plastic wall with such force that I'm surprised the wall don't shatter. When I see the culprit, I stop and just stand there, shaking my head.

"Oh, hell no."

"Hey! Hey, you two. Get me out of here, and I will be forever in your debt."

Standing on the other side of the plastic cell is none other than the large, massive leader of the Raiders: Busher. The one who'd captured us in the mountains, threatened to sell us for profit, and then tried to turn us in to the Prezedant for the reward money. The last I'd seen of him; he and his men had been immobilized by Po and his campsite overrun with Army. I guess I know how that ended. He looks worse for wear. His long ropes of hair are now gone, shaved entirely off. The welts and bruises covering his bare torso—some old, some still fresh—leaves no doubt as to what he's undergone during his capture.

"Get you out?" I say. "You gotta be kiddin' me. Why would I help you?" I push my mask back up, so he gets the full impact of my glare. He stares at me for a moment before recognition sets in, and he smiles that wickedly white grin.

"Baby New Blood! I can't believe it's you. Let me out of here."

I ignore his pleading and continue on, as Jax throws him an almost apologetic "Sorry, man," before catching up with me. We open five more cell doors before we reach the end of the line. The occupants sob at us in gratitude as they rush by.

"That's it," Jax says. "Let's get out of here."

Busher is still standing at his wall and starts pounding again the moment we pass by.

"Come on. You have to let me out. You can't leave me here. They will eventually kill me as well, just like the others. You can't let that happen," he pleads.

"Not my problem," I say, turning my back to him. He had no qualms about our lives when he tried to sell us, more interested in his reward than our living or dying.

"Please, I can help you. You are going to need help getting off the grounds. The Army is not going to let you pass without a fight. Hey!" He bangs on the wall again, trying to get my attention. "I can help you!"

Jax pauses and turns my way. "As much as I hate to admit it, Tara, he's right. There's no way we're going to be able to sneak this many people out without being noticed. And he is a powerhouse. He can come in handy."

An internal battle rages before I come to a decision. "Argh," I mutter as, against my better judgment, I swipe his lock and open the door before I change my mind. He charges at me and I back up in horror before I'm lifted off my feet and spun around.

"Hahaha, thank you, baby New Blood. You will not regret this decision."

"I already am," I yell. "Put me down."

"As you wish," he says and does as I say. He then turns and bellows at the prisoners still hanging about in the corridor. "What are you fools waiting for, an invitation? Move out."

I'm not quite sure they understand the sarcasm, but they get the authority in his voice, and they listen.

"That is all of them, Mistress," the oldie says to me as the corridor empties out, leaving just him, Jax, Ben and myself. "The ones that are willing to go anyways. There's nothing we can do for those few."

He motions to the cells where the occupants are either ignoring us or hooked up to those damn blood bags, already too far gone for us to help. So be it.

"Thank you … I don't know your name."

"Kell is what I am called. Forever grateful is what I am to the gods for sending you my way," he says with a little bow.

"Aye, well, you ain't out yet. You might be wishin' you had stayed in your cell before this eve is over."

"Tara, let's go." Jax looks nervously over his shoulder, watching for any sign of more soldiers, and I grab Ben's hand.

He has remained strangely quiet throughout everything, looking too shocked to do much of anything, but at my touch, he startles and his brown eyes search mine.

"Tara, what's happened to you? Why is the big one callin' you New Blood? What does that mean?"

"I'll answer all your questions later, Ben. I promise. But right now, we gotta go." He seems to accept that, but I can't help the little bit of doubt that creeps into my heart at how accepting he will be once we get out of here. If we get out of here.

———•———

The raider leader is more helpful than I would have believed. I thought for sure he would have been the first down the shaft, but I'm surprised to find him holding the heavy, metal door open as the other prisoners take their turn climbing into the vent-like hole in the wall. Sitting on the edge and then pulling their legs through, they slide quickly out of view, so I reckon there's no other way to go but straight down.

We don't move fast enough though. There are at least ten of us left when we hear the unmistakable sound of heavy boots making their way rapidly down the metal stairs. The Army's on their way.

"Ben, you're next." I try to push him toward the hole, but he resists.

"Not without you," he says, but the big man isn't having none of it. Without another word, he picks Ben up and literally stuffs him into the hole, and he disappears from view, the sounds of his protest echoing in the vent.

I hear the soldiers getting closer. I look back at the door behind us.

"That lock ain't gonna hold 'em for long. Keep movin'," I yell at the prisoners.

Without a word, Busher starts pushing the heavy, metal table—holding what I now know to be torture devices—in front of the door, trying to buy us enough time.

The heavy thud of footsteps echo as they rush the gray room on the other side of the door. Come on, just four of us left. We can make it.

It doesn't take them long to find the other guards in the locked cell and figure out where we are. As Kell disappears down the hole, a face appears in the window, and the soldier's eyes open wide as he starts yelling. I see the light on the lock turn green, and the heavy, metal table starts bucking as they try to force it open.

"Go, Tara!" I don't argue Jax's command; there's no time.

I jump into the vent head first and start sliding down the metal ramp. I hit the ground with a thud and roll to my feet. It's so dark, I can barely see Ben in front me, but he takes my hand.

"This way," he says, but I yank back.

"No, we gotta wait for the others." I hear the terrifying sound of slug fire echoing down the chute. The soldiers were inside now and shooting at Jax and Busher. Oh, gods, Jax!

A blood-curdling yell precedes the body that falls out of the vent followed by another body moments later. They just lie there, not moving.

They're dead, I think frantically, but then I hear a low groan coming from underneath the pile.

"Get this … elephant offa me."

It's Jax. He's still alive, I think. He's squished underneath

Busher, just an odd leg sticking out. I push at the big man, and he struggles to his feet, freeing Jax. I grab his hand and pull him upright.

"You oka—"

But he cuts me off, winded. "No time … right behind … go."

I understand. We run.

The moss-covered stone floor is slippery under our frantic feet and running blind makes it even worse. The rock walls around us dictate which way we go, but I can feel a cool breeze on my face, so I know we're heading for some kind of opening. I'm just not sure what's going to be waiting for us when we get there.

The single passageway suddenly becomes two, and I pull up short, the others nearly running me over before managing to skid to a stop.

Which way? Oh, gods, I can't tell. Which passageway is the breeze coming from? My panic threatens to overwhelm me until I hear a whispered voice from the left passage.

"This way, Mistress."

Kell is motioning to us furiously, and we take his advice. We go left, the breeze on our faces growing stronger the closer we get to the light at the end of tunnel. The sliver of light starts to widen, and I suddenly realize what it is. Moonlight. We're almost out of the cellar. I can hear the shouts of the Army behind us, still in pursuit, but we don't look back. *Focus on the light,* I chant over and over in my head, expecting at any moment to feel a slug rip through me. It doesn't happen though, and we finally stumble up the stone steps that lead out onto the rolling back-grounds of the estate. It takes me a moment to orient myself before I notice something that almost makes me sob in relief. Doors. There are two huge, wooden doors lying on either side of us, just begging to be closed.

"Doors!" I yell and right away, Busher starts hauling on one while Jax and I yank on the other. They are heavy as hell, but once we get the momentum going, they start to swing shut with the force of a rockslide. Just in time, too, since I swear I see the whites of the soldier's eyes about to follow us up the stone stairs. We pull the heavy, metal latches across the doors and lock the guards in, their banging and shouting absorbed by the thick wood.

We made it. We're outside. I have no idea if the doors will hold the soldiers for long or if they have another way to get out and continue the chase. Hell, there could be another bunch around the corner just waiting to capture us, but for now, we're safe.

As my eyes adjust to the moonlight, I can see the other prisoners running, spread out over the rolling hills like scattering sand biters. I truly hope they make it out.

"What now?" Busher asks, and I peer at him through the gloom. Why is he even still here? But I don't bother to question it.

"The barns," I say. "I dunno how much time we have before the alarm is sounded up here, but if we can get to Talbert and Beanie, they might have managed to find us another way out—"

"There they are!" We hear the yell a split second before a gaggle of guards appear from around the corner of the main house.

"Damn, that was fast," Busher cusses under his breath.

"Go!" I yell, and we run once more, the soldiers' voices carrying their threats to shoot at our backs if we don't stop. The barns aren't that far away, but they may as well have been on the other side of the city since we're not even halfway there when Ben collapses on the ground.

"Ben, get up," I say as I grab his arm, practically dragging him to his feet.

"I cain't," he pants.

"You can. *Now move!*" I yell right into his face. We will not be caught. We will not have gone through everything tonight for nothing.

"Go on … without me," he says as he cradles his injured side.

"Fat chance," I say as I throw his arm around my neck, forcing him to move.

"Shizen," Jax cusses at us loudly as he runs back and props Ben up on the other side. We drag him, his feet barely touching the ground.

The sound of slug fire whizzes by my ears. They are really shooting at us.

"Keep going," Busher yells as he pulls one of the guards' iron shooters out of the small of his back and starts returning fire over his shoulder as he runs.

I hear another round of shots and then Jax's, "Ugh," as he stumbles forward a bit.

"Jax," I cry, but he doesn't stop.

"I'm okay. Keep going."

I know *he* is there before I even hear him. The cold, invading fingers prick at my mind, and I swear every other sound suddenly just … stops. I can't hear anything: the soldiers' shouting, Ben's painful gasps, my own pounding heart, nothing. It's like I've gone deaf.

"New Blood." There's a piercing whisper in my head, and it brings me to a standstill. Ben and Jax stumble at my sudden stop and then look at me like I've gone mad. I can see Jax's lips moving. He's yelling at me, and Ben is calling my name, but I hear none of it.

"Turn around."

It's like my body isn't my own, and I'm powerless to do anything but what the voice demands of me.

"Ah, there you are."

Now that we have stopped running, the soldiers quickly catch up and form a solid wall around us, shooters pointing at us from every direction. Moments later, the wall starts to part like a sea of grass pushed aside by the wind. He seems to almost glide through them instead of walk, and I'm acutely aware of his intense satisfaction at finally finding me. He stops almost in front of me, and I feel the cold tentacles burrowing their way into my brain.

This close to him, I can feel his power, his Chi, radiating off of him, and the intensity makes my gut churn. What in the world made me possibly think I could compete with such power?

"Well, then, we've had quite the little dance tonight, haven't we?" He smiles at me, and I almost feel myself smile back at his pure magnetic pull. "You are quite the temptress, teasing me with little tidbits of your Chi. Imagine my surprise earlier when I felt your presence in the ballroom. Oh, the healer tried her best to conceal you, and she almost succeeded, but yet here we are." He shrugs and lets out a delighted laugh. "I am so happy to meet you."

Face to face with him finally, I feel my intense hatred bubbling in my gut and start spreading over me in waves. I want to rip his heart out for Lily's death. I want to scream at him, damn him to hell for my ma and Grada and Rivercross and for every other innocent soul he has ever made suffer. I do none of that. Instead, all I can do is stand motionless as he peers into my eyes and then touches my chin lightly, moving my face from side to side. He pushes the mask up, revealing my whole face, and my knees almost buckle at his touch.

"Hmmmm, do I know you?"

"Get away from her," Jax snarls and leaps at him, but with a simple wave of his hand, the Prezedant sends Jax flying across the grass to land in a heap about five arm spans away. Holy mother of gods! How does he do that? I'm unable to go to Jax to see if he's okay, but I see him struggle to his knees out of the corner of my eye. At least I know he's still moving.

He doesn't even look Jax's way; he is still studying my face intently. Suddenly, his dark eyes go wide with awareness.

"On all that is holy … is this possible? You have to be. You look so much like *her* it cannot be a coincidence. You're the child, Tara."

For a brief moment, his shock and excitement are underlined by another emotion, one that I'm sure I must be mistaken about. Surely, I had to be wrong but for just that one brief little moment in time, I swear I detect fear. What possible reason would he have to fear me? I'm no threat to someone this powerful. And how the hell does he know my name? Just like that, the sensation disappears, and he rubs his hands in glee.

"It is you! What a glorious day. All this time looking for you, and you walk right into my home. The irony in that does not go unnoticed."

"What do you want from me?" I croak, each word an effort to force through my immobilized throat. He takes another step closer to me, and I can see the gold sparkles that have fallen off his mask and scattered all over his unlined face, the colored lights reflecting off them almost mesmerizing. He pushes his own mask up then as if to study me better. I am vaguely aware of how normal he appears—good-looking even. I surely thought evil would have looked much different than this.

"Why, what I want from every New Blood of course: your power. And yours, I'm sure, will be doubly sweet." He looks me up and down with disappointment in his eyes. "I truly thought a child of Rease's, well, I thought you would be more of a challenge." He waves a hand at me in dismissal and turns his back to me.

"Take her to the lab, and get her prepped," he says to a soldier who comes to attention at his words.

"Yes, sir," the soldier barks and nods at another who is off to my side. The other soldier moves into view, and I notice right away what he's holding. The white needle object I remember from Littlepass. The serum.

"And the rest of them, sir?" the soldier asks.

"The rest?" the Prezedant says like he can't quite understand why they would bother him with such a silly question. "They are not important. Shoot them."

The words freeze me to my core. No. Jax. Ben. I'm not

about to watch them die too. There's no way they are all dying tonight for nothing. I have to do something. As if Lily is standing next to me, her same words again echo in my head.

"Apply your Chi, Tara."

I don't know how I do it. Maybe it isn't even my own doing. I'm not sure if I break away from his power, or he considers me to be so weak that he releases me. Either way, my body falls under my own control once again. I can move. Come on, Chi. Don't let me down.

I feel the fire immediately start spreading through my veins, the tiny, weak flame sparking into a raging inferno. I see everything happening around me, but just like every time before, it's like I'm watching it from off to the side, like it isn't me doing any of this.

I watch the soldiers raise their shooters as the Prezedant turns his back to me. I see Busher slowly raise his shooter to fight back. I can see Jax trying in vain to reach the soldier about to inject me, and Ben looking at me with such confusion. But none of it has time to register. All I know is I need to stop the executions that are about to occur.

The soldier holding the serum comes at me, and I grab his wrist, snapping it back. Ignoring his scream of pain, I catch the needle as it falls out of his limp hand and leap at the gold-suited back. The roar of an unearthly wind whips by my head but not a hair of mine is blown out of place. It's like the wind somehow just takes me with it, like I'm a part of it. But it doesn't go around the soldiers. They are pushed through the air like leaves in a breeze, flying backwards with an unseen, mighty force. I get a quick glance at the

Prezedant's shocked face before I plunge the serum into his neck an instant before he, too, is blown backwards. It doesn't last long. One moment, they're there in front of us, and the next, we are alone. A couple of shooters lying at our feet are the only indication that we'd been surrounded. The soldiers and the Prezedant are scattered all over the grounds, spread out like the petals of some dead flower. I can see some of them struggling to their feet, but it's the one in gold that my eyes search for. He yanks the needle from his neck and wobbles to his feet, but he's having troubles. Apparently, the serum affected him just as well as the rest of us.

"What the—?"

Busher's words are cut short as an explosion rocks the ground under our feet, and a dust cloud mushrooms at the rock wall near the gate. From out of nowhere, a carriage flies towards us at such a breakneck speed it goes up on two of its side wheels, nearly toppling over. It crashes back down on all fours, and Beanie flings open the carriage door, nearly flying out with the effort.

"Get in!" Talbert bellows from the driver's seat.

He doesn't have to say it twice.

I'm not sure who grabs me, but I'm yanked off my feet and forcefully thrown into the waiting carriage. Bodies pile in on top of each other, so squished I can't tell who owns what parts. Talbert must figure we all made it inside; however, and the carriage jerks to a start. And not a moment too soon. I hear the Prezedant's furious roar of, "Stop them!" an instant before the sound of shooter fire erupts around us.

I peer up at Beanie from my cramped position on the floor.

"How we gettin' out? The gate," I say, but he just grins at me and laughs in pure glee.

"The explosion, Mistress. There ain't no gate to worry 'bout now."

I can't believe I'm thinking this, but these two idiots are actually starting to grow on me.

CHAPTER ELEVEN

The Allies

———◆———

"**M**ack!" I yell in panic and try to bolt upright, but I'm still weak and pinned under the sea of bodies. I can't move. "Everybody get off me," I cry as I start pushing.

Easier said than done. With Talbert driving like a madman and the carriage all over the road, we're rattling about something fierce. Finally, the weight is lifted, and Jax pulls me up off the floor to sit between him and Ben. I kind of do a double take as I see old man Kell sitting on the other side between Beanie and Busher. Where the hell had he come from? Had he been with us all this time?

"Mack?" I say again, but Beanie shakes his head.

"We ain't heard from the Captain, Mistress," he says.

"What? Then we gotta go back. We cain't leave him there. We gotta get him and Tater outta there."

"Mack can take care of himself," Jax says and braces himself as we take another sharp turn. I fall into Ben and squish him against the wall. "Besides, he told us not to wait for him. Riven is still back there, too, so it's not as if he's on his own. He said to get you out of there, and that's what we're doing."

He winces, and I notice he's cradling his left arm. There's blood seeping through his fingers.

"Jax, your arm. Are you hit?" I say, trying to look at it, but he slaps my hands away.

"I'm fine … just a flesh wound. Nothing I can't handle. I think your boyfriend over there needs a little more attending to than I do. He's not looking so good."

Jax is right. Ben's face is stark white, and he looks bewildered, like he's not quite sure what's happened. But as much as I am afraid for how Ben looks, I'm more concerned with Jax at the moment. Don't look like just a flesh wound to me. Ripping off a piece of my now badly tattered dress, I snap at him, "Jacket off."

He stares back defiantly, but the determination in my face soon has him working his arm out of his jacket. The sticky sleeve underneath is already torn by the slug, so I rip it the rest of the way and start a little at the amount of blood. I study the wound more closely, and I see he's right; the slug did just wing him, but it has gouged pretty deep. He's going to need it cleaned and something to stop the infection. Right now, all I can do is wrap it tight as he stares ahead, face etched in stone.

Talbert don't show no signs of slowing down, and the carriage rocks unsteadily once more, almost causing me to fall into Jax's lap headfirst. Why is he still driving like a madman?

"Is the Army followin' us?" I snap at Beanie, and he yells at Talbert loudly.

"Anybody followin' us?"

"Clear fer now," Talbert hollers back. Some of the knots in my belly lessen. I had probably rattled them pretty good, but they won't stay off our trail for long. Now if only they had been rattled enough for Mack, Riven, and Tater to get out of there as well.

"I have to say, baby New Blood, that was an impressive show back there. Your powers have strengthened greatly since the last time we met."

The giant's words pull me away from my worry about the others.

"Why you talkin' to me?" I growl. "I don't even know why I let you outta that cell. And stop calling me New Blood. I have a name you know."

"Ha!" His laughter booms around the carriage, and he rubs his stubbly head with one of his massive hands. "You still haven't lost any of that sass, I see. You let me out, *Tara,*" he over emphasizes my name, "because you are naturally goodhearted as all of your kind are. It's inherent to you. You cannot control your kind nature any more than you can control your destiny."

"As all of my kind are?" I stare at him, dumbfounded. "What kinda bullshite have you people been told? In case you ain't noticed, you big galoot, the Prezedant is a damned New Blood. I could feel his power just as plain as I can feel this bench I'm sittin' on, and trust me, there ain't nuthin' goodhearted or kind-natured as far as he's concerned."

This seems to shock them all. Seriously? Haven't they ever wondered why the Prezedant was so damned strong and said to be immortal? He was every much a New Blood as I am and a hell of a lot stronger. Why the hell did somebody not already know this?

My admission seems to be too much for Ben to handle. He sits upright and glares at me like everything is all my fault.

"What is happenin', Tara? Who are all these people? And what happened back there? What you did … your hair..."

He trails off, and my gut wrenches. How do I explain it to him? How do I even begin?

"Ben," I plead, reaching for any way to explain, but Beanie interrupts.

"Ben?" he says in delight, making the connection. He laughs maniacally as he grabs Ben's hand and pumps it up and down.

"You did it then. You found him, Mistress! What about Lily? Did you not find her?"

At the mention of her name, the tamped-down grief overwhelms me, and I hold my stomach as a sharp pain slices through it only able to answer with a shake of my head.

Beanie don't bother asking for any more info; he can tell from the look on my face. His own face falls, and he looks like he is about to cry. *Please don't,* I think frantically, *'cause if you cry, then I won't be able to hold it together.* Talbert's unexpected bellow from outside saves me from a complete and utter meltdown.

"Brace yerselves," he warns moments before we hit a bump, and the carriage seems to sail through the air. We come down hard, and I fly out of my seat, striking my head on the top of the carriage so hard black spots swim before my eyes. The carriage starts bucking and twisting wildly, jarring us so much it feels like my bones are going to shatter, but still we don't stop. What the hell is going on?

When we finally do stop, it's so abrupt I don't think it's by choice. The carriage now leans badly to one side, and I would say our stopping has more to do with one of the wheels breaking off. The lack of movement is followed by utter silence. Not sure if everybody is still in shock at my admission or has all been knocked senseless like I was. Where are we? Are we safe? Or will we open that door to find ourselves surrounded by the familiar brown robes of the Army? I reckon everybody is thinking the same as me since not one of us makes a move to open the now barely-hanging carriage door.

"Everybody all right?" I whisper into the silence, but I don't get an answer before the door is suddenly yanked open. It screeches in protest as it comes completely loose and falls off the carriage to hit the ground with a dull thud. I suck in my breath, expecting the worst. The sore-covered, grinning skull of Talbert fills the gap.

"An' that, mates, is 'ow you pull off a great escape." Then, without missing a beat, he eyes Busher up and down. "Oi, yer a big 'un then, ain't ya."

I can't help it; I lose my shite. I'm not sure if I'm laughing, crying, or dying, all of my emotions bleed together, and I start shaking uncontrollably. My teeth chatter, and I cover my head with my arms and rest my elbows on my knees, trying to gain control of myself.

"Tara," Jax says, his voice filled with worry, but I answer him right away.

"I'm fine," I say. "Ben?"

"I'm alive," Ben answers quietly, and I close my eyes in relief.

Did we really and truly just pull this off? I take a couple of calming breaths and pull myself together.

"Well, come on then. Move it already. We ain't safe yet. We still got a ways to go," Talbert says.

Talbert is right for a change, and we start piling out of the now-defunct carriage. I don't know where we are. The moon overhead provides enough light so that I can see we are in a little clearing alongside a fair-sized river. Talbert has somehow managed to get us off the road and on the other side of a grove of trees all in one piece, albeit the carriage is worse for wear. I was right; one of the wheels has come clean off. We're not going any further in that. Why did Talbert purposefully take us off the road? Why aren't we still moving and trying to put as much distance between the Prezedant and ourselves as we can? Sure, I had slowed him down for a bit by jabbing him full of serum, but they'll be in pursuit soon enough.

"Come along," Talbert says. "No time for introductions. Take a bit to make sure all yer parts are still attached eh, and then move along. We 'ave people to meet. Beanie, you take up the rear."

"Stop," I yell at Talbert, and he looks at me in surprise. Then, lowering my voice, I continue, "Why did you bring us here? Why ain't we sticking to the plan? How did you two manage to create that explosion back there? That wasn't part of the plan."

Talbert and Beanie glance back and forth between each other.

"Ya didn't tell 'em, Beanie? Ya was supposed to tell 'em," Talbert accuses, but Beanie just shrugs his shoulders in defense.

"There weren't no time, Talbert."

"Yer only job wuz to tell 'em the plan while I got us outta there, an' ya didn't even do that right."

"I tried, but I wuz so excited to see young Ben here, and then Mistress told me about Lily, and—"

"One job, Bean, an' I still 'ave to do it myself. Ya always get sidetracked; ya need to learn to focus."

"But Talbert—"

"Shut up!" Jax, Busher and me yell the word in unison, and the two arguing idiots look at us in surprise, like they have no idea why we would be so worked up. I rub my temples. Not only is their bickering making my head ache even more, but it's also making me revise my earlier opinion on these two.

I speak directly to Talbert. "Just tell us what's goin' on."

He sends another disparaging look Beanie's way before answering me.

"Good enuff. Ya know 'ow we wuz supposed to explore the estate and find other ways out if need be? Well, there weren't none. That 'ole monstrous place is surrounded by that rock wall, guards posted every ten armspans. Ain't no way out lest they want ya to leave. So Riven an Beanie an me, we wuz wrackin' our brains tryin' to figure out a plan jest in case the first backfired, which it did," he pauses, and I urge him on with an impatient wave of my hand. Tell me something I don't know. "Well, we almost shat our britches when a couple of guards start comin' our way an' cornered us in the barn. I thought fer sure we wuz goners eh, Beanie?"

Beanie nods and echoes, "Goners," followed by that mad, disturbing laugh, which I have come to realize is just a nervous tic. Don't mean he's any less crazy though.

"But ya coulda knocked us over with a feather when we see who it is. That one from the sanctuary … the guard at the gate …" he trails off, searching his brain for the name.

"Flip?" I say, and he points a bony finger at me.

"Right ya are. Apparently, Mack 'ad called in backup jest in case the first plan didn't go all quiet like. 'E said knowin' you, Mistress, well, the Captain's a smart feller, 'e is. Flip an' Lily's second in command … Zoe. They wuz the ones who blew the gate. It wuz them. All we 'ad to do wuz get you out, Mistress, and then meet 'ere at the spot on the road they marked. "

It was starting to make sense. Woulda been nice of Mack to tell us about this plan B, but I won't judge him too much since it had just saved our arses.

"Where do we go from here? It's not like we can go back to Mack's now. I'm sure they had to have recognized Mack's house emblem on the carriage and known where to start looking for us," Jax says, but his words make me panic.

Finn and Cat were back at the house. If they go looking for us, they are sure to find them.

"Wot 'mblem?" Talbert says, laughing, and I glare at him.

Why is he finding this so funny? But then I take a closer look at the carriage. This isn't the same carriage we arrived in. As a matter of fact, it has the Army crest on it. It's one of the Prezedant's carriages.

"I borrowed one of theirs fer us, leavin' Mack's fer 'im an' Riven. The captain is just gonna git in 'is carriage and drive outta there, no worry, no fuss. Durin' the kerfuffle that Zoe and 'er friends are sure to 'ave caused by now, they ain't gonna realize that Mack's kin are missin'. Ain't no way fer 'em to tie the captain to any of this. An' if any of 'em did manage to follow us, then they will be searchin' fer one of their own wagons, and that's the reason why we's ditchin' it 'ere in the woods."

Could it have really worked out so perfectly?

"But the Prezedant, he knew my name," I whisper it since I don't want to admit it out loud. "He called me by name; you all heard it. He knew who I was."

"He knew you were the New Blood he's been searching for years for," Jax says softly. "He doesn't know to connect that with Mack's niece, Sara. While you were Sara at the ball, you wore a mask. Right up to the end, you wore your mask. Barely any of them saw your face. There were hundreds of people at that ball. If we're lucky, it will take them a while before they connect the pieces at least and give us time to collect Finn and get out of here."

I want to believe Jax's words. I really do. But I can't help the nagging feeling that something isn't right. That this was just a bit too easy, and we are missing an important piece of the puzzle.

"Can someone please explain to me what the hell is goin' on?" In spite of the filthy clothes and the matted hair and the blood-stained tunic, Ben is staring at us all with that stubborn, mule-headed look I remember so well.

Not now, Ben, I think. *This isn't a good time for your stubbornness to rear its head.* His confused eyes seek me out.

"I ain't takin' another step until you explain some things to me, Tara. How do you know these people? Why is the giant there callin' you a New Blood? What the hell is that? And why is that madman after you? How does he know you? And how did you do that ... thing to help us escape? I don't—I cain't," he stammers, his voice rising with each word, echoing with anger and frustration.

"Ben, please quiet down—"

"No! I ain't movin' 'til I get answers. What is happenin'? *What is happenin'?*"

The blow Jax gives him really isn't all that hard, but in his weakened state it's enough to send Ben stumbling back on his arse.

"Shizen, Jax," I hiss as I rush to Ben's side. "Have you lost your damn mind?"

"Somebody had to shut him up," Jax retorts as he flexes his hand. "If there is Army on our trail, this fool is gonna lead them straight to us with all that yelling."

He's right, I know, but that doesn't make what he did okay. I try to help Ben to his feet, but he pushes my hand away and stands on his own, rubbing his jaw and glaring daggers at Jax. He seems to be all right, and he's at least quiet now.

"Ah, hate to break up this little bit of entertainment,

people, but someone's coming this way." Busher motions with his chin towards the river behind our crashed carriage.

He's right, sure enough. There is a light slowly making its way down the river. Shizen. Should we run? The light starts doing this weird thing where it blinks quickly, then pauses, then blinks again, like someone was turning it off and on on purpose. Talbert lets out a sigh of relief.

"It's okay; it's who we's waitin' for," he says and then answers back with a low whistle that carries on the night wind.

Talbert says it's okay, but I can't help the way my heart is beating out of my chest as the hazy, black blob in the water gets closer, and I make out the shape of people. There's two of them at least, and they glide silently up to us on a flat-bottom barge. Someone throws a rope, and it smacks Busher plum in the chest. He grabs it and ties it to the broken-down carriage, securing the barge so it doesn't float away. The person holding the light steps off the barge and holds it up, searching our faces. I squint into the light at first before my eyes adjust, and I see her face. Zoe.

She steps up to me and grasps my fingers tightly, giving my hand a little shake.

"Tara, good to see you."

"You as well, Zoe, and thank you," I say with all the heartfelt gratitude inside of me. She nods and then looks around expectantly at the rest of them. I know whose face she searches for.

"Lily?" All of her hope is conveyed in that one word, but I shake my head in sorrow. Her eyes close for a moment as grief crosses her face. But just as quickly as it came, it is gone, and when she speaks, her voice is brisk.

"Let's move. I have another carriage waiting upstream to take you back to Mack's where you must get the boy and get ready to move out quickly."

"But won't we be stopped? Won't the Army be searching the carriages on the road? They ain't gonna let us get away so easily."

She shrugs. "They won't be searching for a while. We left them pretty disorganized. A search party will take a bit to get together, more than enough time for us to get back. Besides that, we are on an island with only one way on or off. He knows you will eventually have to come to him if you wish to leave the island."

She has a point.

"How *are* we gettin' off the island?" I say.

She hesitates.

"Zoe?" I insist.

"We … are not sure yet," she says. "We arrived the same way you did—in Riven's wagons—but with the knowledge that you are now on the island, any travel on or off will undoubtedly be brought to a standstill. There's no way they will allow the bridge to remain open and take the chance of you escaping."

"Then we are still trapped," Busher says hopelessly.

The old man, who had remained totally silent up to now, approaches me and gives me another little bow.

"Seems like, Mistress, destiny has thrown us together, it has. I may be of assistance. Before becoming prisoner 3026, I was what you would call a mover of unattainable items from this side of the island to those much less fortunate people on the other side."

I don't quite follow, but Jax is quick on the uptake.

"You were a smuggler," he says. "So you know of another way off the island?"

He nods his gray head. "I do."

Me and Jax grin at each other over the oldie's head, but Busher isn't as convinced.

"Hold on, you two; don't get too excited. I've seen what happens to a lot of these prisoners while in the Prezedant's care. They get real mixed up sometimes … know what I mean?" He points at Kell and then swirls his finger in a circle at his own temple.

"You know of another way for us to get off this island then?" I say quietly, and Busher stops his swirling to study me.

"Then again, I didn't turn into a raving lunatic while imprisoned, now did I?" he says and clamps the smaller man's shoulder with his beefy paw. "Lead the way, little man."

Hmmm. That's a matter of opinion, I think.

———

Mack's house is ablaze with lights upon our approach, but nothing seems out of the ordinary. It appears Jax was right and the Army didn't connect me with Mack, not yet anyways. As soon as Zoe brings the carriage to a stop in front of the doors, Finn comes barreling out, almost tripping over his own two feet in his mad rush. He must have been waiting right at the door for any sign of us. He aims straight for me as soon as I get out the carriage, but skids to a stop as soon as

Busher gets out behind me.

"Whoa … what the shizen is he doin' here?" he stammers. His surprise turns to all-out confusion as Kell quickly follows, and then to concern as Jax lands with his bloody, bandaged arm.

"Jax," he cries.

"I'm okay, Finn," Jax says, his voice reassuring as he ruffles the boy's hair. "Is anyone else here? Mack or Tater?"

Finn shakes his red head. "No, you're the first ones back." His face lights up in delight as Ben is the last out of the carriage. "You did it then. You got Ben."

Ben, much to his credit, doesn't show surprise at the boy's reaction to his presence. Then again, he doesn't show much of anything anymore since Jax had punched him at the river. It's like he's just accepted what's happening, or he's to the point where he just doesn't care anymore. I can't tell. All I know is at least he's stopped yelling and demanding answers. Not for the first time since we found him do I have a sneaking suspicion that Busher was right. The Prezedant's prisoners do get mixed up in a way because this isn't the Ben I remember. But I will have to deal with that suspicion much later when there isn't any fear of being caught and killed by the Army.

We trickle into the house to find Coral and Duchess hovering anxiously. Duchess squeals in dismay as soon as her eyes fall on my frazzled appearance.

"My dress," she cries, and her hands fly up to cradle both sides of her face in complete dismay.

I look down at myself. I guess in all the excitement, I hadn't realized the damage, but from what I can tell, the dress is past salvageable. Most of it is missing from the knees down, torn away from fighting in it, stepping on it, and using it for bandages. The part that is left is mud-splattered and stained a rust-brown in spots; Jax's blood, I'm guessing. I look at Duchess with a sheepish smile and shrug my shoulders.

"Sorry?"

"What on earth happened to you all? Who are these people with you? And where is Tater?" Her eyes travel over us, searching in vain for the half man.

"Tater is fine. He'll be along shortly with the others." I hope, but I keep that last part to myself. "We have to move though. Coral, go to the kitchens, and pack as much food as you can in as many sling bags as you can find. Finn, get Cat. We have to go."

"Ahhhhh, man, again? But I like it here."

I ignore his whining and turn to the others.

"Jax, take Ben and get him into some fresh clothes. He cain't travel in that prisoner garb; it will be a dead giveaway if we're seen. Finn, see if you can find anything that can fit Kell here. Busher—" I look the big man up and down. "Hell, we ain't got anything that'll fit you. Duchess, get Busher a blanket and cut a hole in it. At least it'll be something to cover his wounds. Zoe, Mack has a collection of weapons in his study, that door on the left." I point with my chin. "Now, everybody move and meet in the study as soon as we can."

I don't know if it's authority or desperation they hear in my voice, but to my surprise they all obey me and scurry off. I'm about to do the same. I can't wait to get this stupid corset and what's left of this dress offa me. I don't even make it out of the hallway, though, before I hear rocks crunching under approaching hooves through the still-open doorway. I rush to the door, hoping against hope that it's Beanie and Talbert. There hadn't been any room for them to travel in the second carriage with the rest of us, so they unhooked the horses from the first carriage, planning to ride them here before setting them loose to find their own way back. Only it isn't Beanie and Talbert I find riding up the path, and my stomach lurches in fear. The horses approaching carry the brown-robed soldiers that I didn't for the life of me want to see right now. The Army had found us.

CHAPTER TWELVE

The Tunnel

—◆—

"**Z**oe!" I yell frantically over my shoulder, not taking my eyes off the door. I don't have a shooter, and I lost my knives somewhere during my flight, so I have nothing I can hold them off with. Shizen. How had they tracked us down so fast? Jax had to have been wrong, and they knew who I was all along.

Zoe comes running and skids to a stop beside me. "Damn."

She pulls her shooter, but the lead rider leaps off his horse and quickly covers the distance to where we stand. Ascending the steps in almost a run, he finally pauses as he spots us, putting his hands up in the air and pulling the wrapper from his face with a quick jerk.

"It's us," Mack calls out, and I let out a huge sigh of relief as I recognize the face underneath. The other riders unmask as well, and I'm glad to see Tater and Riven safe and sound. The other I don't recognize but assume he is to be trusted since they had brought him along. Mack and Tater hurry inside, leaving the other two remaining outside on watch. Good idea, don't know why we didn't think of that. Mack greets Zoe warmly, his hand on her forearm in a silent gesture of gratitude.

"Lily—" he starts, but Zoe cuts him off.

"Tara has let me know. She died for what she believed in," she says, but that don't help the grief and guilt in my heart none.

Mack nods, and his gaze falls on me.

"You made it out," I say, but his one eye reflects the relicf we both feel at seeing one another again.

"Barely," Tater whines as he brushes past, removing the Army wrapper and tossing it aside in disgust. The trousers he's wearing are much too long, and he trips, almost sprawling at my feet before turning his angry glare on me. "I am not quite sure how your quiet little escape plan escalated into this all-out extravaganza of a debacle, but you sure have them riled up. He's not letting anyone leave other than his own men sent out to search for you of course, hence the disguises. Every single guest is being detained and questioned for any information on you, young lady. We barely made it out ourselves ... wouldn't have if not for Mack's quick thinking. The Prezedant is very aware that you had to have been included on someone's invitation, and I fear to say it won't be long until he links you to Mack."

Mack crosses his arms and grunts in agreement. "Tater is correct. We can't stay here much longer. But where we are to go, I'm afraid I haven't quite figured out yet."

"We have a plan—" I start to say, but Tater suddenly cuts me off with a yell of terror as he flattens himself against the wall, and I whirl, expecting to see the Prezedant himself standing behind me.

"Arrrrghh! What in damnation is that gargantuan doing here?"

Busher wanders into the hallway, the red and yellow wool blanket he now wears, making him look like some giant ball of fire. Duchess had done what I asked, and his bald head now sticks through a hole cut in the blanket while his massive arms poke out on either side. The blanket is pulled in at the waist with a piece of rope, creating a cloak of sorts. He looks utterly ridiculous, but it doesn't seem to bother him none.

"Hello, little storyteller," he says jovially, picking Tater up and bouncing him up and down, much to Tater's vexation. The half man's continuous cries of part fear, part disbelief soon bring everyone running. Duchess' squeals of happiness at seeing Tater alive and well compete ferociously with Finn's whoops of delight. It's enough to bust an eardrum. Even Riven sticks his head through the open door to see what all the hullabaloo is about.

"Busher, put him down," I yell at the giant over the din.

Busher ignores me at first, but when Cat barges into the hallway wanting to get in on the action, he hollers in complete terror, "Devil Cat!" He sets Tater down in front of himself like a shield against the beast. Tater makes a break for it, only to be squashed again as Duchess tearfully pulls him into her own embrace, and he disappears amongst her ample cleavage. And if it isn't already crowded enough, Beanie and Talbert finally arrive, adding their boisterous shouts to the already noisy room.

"You were saying?" Mack whispers in my ear as he pulls me aside, away from the ruckus of hollering and greetings, Finn's voice louder than the rest of them combined as he tries to assure Busher that Cat isn't going to eat him and not to shoot her.

I spot Kell amongst the now crowded hallway and pull him along with us as Mack, Zoe, and myself make our way to Mack's study. We need to talk, and there's no way to do that with all that ruckus going on. I'm not surprised to see Jax squeeze through the door behind us, but Ben shocks me a little. I didn't think he was aware of much happening around him, but the little grin he gives me lights a spark of hope in my chest that maybe he's gonna be okay after all. It somehow makes me feel better.

"This is Kell," I say, motioning to the old man. "He was one of the prisoners we let loose this evenin' along with Ben and the giant out there. Long story short, Kell says he was a smuggler, and he knows another way off the island."

"Is this true?" Mack asks over his shoulder as he searches the wall-full of books for something. He finally finds what he is looking for and pulls it out. The map of the city.

"It is. A few years ago, my fellow runners and I, stumbled onto a tunnel underneath the water way that runs from Royal Island to the outer city. Not sure what it was originally used for. It is old; we know that much. Some of it has fallen in over time, but the structure is still fairly sound and passable. Well, for souls of normal stature; I'm not sure the giant out there will be able to pass through without issue."

"And where does this tunnel lead?" Mack asks as he pushes everything off his desk to the floor, so he can spread out the map. "Does it go underneath the outer walls? Will we be able to leave Skytown through the tunnel?"

Oh, please, please, please let the answer be yes, I think in my head. *Please say we will be able to escape this foul city altogether.* But as usual, the gods don't answer my prayers.

"No, afraid not. It ends ..." He goes to the map and peers at it and then points with a bony finger, "... here. In the abandoned area of the city next to the manufacturing district. Well, abandoned as far as the Army knows. There are a few squatters and poor souls scattered throughout there. Though we give 'em enough food and necessities to buy their silence, they will not squawk if we come through there."

Not what I wanted to hear.

"So we are off the island but still stuck behind that damn wall," I say to Mack. "That ain't gonna do us much good."

"Not like we have a lot of choice or time right now," Mack replies. "Everyone needs to be ready to move soon before any soldiers start looking this way. We'll worry about getting off the island right now and out of the city later. Where is this tunnel at, Kell?"

The oldie shrugs. "I'm afraid I have lost my sense of direction in our mad dash here, so I do not know the distance." He peers at the map again. "There, the hall of worship located near the south side of the island. It's not in use any more, hasn't been for about twenty-five years now. The Prezedant had the statues of the gods removed long ago and replaced with statues of himself. That's how the tunnels were discovered, oddly enough."

Mack nods with a slight smile. "I know of it. Let's move out as soon as possible. It will be a few hours' walk for sure since we will have to stick to the woods and off of the main roads. No doubt road blocks will be set up this evening and every carriage searched thoroughly."

A few hours' walk. I look at Ben, wondering if he'll be able to make the trek. His injured side had almost gotten us captured back at the estate. How would he handle a few hours of walking? Will he slow us down? Like old times, he smiles at me like he already knows what I'm thinking.

"I'm okay," he says firmly. "I can do this. If only to finally get somewhere safe so as you can give me some damn answers."

I laugh. I can't help it. It was like the smart-alecky old Ben is finally back.

"Well, you did say that you wanted to see what we would find outside of Rivercross," I tease, and he chuckles in response.

"I did, didn't I? I guess the old sayin' is true and be careful what ya wish for."

My laughter dies off as I see Jax watching us with the weirdest expression on his face. His arm. How could I have forgotten?

"Jax, how's your arm? Has the bleedin' stopped? You gonna be able to make this walk?" I ask, but he just gives me a curt nod.

"Don't worry about me, seems like you already have enough to worry about. I'm fine." And he brushes by me in such a hurry to leave the study he nearly knocks me over.

Shizen, what have I done to put that stick up his arse now? That man is more confusing than Tater's rambling some days, and that's saying something.

"Well, we know our destination. Supplies should be our concern right now. Zoe, divvy out the weapons from the cabinet over there. I don't have enough shooters for everyone, but there should be enough blades to go around. Tara, food—"

"Already on it. Coral is packin' slingbags from the kitchen as we speak."

"Excellent." He reaches into a drawer in his desk, pulls out a fair-sized sack and tosses it on the desk. It lands with a loud clink, and I know right away it has to be coins. "In case we need to pay our way out of the city. Now, we should move."

"I agree, Captain," Kell says. "But a word of advice. You should all maybe change out of those Army uniforms. Where we're going … those are probably not the best idea."

———•———

We make the trek mostly in silence, the fear of our voices carrying on the wind and being overheard by any searching Army very real. More than once we sink down into the shrubbery and behind the trees, hiding in wait as units of soldiers pass by dangerously close on the roads above us. They aren't giving up this search anytime soon and they're out in full force.

The walk isn't easy. The wooded floor we're walking on is covered in stumps and tangled with thick roots, tripping us with almost every step in the dark. When we're not stumbling, we're being stuck in the muck and mire of the muddy swamps. Lucky enough, I had switched to my boots before this hike, but Duchess, well, I can hear her crying over the ruination of her shoes and dress more than once. Foolish woman. Why didn't she have enough smarts to change before we left? I feel bad for her as she stumbles once again and falls face-first into a real boggy patch. But when she finally struggles back to her feet covered in goop and looking like some swamp monster, I can't help but snicker just a little.

"I heard that," she hisses loudly. "Stop laughing. I hate you. I hate you all. I shouldn't even be here!"

I stop laughing real quick. She's right. None of them should be here. My old friend, guilt, comes to visit once again. Everyone here is running for their lives because of me. Lily gone because of me. Coral and Mack displaced from their home because of me. The burning guilt grows in my belly and works its way out. But before it can overwhelm me with its maliciousness, a warm hand finds its way into mine, and I glance over to find Ben walking beside me.

"I think I forgot to say this, but thank you for savin' me. Savin' all of us."

A few simple words, a squeeze of my hand, but it does more for me than he will ever know. It makes the guilt lessen a little, so I can push it to the back of my mind. So I can go on and not be consumed by it. And that what we did tonight … it was the right thing to do.

We reach our destination without incident, and Kell leads us through the decaying ruins surefooted. He, at least, knows where he's going. We pass through a crumbling entryway at the front of the ruins, pushing aside the vines and spiderwebs, and down a double-wide stairway to a large central room. At one time, it must have been a focal room, the remains of a clock tower still very much in evidence. Now, however, it's overrun with weeds, and strangling bramble bushes grow out through the hole where the clock once sat. I wonder what its purpose had originally been. Kell said it once was a worship hall for those that still believed in idolizing the gods, but you can tell it had been built long ago by the settlers, probably for a much different reason. A cold shiver passes over me as I look around the massive, empty space, and I swear I can all but hear the echoes of the souls that had occupied this place ages ago, but long since passed on.

"Over here," Kell motions, and I shake off my trepidation as we follow him across the wide space. He approaches a more recently-placed statue of the Prezedant. It looks to be a duplicate of the one in Littlepass's town market. He steps around and squeezes into the narrow space between it and the wall. The wall looks like what it's supposed to be: a solid wall. Where the hell is the tunnel?

I watch, curious, as Kell runs his fingers over the surface, and then, satisfied with what he finds, asks for a blade. Jax gives him his knife, and the old man jiggles it in a crevice for a bit before we hear a slight click, and a gap forms in the rock wall. He pushes on it, opening it a bit further to reveal complete blackness.

"How the hell did you find this, Kell?" I ask, impressed

at the ingenuity of it all. It would not be something easily found.

The old man chuckles. "It didn't always look this way. When we found it years ago, hidden behind a tapestry, it was exactly what it was meant to be … a door. But when we realized where it led and its implications, we knew we had to keep this a secret. A stone-layer ally of ours altered the door to blend in with the wall surrounding it. Very simple really, instead of a door knob, it has a latch that can be depressed with the tip of a blade, if you know where to look, of course. And thus our smuggling route was born. It has been the difference between life and death at times over the years for a lot of people in outer Skytown. And a way to support my family until I got caught."

Zoe steps past us all and peers at the wall curiously.

"Show me how to activate it, old man, since I will have use of it later," she says, and he does as asked, but her words bother me.

"You're not goin' with us, Zoe?" I ask, and she shakes her head.

"I will join you shortly, I hope, but I still have people here that I had to leave behind. I need to meet up with them and get them here. I'll bring you news of the Prezedant's movement as soon as I can."

I don't like the idea of leaving her behind, but Zoe is Zoe. There's no telling her what to do.

"Gods speed," I say to her as she says her goodbyes and retraces her steps back into the night.

"Well, then, shall we get going?" Kell disappears into the hole, but moments later he reappears, holding a lit torch. I wince at the unexpected flame.

"This way." His whisper is met by Tater's grumbling, "Underground again?"

The half man truly did seem to have an aversion to underground cellars, no idea why. But he takes his turn just as well as the rest of us as we climb through the opening.

"Watch your step," Kell's disembodied voice floats back at us from the flickering flame up ahead. "There are six stairs down, then you will be on the tunnel floor."

I feel my way with my feet, counting in my head as I go down. Finally, I hit bottom, and I can see Kell through the blackness, illuminated by the glow of the flame.

"There are more torches over there," he says.

He points with his own torch to a makeshift table propped against the stone wall, and I grab one along with Mack and Busher. Four torches in all. It will suffice.

"Before we start our journey, I must warn you; we will not be the only creatures in this tunnel. There are rodents and spiders of some size that live down here, but they're usually scared of the flames. Just be on the lookout."

Usually? I think, a little panicked by Kell's words. He tells us that now? I grip my torch a little tighter and pull one of my knives out of its sheath, keeping it handy.

"Finn, stay close," I say to the boy, and he heeds me by sticking to my back and holding the metal baton I'd given him back at the house for his protection. It's not much, but it's enough to beat off a rat if needed. Ben falls in step behind him, watching our backs while Jax relieves me of the torch. I don't argue. Don't think my arms have regained enough strength to carry it far anyways.

The light-bearers spread out between our ragtag bunch trying to provide as much light as possible, but we're lucky the floor of the tunnel is pretty even. Now that my eyes have adjusted to the low light, I can see more of where we are. The tunnel kind of reminds me of the tunnel in the dead city where we'd found Talbert and Beanie. This one isn't as big as the one Orakel and her people had lived in and not in near as good a shape, but it seemed to still have the rounded, tiled walls. Most of the tile had already fallen off and crumbled away, but some of it still clings stubbornly to the walls, refusing to let the dirt fight its way through.

We trudge by other old tunnels off to the side, but they had caved in long ago, filled with dirt and rock, totally impassable. It scares me something fierce. Why is this one still useable? Why hasn't it crumbled by now? The way my luck is going, it probably would happen today while we are down here, burying us all alive. *Stop it,* I scold myself, my exhausted mind playing out all kinds of scenarios in my head and making me think horrible thoughts.

Some areas we come upon are partially blocked, the dirt forcing its way through, demanding to retake its territory. The rest of us manage to bypass these areas no trouble, but Busher has some difficulties. At one junction, as he squeezes his body through the jumble of rock and debris, I swear I can hear the ceiling above our heads groan in protest, like he's disturbing its precarious balance.

"Don't you dare," I whisper fiercely at the tiles and beams above our head, and they seem to listen. They stay put.

We must have been walking a good hour or so when a shrill scream from Duchess or Coral, I'm not sure which, almost makes me jump from my skin. I'm already agitated enough with the dark and the crawly things and the idea that's stuck in my head of us stumbling on some scorpiants down here as well, so the fool screaming grates on me something fierce.

"Something just ran across my foot! I hate this place. I hate it." Yep, it's Duchess alright. Tater is doing his best to calm her down, but she keeps yelling.

"I can't take it anymore. I hate being down here. I need to get out."

"Duchess," Tater says.

"Don't you 'Duchess' me, Winston Phillip. This is your fault. You got me mixed up in this … this catastrophe," she screams.

"Please calm down. This is not helping."

"No, I will not calm down. I will not. I will not!" She's stamping her foot with each scream. Her voice pierces through my skull like a knife and hits every raw nerve, and I can't take it anymore. Lunging at her, I hold the tip of my knife to her quivering chin.

"Shut your pie hole," I growl at her in the ensuing silence. I know everyone is staring at me in shock, but I can't control the angry words pouring out of my mouth. Her chin stops quivering, but I think it's more so from the fear of hitting the knife tip underneath it. She falls silent. "Or I swear on all that is holy, I will knock you senseless and have Busher carry you the rest of the way. Am I clear?"

Her eyes have gone wide at my attack, but at least she stops screaming. I watch as her eyes fill up with tears, and I'm consumed by guilt, but however cruel my actions may be, it seems to have worked. She takes a couple of deep breaths and nods her understanding at me.

"Okay then," I say as I pull my knife away and glance around at the others. "Whadda you all lookin' at? Let's keep movin'. Kell, how much further?" I snap at the old man, and he jumps a little in fear.

"Ah," he seems unsure how to answer me. "Not much, I do believe. Almost there."

"Good," is all I say, but I keep to myself how glad I am of that fact, and how close I am to losing it just the same as Duchess. I won't admit it to any of them, but I had to shut her up quickly else I would have become just as much a raving lunatic as her. We can't get there soon enough.

Kell hadn't lied. It isn't long before we come to a branch off from the tunnel we're in. A faded, dirt-encrusted sign still managing to hang on above the tunnel entrance simply says, "E."

"This is it," Kell says. "In here."

A slight incline and then another set of badly broken steps leads us out of the confining tunnel. We now find ourselves in what looks like the remains of a building that has kind of fallen in on itself, so that the hole we had just crawled out of is covered by a maze of twisted beams, rock, and 'crete. If you didn't know what to look for, there's no way you were gonna find that entrance on your own.

"Watch your step," Kell says as he leads the way. "Lotta sharp pieces here."

We heed his words.

There's no roof left whatsoever above our heads, which allows us to see straight through to the outside. The pale moon hanging in the night sky outlines the dark shadows of the few half-standing sky towers poking outta the mountains of metal and 'crete that litter the whole area. Not a bit of shrubbery or greenery to be seen. We definitely aren't on Royal Island anymore.

"Over there," Kell whispers in the quiet darkness. "The second building on the right. That's where we're headed. That's the safe house. Quickly now."

At least this building looks to be in better shape than what we'd just passed through. A solid steel door stands between us and the inside though, and I'm surprised as Kell politely knocks on the door like we're just here for a neighborly visit. In answer to Kell's knock, a peephole opens, and a beady eye appears, studying us.

"Who's here now, eh? State yer business."

"Harry, it's me, Kell. Let us in."

"Kell? Ya lyin' bastard, Kell is dead he is. Taken by the Army months ago. Whoever you are, take yerselves away before I shoot the damn lot of ya."

The tip of a shooter pokes out through the peephole, letting us know that Harry means business.

"It is me, you fool. I've escaped, look closer."

The blood-rimmed eyeball fills the hole as Kell steps closer. Then the peephole slams shut, and we hear a slight kerfuffle from the other side of the door. Silence follows. The door doesn't open, and I think they've just given up on us. They're not going to let us in. We stand in silence, looking at each other and shuffling our feet.

"Maybe we should move on, Kell," I say finally. "They ain't gonna let—"

The door flies open, and we find ourselves looking down the barrel of no less than five shooters. Safe house my arse.

"Shawn," Kell says, almost falling through the door, but the younger man he addresses doesn't seem to be as pleased as the old one and blocks his entrance.

"What is the meaning of this, Kell? Why have you brought this group of intruders here in the middle of the night? And is that … is that a devil cat? By all that's holy."

The younger man's shooter aims Cat's way, and Finn immediately jumps in front of his beast, protecting her with his own scrawny body. But that's not all. The shooters pointing our way raise all of our hackles, and our own weapons are lifted in our defense. They're not taking us down without a fight.

"Stop! Stop it. All of you lower your weapons." Kell steps in front of Busher and the two others he's staring down with an angry growl.

"Give me a reason why," Shawn snarls at us all.

"Because we are all on the same side. These people are not your enemies, Shawn. In fact, they are fugitives from Royal Island … outlaws … allies. They helped me and numerous others escape this evening from certain death, so I am indebted to them. And as your father, I demand you show them the respect they deserve."

Father? Didn't expect that.

The safe house is no more than one massive, open room with people lurking apprehensively in every shadowed corner. Fires burn in metal barrels, creating the only light since every window has been covered over with tarps or sheets of tin. The whole floor is scattered with old relics. Broken down, saggy chairs and musty smelling pillows and mattresses scattered haphazardly all over the place, abandoned quickly at our unexpected arrival. There doesn't seem to be no rhyme or reason to the room, the possessions, or the people in it. But they do have one thing in common. They're all staring at us right now like we carry a death plague. It's eerily quiet in the room; the crackling and popping of the fire the only sound to be heard.

We keep staring each other up and down, no one wanting to be the first to accept the other. Finally, the young man sighs and lays his hand on the oldie's shoulder.

"It is good to see you alive and well, Kell. We thought … I thought, we would never meet again."

The old man nods and closes his eyes as he shakes his son's arm.

"I, as well, boy. But these people … this girl saved me as well as some of the others you see before you."

"It wasn't just me," I say quickly. "Everyone here had a hand in the rescue." I don't want to take responsibility for it all.

Kell shrugs. "Be that as it may, you have struck a blow to the Prezedant this evening, one that he will not quickly forget."

The young man, Shawn, regards us for a bit through narrowed eyes. Finally, a smile cracks his stern demeanor, and he yells out to his people.

"Very well then. Let us welcome this group of weary travelers, for not only have they returned my father to me alive and well, but they are said to be enemies of our enemy. Any foe of the Prezedant is most welcome here."

This seems to be what they are all waiting for. Almost as one, his people surround us, clapping Kell on the shoulder, smiling at us, and even a few braves ones going as far as to pet Cat. They are a motley bunch—children, men, women—but they all have one thing in common. Their sunken cheeks and gaunt frames tell me they live a harsh life. Theirs is not a life filled with masquerade balls and choc-a-let.

"Come, come, sit in front of the fire. Warm yourselves. You all must be cold and tired. I'm afraid we don't have much in the way of food right now, but there are some boiled greens left over that you can help yourself to."

A lumpy chair is pushed against my knees, catching me off guard, and I fall back into it. Its innards are coming unstuffed, and I can feel springs poking into my arse, but I'm grateful just to be sitting. I pull the slingbag off my shoulder and catch Mack's eye. Is he thinking the same as me?

"We have food," he says as he offers his own slingbag to Kell's boy. "It isn't much, but you are welcome to have it. Consider it a payment for our passage."

I offer up mine as well and so does everyone else carrying a slingbag. Everyone, that is, but Duchess. Tater nudges her arm, but she shakes her head.

"No, I may need that. No," she snaps as Tater pulls it off her arm and tosses it into the pile already on the floor. "I may have needed that," she whines, but at seeing everyone's eyes on her, she straightens her back and fusses with her ruined hair. Not much she can do with that rat's nest at the moment, but I don't have the gumption to tell her that right now.

Our offer is met by silence. Numerous eyes watch us warily as if suspecting a trick.

"Please, the offer is sincere," Mack says gently.

He doesn't have say it again. At Shawn's slight nod, hands grab for the bags, and we hear the "ohs" and "ahs" as each new tidbit of treasure is pulled out. Dried meats, cheeses, breads, oranges, each morsel is studied eagerly, and I can almost hear their lips smacking in anticipation.

"Thank you for your generosity," Shawn says.

The feast is quickly divvied up and shared with our own exhausted crew. I'm surprised to find I have any sort of appetite left after tonight's events, but I devour the food just like the rest of them. The tension in the room seems to have melted some with the full bellies and quenched thirsts, and I find myself finally starting to relax. Shawn studies us through the flames of the barrel fire as he sits casually in his own chair, a pipe gripped tight between his teeth, giving off a pleasant aroma.

"Now please, just like everyone else I'm sure, I'm dying to hear your story of this great rescue."

We talk for hours, seems like, as Kell relates everything that happened—to his son, and the rapt audience. Tater can't help but jump in at times, like the storyteller part of him just can't stand to be left out. I'm glad Kell leaves out my New Blood part of the story. I'm not willing to share that side of me with these strangers, and I'm not really sure how they would react. But finally, the talking is over, and I'm more than happy to be led to makeshift beds. Even the lumpy chair was starting to feel like a torture device.

Ensuring Finn and Cat are settled in before making my way to my own allotted sleeping quarters, a groan erupts from me as I sink down into the lumpy mattress. The evening's events had taken their toll on me, and it feels like I haven't slept in days. But sleep isn't meant to be an option right now. Just as I'm about to close my eyes, a shadow falls over me, and I peer up into Ben's face.

"Hey," he says quietly as he plops down on the mattress beside me, and I groan once more in protest as I sit up, my back against the wall.

"Hey yourself," I say.

He joins me against the wall and pulls his knees up, propping his forearms on them.

"You know, I keep thinkin' I'm dreamin'," he says as he scratches the yellow whiskers at his chin. "Like this is all some bad dream, and I'm gonna wake up back in Rivercross. Like none of it ain't gonna be real."

He really wants to do this now? But I don't argue. I simply wipe the sleep out of my eyes with my hand and get ready to talk.

"Yeah, I know what you mean," I say gently. "I've gone through that."

He looks over at me, and his eyes fill with profound sadness.

"But it is real, ain't it? Everybody is … gone."

I nod past the sudden lump in my throat.

"Ma and Pa, your grada, Lou, Molly..." he trails off. "I knew they were gone; I seen it happen. Yet there was this tiny part of me that was hopin' you were gonna tell me they were all okay."

The shake of my head is all he needs as confirmation. He closes his eyes, and a grimace of grief crosses his face, causing my own wave of pain. I grasp his fingers and entwine them with mine; little comfort I know, but it's all I can give him.

Finally, he opens his eyes again, and they're filled with tears. He gives them a quick wipe with the back of his sleeve and swallows his sorrow.

"I didn't know what happened to you. I couldn't find you anywhere. We tried to fight back, but they started shootin', and I … I was so scared," he whispers that last part. "But then, when they had us all lined up by the river and you weren't there, I thought, 'Good, Tara got away. They ain't gonna find her,' and it was that thought that got me through these past months. That maybe you were okay."

My heart hurts for my kin and for Ben, how scared they must have all been. I feel a sudden flash of anger at Grada for what he did. If only he had let me be, I might have been able to do something. I might have been able to save them with my Chi. But it disappears as quickly as it came. No use crying over something that is long past.

"Grada saved me. He knew what they were. He knew it was the Army. He knocked me out, hid me in the cellar. By the time I got out, everybody … everybody was gone. I was so heartsick. I just wanted to lay down and die, too. But then Molly, she stayed alive long enough to tell me they took you and Jane and young Thomas. And I just knew I had to find y'all and get you back." I let out a bitter little laugh. "Ben, so much has happened since then. I cain't … I cain't even begin to tell you everything. My meetin' up with everybody here, being captured by the raiders, and then the Army. Seein' for myself all the despair and grief that exists livin' in a world run by the Prezedant. The things he does ..." I don't need to explain since I know Ben has seen firsthand what I'm talking about. "Losin' so many people because of that madman. It's nuthin' I coulda ever dreamed of in any night terror."

I toss him a sidelong glance, my heart beating out of my chest for what else I'm about to say.

"Findin' out I was a New Blood."

"Aye, about that," he says. "The giant over there keeps callin' you that, but well, what I saw you do to help us escape, I ain't got no way to describe it. Even your hair, I could swear it was givin' off some kinda light. Was I seein' things? What's happened to you, Tara?" I can see the confusion in his brown eyes, and it tears at me.

"I—" There's no easy way to say it, I reckon, so I may as well come clean. "I'm a mutie. A New Blood others call me, but a mutie just the same. I can do things ... have done things, no normal person should be capable of. I cain't control it, well not yet anyways, but I'm gettin' better at it. I have this force in me, this power that they call Chi or ..." I search for the word Lily had used, " ... bio energy. It makes me stronger, and I can use this energy to control other things around me, like the wind or sand. And I was told only those New Bloods that are the strongest are of the light. The glow that happens with my hair..."

I fall silent since by now Ben is staring at me like I just grew another head. I know it all must sound crazy to him. Even I find what I'm saying hard to swallow, and I lived it all.

"You're a mutie?" he says, and I can feel my gut clench at hearing those words come from his mouth. I brace myself, waiting for the look of disgust or revulsion or fear. Instead, he grins. "I knew it! I knew there had to be something strange about you. There ain't no way you coulda beat me at everything while we were growin' up. You were always faster, stronger, but all this time, you were cheatin' because you had an advantage."

The relief at his reaction almost overwhelms me. He's not freaking out. He's actually teasing me. That's good, but I'm not done with the confession. Not yet.

"Ben, I don't think you understand. I'm a New Blood … something the Prezedant badly needs. I'm the reason the Army came to Rivercross. I'm the reason you got taken and imprisoned and tortured. I'm the reason why everybody died."

Saying all that out loud, admitting to it, it almost kills me, but I don't get the reaction from him that I expect. Instead of looking at me like I'm some kinda of hideous monster, he just squeezes my hand tighter.

"No, none of that was your fault. You loved everybody as much as I did, and you would never cause 'em any harm. That was all *his* doin'. The Prezedant is the one who did all that. I don't care what the others call ya or what you believe yourself to be. To me, you are still my Tar-Tar."

His words are simple and to the point, but I hear the honesty in them. Stupid tears fill my eyes and I dash them away before he can see. He doesn't blame me. Feels like this great weight is lifted from my chest, like I can breathe again. All this time, worrying about what Ben would think of me, if he would blame me. But he doesn't care. To him, I'm still just me. I want to tell him how grateful I am at his acceptance, how thankful I am for his unconditional love, but like usual the words don't come. All I can do is smile at him like some idiot.

"What about Jane and young Thomas then? Have you found them, too?" he asks suddenly, and I so badly want to give him what he wants to hear, but I just shake my head no.

"I cain't find 'em anywhere. I was hopin' you would have some clue to their whereabouts."

He mulls over his next words. "I may know something. They were dropped off before I got to the iron mines. The city where you first found me."

"Littlepass?" I say, and he nods.

"Before I was taken to the mines, we stopped at this tavern just inside of the gates. I don't know if they were left there or taken somewhere else, but I know they were taken inside and never came back out."

I can feel my heart skip a beat. Are they still there? Had they been sold to the tavern owner? Was it possible that I may be able to find them like I found Ben? The prospect fills me with excitement.

"We have to go back and see," I whisper, and he nods his agreement.

"If we find 'em, promise me we will all leave and go back to the sand lands. Get away from this mad world."

"Finn and Cat, too," I say, and he shrugs.

"Take whoever you want. Well, maybe not the jackass that hit me. Him I can do without. But I truly want to put as much distance between us and this side of the mountains as we can get. Promise me?"

I'm a little taken aback at his urgency and his aversion to Jax, but I nod in agreement anyways, and the worry on his face turns to relief. In a typical Ben move, he pulls me into a bear hug at my wordless agreement and rests his chin on the top of my head, holding me tight to his chest.

"I'm so thankful you're alive, and that you found me. Now, we just have to find Jane and Thomas, and everything will be okay."

It feels normal to be in his arms. Like somehow I'm back home, where I belong. But I can't help this nagging feeling that something just isn't right. Even though Ben has only expressed what I myself have been wanting for so long—to find my kin and escape back to the sand lands—it feels like I've just promised him something that I'm not going to be able to fulfill. Like my part here on this side of the mountains is far from over. My guilt makes my response intensify, so I hug him back a lot tighter than I would normally have done, hoping he doesn't notice my unease.

The hackles on my neck rise, and I glance over Ben's shoulder. Jax is leaning against the far wall and watching us intently, his face a mask of anger. How long has he been watching? And did he hear me make my promise to Ben?

He catches my eyes and his expression shifts, replaced by calm detachment before wandering off to the door-less exit on the other side of the room and disappearing from view. Yep, he'd definitely heard everything. Gods, that man is getting pricklier by the hour.

I pull away from Ben and whisper at him, "We can talk more later. You should rest."

"Aye, I'm pretty beat. And this mattress feels mighty comfy. Cain't believe you even got a mattress. Think I'll just lay down here if you don't mind. You can have my blankets on the floor over there." He motions with his chin to the other side of the now snoring Finn, and I laugh at his nerve.

"Jackass," I mutter to his back as he flips over to snuggle down into *my* bed. All I get in return is a middle finger salute. Just like old times.

I head for the blankets piled on the other side of Finn, tripping over Cat, who gives me an irritated growl. But Jax's odd behavior keeps gnawing at me, and I have the urge to follow him to find out why he reacted so strongly to what he'd overheard. None of it should surprise him any. I just don't get it. And the flesh wound he'd suffered in our escape really did need to be looked after, and I know he hasn't done a thing about it. I guess it's up to me. Tracking down Tater and Duchess, I get from them the few things I need before heading off to find Jax.

The exit he'd gone out of leads to a set of 'crete steps that look like they've seen better days, but they're still passable. They only lead up, so I guess I know which way he went. A couple of narrow windows sit high up on the walls, allowing some moonlight to filter through, so at least I'm not stumbling about in complete darkness. The stairs lead to another floor and then abruptly end. Can't climb any higher, so he has to be in there somewhere.

This floor is a bit trickier to navigate than the one below. Parts of the ceiling had collapsed in over time, and metal beams and rods poke outta slabs of 'crete, creating pitfalls of danger. I can see why the group has decided to keep their living quarters confined to the floor below us. One side of the building even has a whole piece of wall that is crumbled away so as you can look out over the ruined city below. This is where I find Jax. He sits on the partial wall in a patch of moonlight, hunched over, and his hands hanging loosely between his legs like he had the weight of the world on his shoulders. I observe him in silence for a bit, before he speaks, startling me with his awareness.

"For someone who's supposed to have 'special abilities,' you have the stealth of an elephant. I could hear you coming from leagues away."

"Well, it ain't like I'm *tryin'* to sneak up on you," I say to his back.

"Then why you just standing there?" he says, and I huff at him in annoyance as I join him and hop nimbly up onto the wall.

"Why you up here instead of sleepin'?" I say. No beating around the bush.

He turns his head to look at me in the moonlight.

"Just needed to clear my head. Question is, why are you? The last I saw of you, you were pretty entwined in golden boy's arms. I'm surprised you were able to tear yourself away."

"He has a name," I snap, his words irritating me something fierce. "Stop callin' him golden boy."

He gives me a slight nod. "Noted." He turns away again. "So why are you following me?"

"Well, for one thing, I'm worried about your arm. You really need it cleaned and some fresh bandages on it." I hold up Tater's tin flask and the piece of material from Duchess' tattered dress in front of me like a peace offering.

He stares back stubbornly at first, like he isn't going to let me do it. I sigh at him in irritation.

"Listen, I know bein' a bullheaded jackass is just your nature, but don't be a fool, Jax. You cain't afford to let it get infected."

Without a word, he hops off the wall and yanks the tunic over his head, bearing his chest and wounded arm to me. I feel a jolt deep down in my gut. The sight of the smooth skin of his chest and stomach stretched taut over the bulky muscles underneath makes my heart quicken and my mouth go dry. There is a long, pink scar running horizontally just below his left shoulder, and I have to stop myself from reaching out and running my fingers over the puckered skin. *What had caused it*, I wonder. Does it hurt? I'm not even aware I'm staring like a fool until he says dryly, "So you gonna change the bandage any time soon before I freeze to death? It's not exactly what you would call a balmy night."

A hot flush fills my cheeks, and I tear my eyes away from his bare body, focusing on the blood-soaked bandage instead. What the hell is wrong with me? Not like I never seen a man without his shirt before. I busy myself with untying the bandage I'd placed there earlier to hide my confusion. Dried blood has the cloth sticking to the wound.

"This is gonna hurt," I say just as I yank the bandage off, not giving him time to brace himself.

"Shizen," he hisses, telling me I'm not wrong.

Right away I feel bad for my rough treatment, so I warn him before I attempt the next step. "This is gonna hurt even worse."

I unscrew the cap from Tater's whiskey. I wait for his nod

of consent before I pour the alcohol over the gash on his arm. His sharp intake of breath his only reaction. Satisfied I'd doused it enough, I start wrapping the wound again with the clean cloth. He watches me silently from hooded eyes as I secure the knot.

"Is it too tight?" I ask, but he shakes his head no and shrugs back into his tunic.

We're quiet for a bit, both of us staring off at the full moon before I finally say, "You're welcome by the way."

His profile in the moonlight looks like it could have been chiseled from stone.

"I didn't ask for your help," his words are cold, and I swear my mouth falls open in disbelief.

It pisses me off something fierce.

"Well, forgive me for caring if you lost your damn arm to infection," I say as I snatch up the discarded bandages and Tater's tin. "I don't even know why I bothered really since earlier you looked like you were gonna knife me in the back. I should have just let your damned arm rot off."

He doesn't respond; he just continues to stare ahead. I slam the tin down on the half wall in frustration.

"Honestly, I don't know what I do to you at times to make you so angry. Why are you always so angry at me?"

"Angry?" he finally responds as he turns to stare at me. "I'm not angry. What makes you think I'm angry? Nope, no anger here," he says.

"Really?" I say in total confusion. "'Cause you coulda fooled me by—"

"Yeah, I'm angry! Actually, I'm way past angry. I overheard your conversation with golden boy down there. But you probably didn't realize anyone could overhear since the two of you were so wrapped up in each other the damned building could have fallen down around your ears, and you wouldn't have noticed. Seriously? After all we've gone through, all we've seen. All your training. Lily and all the other deaths, all in vain. You're just going to give up and run off with *Ben*," he spits out the name, "like none of that ever happened? Like none of it means anything?"

I'm not prepared for the vicious attack, but it doesn't take long for my own ire to rise to the occasion.

"How dare you say Lily's death don't mean anything to me? How dare you." I step closer to him, pointing my finger in his face. "If you must know it feels like there's a big hole torn in my heart, and I'm slowly bleedin' to death. Feels like I'm bein' eaten from the inside out with guilt because another person has died for me, and for what? I didn't ask for any of this. I cain't stop any of this. I told y'all that from the get go, yet y'all have put this faith in me that I don't deserve and sure as hell don't want. I've faced the devil himself up close, and guess what? He's a hundred times more powerful than I will ever be. So yeah, forgive me if I'm thinkin' about runnin' away from it all and escapin' certain death at the hands of that madman."

We're pretty much nose to nose now, and my hands are gripped at my side in fists. I feel the need to lash out, to let out some of this growing fear that has been festering in my gut since my run-in with the Prezedant. Jax glares back, both of us breathing heavily with our anger.

Suddenly, his face softens, and he whispers, "Oh, hell," before his lips crush mine in a punishing kiss.

I try to step away from his onslaught, but I hit the wall, and I'm trapped as his hands slap against the 'crete on either side of me. His lips are fierce and hot, and one of his hands grasps the back of my neck now, tangling in my hair and preventing me from moving away.

A slight whimper escapes from the back of my throat, and as if he hears, the kiss softens and becomes more of a caress than an invasion. The hand that I had raised to slap him with instead clutches a handful of tunic and pulls him closer. What am I doing?

The kiss deepens as both his hands tangle in my hair now, almost as if he's scared I'll run. I'm not going anywhere. You need oxygen and strength to run, and I possess neither of those at this precise moment. My body has gone weak, and I feel faint from the lack of air, but still I draw him closer.

I take the opportunity to breathe as his lips finally leave mine and move slowly down my neck, gently nipping at the sensitive area and then fluttering along my jawline before capturing my mouth again. A delicious heat sweeps through me at his feathery touch, threatening to melt my innards. My legs turn to liquid, and I grab at him with both hands now to just try and keep myself upright. He leans into me at my response, nudging his knee between my thighs, and I delight in the heavy weight of his body pressed against mine, pinning me to the wall. I can feel his physical want and desire for me, and it fills me with an indescribable headiness. I've never felt this way before. I want to surrender myself to him. To give him everything, body and soul, right here under this beautiful, moonlit sky.

"Sky!"

I'm unaware I cry the name out loud until he stops, staring at me in complete shock. His lips linger for a brief moment on mine before he pulls away, and I actually whimper in protest. I can't help myself. I can still feel my need of him strumming through my body.

"Jax?" I say through swollen lips as he steps back from me.

He takes a tortured gulp of air. He runs an agitated hand through his hair as he watches me, his eyes still glowing with want.

"Why you playin' this game with me?" I whisper, the shame of my wanton reaction to his kiss radiating waves of heat of a different kind over my body now.

"I'm-I'm sorry, Tara," he stammers. "I'm not playing any game, I swear. There's nothing I want more at this moment than to be with you but—"

"But you have a betrothed," I finish for him bitterly, thanking the gods in my head that at least one of us had the sense to pull away before we'd done something we would both probably regret.

"She doesn't deserve this from me," he says. "I'm sorry; I had no right to do that."

There is regret in his tone, and I wonder for whom it is meant. Regret for kissing me or regret for what he was about to do to Sky? Doesn't matter. I don't want to know. What I'd felt for him just moments before quickly dissolves and turns into humiliation and anger. I can't believe I'd responded to him in that way. And he had shut me down. Again. What the hell is wrong with me?

I turn to leave, but he grabs my arm.

"Tara, wait—"

I shake his hand off like his touch is burning me and snarl at him over my shoulder, "I am only gonna say this once. You ever touch me like that again, and I will slice your bits off and serve 'em to Cat for supper. Understood?"

"Understood," he says, his voice miserable.

I walk away, my back rigid against his stare. I get it, I do. We had wronged Sky, and he's right. She didn't deserve that. So why do I feel like the one with the betrayed, broken heart right now?

The Crimson Legacy series, Book Two

CHAPTER THIRTEEN

The Fugitives

———◆———

The next couple of days pass in a haze. Jax is as good as his word; he doesn't lay a finger on me. Hell, he doesn't come anywhere near me. I catch his gaze on me every so often across the room, but I don't make eye contact. Even just looking at him reminds me of the shame and humiliation I felt at my response to his kiss. But worse than that, it brings back the memory of my intense need for him, the want to feel his lips on mine again. It leaves me frustrated and confused.

Zoe and her crew finally come through the tunnel on the second day, and I'm glad for their appearance since it gives me something to focus on. They bring us the news we were expecting. The Prezedant has realized Mack is a traitor to his cause and that his supposed niece is the New Blood he seeks. It doesn't surprise me none, but it does scare me. Before I was a nobody to the Prezedant, an unknown, faceless New Blood. Now he's seen my face and knows my name. It doesn't sit well.

Zoe was also right about the outer tunnel: it's our only way in and out of the city. It was shut down to any travel other than Army business. The Prezedant isn't taking any chance of us escaping. She said he was going over Royal Island with a fine-toothed comb. Sooner or later, though, he's gonna realize we're not there, and then a sweep of the outer city will begin. We had best be outside that wall before that happens. Although as much as we are wracking our brains, nobody has come up with a way for us to do that yet. Oh, there have been a few ideas tossed around like bribing our way out. But Mack doesn't have enough coin, and there are too many guards. We could fight our way out, but we don't have near enough manpower or weapons. Sneaking our way out at night is a possibility, but again, it would mean overtaking at least twenty-five guards, and quietly enough so we don't rouse the others. And there's the matter of getting the gate open. We could blow the wall like Zoe had done at the Prezedant's estate, but where would we get enough explosives for that? It's not something we can easily come across. Busher keeps insisting if only he could contact his people, then they would have the means to blow the wall and get us out. After him repeating that for about the tenth time, Mack finally snaps at him, "Contact them with what? Smoke signals? Nobody is allowed in or out of the city."

Mack isn't the only one being testy though. We're all a little worn out and irritated with each other from being cooped up, I reckon. My only real time outside of our decrepit safe house is a daily romp about the ruins with Finn and Cat, but we can only go at select times of the day. And we can't go far for fear of encountering the soldiers ferrying the various shifts of workers on their way to or back from the manufacturing area of the city. So instead, Finn and I have been spending most of our time with Ben on the ruined third floor, filling him in on our past few months and our search for him through the mountains. He listens, astounded, but he takes it all in and believes every word. He still refuses to share his horror of the past few months, and sometimes, when he thinks I'm not looking, I see the terror and shadows still etched on his face. I guess we all have our demons that still haunt us.

Being cooped up though, isn't going well. If I have to answer one more question from Finn about how we're getting out of the city, or what do I think is going to happen to us all, or even why the stars sit in the sky at night the way they do, I'm gonna rip my hair out. I understand he's only asking all this shite because he's scared. I know that. But it doesn't give me any more patience on the matter. So it's with great relief when I'm asked by Mack to go on a supply run. With so many extra mouths to feed now, Kell's group's food supply is running mighty low. I'm more than happy to agree. Any excuse to get away from this place for a bit and occupy my mind with something other than my own fears. But then I find out who I'm going with.

"Why does Jax have to go? Why not Ben or Busher, hell,

even Duchess. You. Anybody but him," I growl at Mack.

He doesn't question my anger, but he eyes me strangely with that one beady eye of his. I feel myself reddening under his questioning gaze.

"Do I really have to spell it out for you, Tara? Ben is still far too weak in case you do run into trouble. Duchess and Coral, too, for that matter. Tater is too noticeable for his small stature, Busher too noticeable for his larger one, and I am too well-known in the city. Zoe and her men are already out trying to discover a way to get us out of here. Beanie and Talbert, well, even if they weren't marked, I would still be afraid to send them off with coin. It would probably be spent in an alehouse or brothel other than on supplies. That leaves you and Jax. You two are the least suspect, as strange as that may be. Can I make it any clearer? Or perhaps you would prefer tiny Finn to go with you?"

"Fine," I mutter, knowing he's right about everything. But knowing he is right and saying it out loud are two different things. Jax can go, but I'm not happy with it.

With Kell as our guide to the black market, we head out. Kell keeps up a constant chatter, which is fine by me. It breaks what otherwise woulda been a very awkward silence between the two of us. Between the old man's chatter and having to watch our step so as not to fall in the craters or holes hidden in the piles of debris that litter the old roads, the first leg of our journey passes well enough. It's only when we reach the more populated outer city do we have to travel in a tighter group so as not to be separated. No one pays us much attention though. After our travels through the woods, the half-collapsed tunnel, and sleeping in our clothes on the safe house floor, we are just as unwashed as the rest of them filling up the streets. We fit in. Not at all like my first arrival in this city wearing my fancy cloak and being stared at with all those hate-filled eyes. Now, we look as beaten down as the rest of them here. Like we belong. No one pays us any mind.

I try to keep Kell between us as a buffer, but the old man scurries ahead at times, leaving me within an arm's reach of Jax. Someone from Kell's group had provided me with a battered, old hat, and I jam it down as far as it can go on my head so as to block Jax from my side view.

We walk like this in silence for a bit before he finally says, "Tara—"

"Don't even," I say, cutting him off. "There's nuthin' you can say that I wanna hear, got it?"

He answers me with a stiff nod. We walk a while longer, following Kell as his gray head bobs ahead in front of us through numerous streets and side alleys. Shizen, just how far was this black market anyways? It's a good thing Kell is leading us because I'm lost right now.

"Tara," Jax says again as he grabs my elbow, and I try to pull away.

"What did I—"

"Shut up for just one second and listen, dammit," he hisses in my ear as we keep walking. "Don't look now, but we're being followed and—I said *don't look!*"

He yanks on my arm as I start to swivel my head.

"You sure?" I say, annoyed and a little pissed at myself for not noticing. I had been so intent on blocking out Jax I didn't even spot the tails.

"Aye, been watching them for a while now. They've been

tailing us for the past few streets. I thought at first it was my imagination, but it isn't. They're following us all right."

"Is it Army?" I ask, fighting the urge to look back and find out for myself.

"Not sure. Kell!" he yells to the old man in front of us. Kell pauses and waits for us to catch up. "I think we have company," Jax says, not losing a step. Much to the old man's credit, he doesn't even blink an eye.

"Only one way to find out then. This way," he says and changes direction. We pick up our pace and make our way through the street, past the vacant stares of indifference. Making a sharp turn we find ourselves in an empty alleyway, bordered by a broken wall still high enough to hide us from the eyes of our pursuers. Hurrying past the wall, we take position on either side of the hole we had just come through. We wait to see if what Jax suspects is really true. If they are following us, then they would have no reason to come down this alley other than for us.

We don't have to wait long. A scuffling of footsteps and some low whispering confirms they are indeed searching for us.

"I tell ya, that's them. I recognized 'em from the poster. We gotta find 'em."

"You sure they came this way? There ain't nothing down here."

The other voice sounds confused, and the footsteps stop. *Please, go away,* I pray, trying to sway them with my mind. My gut is filled with panic at the thought of another confrontation. If they are Army, then surely others won't be far behind. My eyes search the far wall for another way out, and I panic even more as I realize we're in a dead end. Seriously, Kell? This was the best you could do?

"They came this way all right. Over there. There's a hole in that wall. They had to have gone that way."

Shizen. Why can't the gods ever grant me one prayer? Just one. I pull my shooter from the back of my trousers as I glance over at Jax. He stiffens and does the same as the footsteps start up again and draw closer. Looks like we'll have to fight our way out.

As soon as they cross the threshold, Jax tackles the first while I jam my boot into the back of the second guy's knee, sending them both sprawling across the dirt floor.

"Don't move," Jax growls as he holds his shooter on them. "Hands above your heads."

They do as he says, and the one I'd taken down peers up at me from his prone position with eyes full of fear.

"Don't shoot. We ain't no threat. We've been searching for you."

"Tell me somethin' I don't know, you piece of Army shite," I growl at him, but it only seems to cause his fear to turn to confusion.

"Army? We ain't army," he answers.

"Lies." I shake my shooter at him to emphasize.

"We can prove it. You're the fugitives, right? The ones the Prezedant's been looking for? I mean, you look an awful lot like the drawings."

I take my eyes off of him for a brief moment to glance at Jax in puzzlement. What's he talking about?

"What drawings?" Jax asks.

"The wanted poster. The—can we stand up now?" the

other asks, and Jax hesitates before he shrugs and motions with his shooter for them to go ahead. I take a step back and narrow my eyes at them, my shooter rock steady.

"No sudden movements," I growl, but I can tell right away he isn't lying about being Army. Their dress is too shabby, their worn and dirty garb similar to what most of these city dwellers wear. Their young, gaunt faces a testament to their little access to decent food. No, they're no soldiers. One of them starts reaching around to the small of his back, and I raise my shooter in threat. He freezes in place.

"Don't shoot. Geez! I'm just reaching for the poster."

He waits for me to nod my consent before he moves again, one hand up in the air while the other pulls a rolled-up piece of paper out of his back pocket and holds it out to us.

"Kell," I say, not wanting to take my attention off them, and the old man grabs the paper. I hear his exhale of surprise as he unrolls it.

"Oh, dear me. You two have to see this," he says.

Making sure Jax has them covered, I glance at what Kell holds up, and I'm speechless to see my image staring back at me. And not just mine. Jax and Mack are there, too. All of us, drawn to perfection by some unknown hand, and the word "WANTED" boldly painted in red above our heads.

"Jax, it's a damn wanted poster. It says I'm a 'dangerous New Blood,' and that you and Mack are my accomplices. There's a 10,000-piece coin reward for our capture." My eyes narrow again at the two in front of us as understanding sets in. No, they're not Army; they're worse.

"You were tryin' to capture us for the reward," I accuse,

knowing full well I'm not going to be taken down by these two fools.

"What? Noooo." The younger-looking one closest to me shakes his head, his eyes open wide in denial. "I mean, yeah, the coin would be nice, but that ain't why we're following you."

"Why then?" I ask.

"Well, like I said, we recognized you from the wanted posters. Jonas, he's got us looking for you all over. I can't wait to tell him we found you."

"You better tell me something soon that makes sense," I snap at the one in front of me. "Or else I'm just gonna shoot you both and not run the risk of you following me anymore."

"No need for that now," the one in front of me cries as he holds his hands up again. "Okay, let's start from the beginning. I'm Peter, and that's Corni. We live here in this hell hole known as Skytown. Jonas is, well, he's our leader, I'd guess you would call him. A rebel leader. We're all rebels, like you."

"We're not rebels," Jax says, lying through his teeth, but I can tell they don't fall for it.

"Whatever, man. Look, we know who you are; we're not gonna turn you in. We've heard stories through the channels, stories of the New Blood and what she's done. Then yesterday, we hear talk buzzing around of some big escape from Royal Island. That the New Blood everyone was talking about was here—in Skytown. And not only had she set free every single prisoner in his dungeon, but had also taken the big man down himself!" The one doing all the talking, Peter he'd called himself, looks me up and down with respect. "Is it true? Did you really stick him with a shot of serum?"

I don't see no need to lie about it, so I nod, and his face can barely contain the grin that spreads from ear to ear.

"I knew it. I knew that shite couldn't be all made up. That is phenomenal. Jonas is gonna be so stoked."

I cut short his gushing admiration.

"Why were you looking for us then? Do you have a way for us to get outta the city?"

"No," he says and looks at me uneasily like I'm about to take his head for that. When I don't react, he continues on, "But Jonas might. He's pretty smart. He's gotten us outta a few predicaments over the years."

"Why?" Jax interrupts. "Why do you want to help us? You know just by talking to us, you could be signing your own death warrants."

The other one, Corni, laughs. "Those were signed years ago, man. We're already dead men walking. With every day that goes by, we're being worked to death making shite for those rich bastards of Royal Island. Starved with never enough food allotted out to us or our families. Never enough fresh water to drink. Being cooped up in this prison he calls a city with no hope for a future. You lot are the most hope we've had in a while. We've heard stories of life outside the wall. Life with freedom and choice. Is it true?"

I'm not sure how I should answer that. Was it a life of freedom or choice? Not really. I mean, before these past couple of months, I would have said yes. But a lot has changed since then. The more I've seen and learned, well, it's obvious no matter where you lived, the Prezedant still managed to have some impact on your life. Still, it was better than being stuck inside these walls as his slaves, I reckon. I choose to simply nod at them. It seemed a hell of a lot easier than trying to explain. My answer seems to please them, however, and they glance at each other eagerly.

"If we help you, will you help us? Will you help us get outta here, away from this prison for good?" Peter says, and I can see the hopeful expectation in his young eyes. It makes up my mind for me.

"If you help get us on the other side of those walls, we will take you with us, yes," I say.

I ignore Jax's quizzical gaze. I can't explain to myself why I should trust these two, so I sure as hell can't explain it to him. It just seemed the right thing to say.

They study each other a bit more, as if not quite sure how to take my words, and then nod as if some unspoken agreement is made.

"Good. Great. We have a place where we meet, away from the eyes of the Army. Canal Bridge. They avoid it like the plague. Meet us underneath on the south side at ten on the hour. We'll take you to Jonas. He's most definitely gonna want to meet you all."

My eyes question Jax. Do we agree to this? Or is it really a trap?

"Kell, do you know of this spot they're talking about?" Jax says.

The old man screws up his face in thought.

"Hmmmm, yes. I do know of it. The boys are right; no Army would dare step foot in that infested swamp. It is as safe a spot as any to meet."

That's all I need to hear.

"So be it. We'll meet you there. And I'm keepin' this," I say as I take the wanted poster and roll it back up again, but one of the young'uns shrugs.

"Keep it. There's plenty more of 'em plastered all over the city. Word of advice, get offa the streets because everybody and their dog is gonna be chomping at the bit to turn you in for that reward."

His words bother me more than I let on. But I know he's right.

"Why ain't you then?" I ask, looking them over in curiosity. "Why not turn us in? That reward would probably ease your burden some, for sure."

"Aye, it would. However, the coin will eventually run out, but this prison will last 'til the day we die," the young one says with a wisdom far beyond his years. "We'll take Jonas your message."

It was quite clear to me now—to all of us really—why the Army avoided Canal Bridge. Kell had failed to mention it was a dump site for all the garbage and waste created by the thousands of souls living in this city. Every picked-clean carcass, every slop bucket, every piece of carrion left over from the slaughter houses ended up here. The smell is almost overwhelming the closer we get to the bridge. The bile rises in the back of my throat and I have to fight the urge to retch up my meager supper. Mack, Jax, and Busher look just as green around the gills, but Kell don't look the least bit affected by it all. The man must have a cast-iron stomach. If the rest of us had known about the specifics of our meeting spot earlier today, I doubt any of us would have come so willingly.

We'd arrived back at the safe house after our encounter today just a few steps ahead of Zoe and her crew. They had stumbled upon the wanted posters as well and had hurried back with the news. Zoe was of the same mindset as us. Having that many more people aware of our presence in the city and looking for us was not good. Before we had been faceless fugitives, but now, with our images plastered all over the city, it increased our vulnerability tenfold. I wondered at first how they had captured our images so perfectly, but then I assumed the Camons and Missus Bodes had been more than willing to help in the creation of the wanted poster. I'm sure Jax's image, at least, was burned into her mind.

And if the wanted poster wasn't bad enough, Mack had brought up the point of the people we'd taken refuge with. What if they were lured by this exorbitant amount of coin and decided to turn us in? And really, who could blame them if they did? If it meant having food in your stomach for a bit, well, I seen worse things done for a lot less. Kell assures us we don't have anything to worry about from his people, but like Mack, I'm not so convinced.

The news of our meeting with the supposed rebels had been met with some excitement and some reluctance. Could we trust them? Could they help us? Busher seemed to think it was a trap while Mack believed they were our only option. After a lot of bickering back and forth, we had finally agreed on one thing: We couldn't afford *not* to meet with them. If it meant a way of escaping the wall, then we have to take the chance.

Ben had wanted to go with us. Now that he was caught up on everything, he felt like he needed to be by my side every hour of the day. Like somehow, he had to protect me. I finally got him to agree that he was needed more here to watch over Finn and Tater and the others. Even with Kell insisting otherwise, we're still not sure what his group is capable of.

We're not going in blind either. While Mack, Busher, Jax, Kell, and myself would go to the meet, Zoe and her crew along with Beanie and Talbert would hide out of sight. Our backup just in case this was some kind of trap after all. Their orders were to come looking for us if we fail to let them know everything was fine with the meet. We're not taking any chances.

Approaching the bridge with hesitation, I pull my wrapper higher over my nose. Someone's already there waiting, blending in with the night, but we don't see them until we're almost on top of them. At the sudden movements from under the bridge, my hand tightens around my shooter, and I'm pretty sure my companions do the same.

The shadows walk out into the moonlight, so we can get a better look. It's the same two boys from earlier today, and I notice right away neither of them have their noses covered like I do. The smell doesn't seem to bother them at all. I guess having a cast iron stomach is a Skytown thing.

They give us a quick once-over, Busher causing them a double take. Finally, the one I remember to be Peter, speaks.

"This way," he says.

We follow them underneath the bridge, wading through a mountain of refuse that reeks so bad my eyes water. Things I don't want to know about squish and crunch under my boots, and every two steps brings a new assault of stench. I start gagging; I can't help myself. And from the sounds behind me, I'm not the only one. I nearly jump out of my skin as, what I first believe to be a mound of garbage, squeaks indignantly at us and scatters at our invasion. The bones of whatever the rats had been feasting on glows obscenely white in the moonlight, and I turn my head, not wanting to see if the flesh-tattered carcass is animal or human.

After walking for far too long in this calf-high river of filth, we're finally directed into a valley hidden between two walls of debris. Situated unexpectedly in the middle of this basin is a slant little building that looks like it's trying its hardest to escape from the stench surrounding it. I reckon it had once been white 'crete, but over the years the walls had absorbed every bit of the disgusting liquids from the squalor around it, turning it a putrid greenish-gray. As filthy as it looks, I can't wait to get inside. Inside has to be better than outside—I hope.

The faint glow of a lantern illuminates the tiny square room we find ourselves in, throwing watery light over the table it sits on and the wooden chairs around it. No one occupies any of the chairs though. They're all on their feet, watching our entrance. After my eyes adjust, I see who shares the space with us. There are about a half dozen or so people, filling the room to overflowing. All men but one, a scrawny, young girl who grins at us with a mouth full of teeth. No more than fifteen or sixteen born years, I reckon. Her horsey smile somehow puts me at ease.

None of us speak at first; we just size each other up cautiously.

Finally, one of the young'uns that led us here says, "See, Jonas, I told you it was them."

The man in front breaks off from the group and approaches me. Instinctively, I step back as Jax moves in, coming between us. But the man doesn't touch me. Instead, he throws me off guard as he places his fingertips to his forehead then loops down with an elegant flourish to touch his chest in the same manner. A form of greeting I assume.

"It is an honor to meet you, New Blood," he says. "I am Jonas."

"Please call me Tara, not New Blood," I say, and he bows his head in agreement.

The other men all follow suit, making the gesture with their fingertips to me. Before Jonas can say any more, however, the young girl leaps at me, and I find myself wrapped in her arms. Too stunned to react, I just accept her awkward embrace.

"I can't believe you're here!" she squeals before Jonas peels her away. She lets him, but she's still beaming at me with all those teeth.

Jonas' soft chuckle hits my ears. "I apologize for my sister's behavior. She is also honored to meet you."

Their behavior startles me but doesn't baffle me any more like it used to. I guess I'm becoming accustomed to people's reaction to my New Blood curse.

"Thank you for agreeing to meet with us," Jonas says,

looking at all of us with genuine relief. "When Peter told me they had finally found you today and that you had agreed to a meet, well, it was almost more than we could have hoped for."

"Your men said you may be able to help us. That's the only reason we are here. Is this true?" Mack, not one to mince words, interrupts my admirers.

"Ah, Captain Mackenzie," Jonas says as he smiles in Mack's direction. "You could have knocked us over with a feather when we found out you were a rebel spy."

"Cut the small talk," Mack fires back. "Can you help us get out of the city or not?"

Jonas and his men look between each other as if assessing how they should answer. Their unease bothers me.

"Easier said than done, I'm afraid," Jonas says, as he returns his gaze back to us and Busher snorts at the answer.

"I told you this would be a waste of time," he says in disgust. "We don't have time for this." He starts toward the door, but the girl's words stop him in his tracks.

"Meela sends her love."

Busher looks gobsmacked as he turns to stare at her in shock. Suddenly, he snarls and moves at the girl, causing all the others of her group to stand in front of her, shielding her from the giant's approach. I don't understand at first what has him so riled, but then I remember. Meela. That was the name of the raider girl I had beaten to a pulp: Busher's daughter.

"What do you know of my daughter?" he growls as he flexes his meaty fists, but the girl doesn't seem to be the least bit afraid of his wrath. Instead, her grin grows bigger, showing more teeth if that were even possible.

"So you *are* Busher. I figured as much since giants are a rarity in Skytown. Meela has been scouring outside the wall for weeks now waiting for news of you. She asked me to help find you. She'll be thrilled to find out you're still alive."

He drops his fists in confusion.

"Meela is here?" he says, and she nods back.

"She's alive." He chokes out as his face contorts into a grimace of relief and happiness, the meaty hands now wiping away the tears sliding down his cheeks. As much as the scrawny girl's words please Busher, they just confuse me.

"How is it you've met Busher's daughter? You said she's outside the wall? You have access to outside the wall? I thought this place was a prison." I don't try to hide my suspicion. Just what is this group up to?

Jonas puts a restraining hand on his sister's arm to stop the flow of words I can tell are about to spill out. The girl reminds me of an older version of Finn for some reason.

"Let me explain. Sometimes, Belle gets ahead of herself." Jonas smiles at her in indulgence, but Mack shows no such patience.

"You people better start talking fast because from what I've heard so far, seems like this has been a waste of our time. If we do not hear something worthwhile in the next two minutes, this meeting is over."

Jonas holds his hands out to us palms up in a pleading gesture. "Please, just hear us out. My sister, as so many other women and children of Skytown, do have access to outside the walls. They are the harvesters. The ones chosen to work in the fields on the outskirts of the city. They choose the weaker and the young to do this since there is less chance of them rebelling against the soldiers who accompany them into the fields. Less chance of them trying to escape. Less chance of them fighting back when they are pulled aside by the soldiers for other ... duties as well."

Belle's scrawny shoulders hunch unconsciously at her brother's words, and she crosses her arms across her chest in a defensive posture. Even if we were to question the validity of what he's saying, Belle's reaction to his words tell me every bit of it is true. Her pain and shame roll off of her in waves, and it makes me physically stomach sick. But at Jonas' questioning, "Belle?" she straightens her back and nods at him to continue. It pleases me to see the girl's spirit isn't broken by the brutal treatment she's obviously suffered at the hands of these soldiers and their "duties."

"It was on one of those days a few weeks ago when Belle had been left alone to pull herself together ... after another attack..." Jonas' words harden, and a vein throbs at his temple, but he continues on, "Someone called to her through the corn field. It was a young girl."

"Meela," Busher says, and Jonas nods.

"She and your people, they followed you all here after they got news of your capture," Belle jumps in, her eyes sparkling with excitement. "They've been watching the city. Trying to figure out a way to get you a message. To find out if you were still alive. I've managed to talk to her a few times while the soldiers are busy elsewhere."

"So my people are outside the wall? You can get them a message?" I can see the plan forming already in Busher's mind, and Jax's eyes catch mine with the same excitement. The raiders are on the other side of the wall.

"Aye, should be able to in some form or other."

"Yes!" Busher roars as he beats his meaty fist into his other hand. "This changes everything, Captain," he says to Mack. "With my people just outside the walls, getting out of here should be a breeze. This changes the whole dynamic of that damned wall."

Busher's words thrill me to no end, but Mack doesn't look as pleased as the rest of us.

"And what's in it for you?" he says to the group in front of us. "Why put yourselves in danger for people you don't know?"

"You promise to take us with you," Jonas says abruptly.

No beating around the bush for him. I already knew the answer, though, since the two young'uns from today had basically told us the same thing.

"We cannot promise you anything." Mack says quietly. "We, ourselves, do not have anywhere to go once we escape this city. Our safe houses have already been found out, most of our allies captured or killed. We have no way to assure any of your safety."

"Doesn't matter," Belle says, and her words catch on a sob as tears fill her eyes. "I would rather face the unknown in freedom than face one more day at the hands of his men—"

Her brother lays a gentle hand on her arm to stop her.

"It's okay, Belle," he says, and she nods, biting her lip to keep the tears from falling. Jonas averts his eyes from his sister back to us, and his look is void of the gentleness he had just shown her.

"We ask only of you to help us escape the city and set us on the right path to a better land. We do not expect for you to shelter, feed, or protect us. We can fend for ourselves. But we can't do this on our own. You lot are our only hope of getting out alive. Together, we can get out of this city alive."

There was that word again. Hope. Only this time, I feel real optimistic about it. Like this time, there is some light at the end of the tunnel—for all of us.

Mack runs a hand through his graying hair and flashes an unexpected grin.

"Kell, run and tell the others everything is okay, but that we will be here for a while yet. We have much to discuss."

CHAPTER FOURTEEN

The Attack

⬦—❖—⬦

C louds move idly across the moon, casting the city in swirling shadows of purple and black. The darkness works in our favor. It's a good night for an escape and not a moment too soon. A restlessness was growing in the city and amongst Kell's people. As much as they insisted the Prezedant was just as much their enemy as ours, looks were starting to fly and insinuations that what was happening in the city was our fault. The Prezedant had tried to terrorize his people into ratting us out with public executions. Men and women were being plucked off the streets for no reason other than to frighten the few they knew had to be hiding us.

Unfortunately, it was working. The deaths and the promise

of more to follow if the people did not give us up was having the desired effect. The murmurings of unrest in Kell's group were getting louder, and we knew it was reason enough to move on. As much as they had helped us, their allegiance was swaying. We knew it wouldn't take long before someone gave us up to save a loved one, and I truly wouldn't blame them if they did, so a decision had been made. In the dead of night, we up and moved ourselves to the garbage house under Canal Bridge. Kell alone had been informed of our intent. He had wished us gods speed on our journey but had chosen to stay with his own people in the city instead of escaping with us.

Needless to say, our people were not happy at seeing our new lodgings. Duchess had fainted on the spot, and Tater had retched up his supper. Even Cat had howled in dismay as the wretched smell hit her, but we don't have much choice. It would have to do until we could make our escape.

Jonas and Belle are true to their word. Belle delivers the message to Meela and the raiders about Busher being very much alive and needing their assistance. As dangerous as it must be and as scared as she must be, she gets every message through: theirs and ours. I can't help but grow a healthy respect for the spunky young woman. She doesn't talk no more about what she and the others endure from the soldiers in the fields, but it shows in her eyes and face as visible as any scar. I know without a doubt she wishes for this escape just as much or more as the rest of us.

Between the raiders' ideas and ours, a plan is made. It's simple enough. The patrol tanks that roam the city every night pass by the gates on the exact hour. At a quarter past the hour twelve, the raiders on the outside would begin their attack on the wall, taking out any guards posted out there. Their attack would be the diversion we would need to sneak up on them from the inside. The wall was designed to protect the guards from an outside attack, but here on the inside, it would be like shooting fish in a barrel. With the guards concentrating on the outside attack, we should be able to pick them off the walls easy enough. The idea of taking so many lives still sits in my gut like a rock, but I know we have no choice. It's us or them. And given the opportunity, I know they would not hesitate to kill any of my crew. It truly is kill or be killed.

We would have to move quick. That would only leave us with a forty-five-minute timeframe to take out the guards at the wall, the ones at the gate, get the gate open, and get everyone out before the next Army patrol showed up. The tunnel that they considered their greatest asset would then become ours. The raiders on the other side had told us they had the means to blow the underground tunnel. With the Army's only passage in and out of the city blocked, they won't have the ability to follow us, at least not right away. We would have time to get away before they would be on our heels. A full-out attack crazy enough it just might work. At least we're all hoping so in our hearts. Time will tell.

Jonas and his crew had not been whittling away their time while we'd been making this plan. The plan hinged on all of us being near enough to the gate to make our escape.

Unfortunately for us, the closest building to the gated tunnel was the brothel. I don't know what Jonas had used for bargaining, or why he believed he could even trust the women that lived in this building, but he gained us access to their lower levels. A crumbling, tiny cellar underneath the brothel had become our assembly point. All evening long, our little band of escapees had been showing up a few at a time so as not to draw attention. Getting Cat here had been the hardest. Not like we could just walk her through the heart of the city. May as well have waved a red flag at the guards at the gate and said, "Here we are, come get us." Jonas had come up with the idea to smuggle her in a garbage cart. No soldier in his right mind would stop anyone and rifle through that slop. She wasn't happy about it, but she let us do it. She still reeks of the disgusting filth she'd been covered in on her journey here. The smell doesn't stop Finn from holding on tight to her as he kneels by her side, keeping her calm in the now crowded room.

Earlier in the day, the room had hummed with an excited energy. Every one of us was eager to finally get out of this hellhole. Now, the closer we get to the hour of our plan, an uneasy silence has fallen over our group; the severity of what we're about to do looms like a swinging axe above our heads. I'm not gonna lie; fear is coursing through my own veins, and a cold, clammy sweat covers my entire body. Thoughts and doubts flit through my head faster than I can keep track of. Will this work? Will we make it out alive? Will the raiders truly be able to blow the tunnel and keep the Army from following us? The more I think about it, the more scared I become.

I pace the room, trying hard to keep in my doubts about our plan. I study the faces of the people standing before me. Some of them I consider my kin now, some of them I just met for the first time today, but feels like I carry the burden of all their futures on my shoulders. I don't like it. Will I be able to summon my Chi to help, or will it fail me? It makes my innards ball up into a knot as I keep circling the little room, anxiously waiting for Jax and Zoe to return from their watch on the gate.

Finn's frightened eyes watch me pace as he clings to Cat, and I swallow my fear. I can tell I'm having an effect on the boy, and I don't want to scare him any more than he already is. I approach him with a forced grin and kneel down to his level. Out of all of them, him being here bothers me the most. He's just an innocent young'un, only in this situation because of me. If something should happen to him …

"You remember what I said?" I say, my words coming out a little harsher than intended. "Once those gates open, you and Cat follow the others and run. Don't turn back for nuthin'. You mindin' me?"

His chin quivers a bit, but his red head nods bravely at my words. Suddenly, he lets go of Cat and throws his scrawny arms around my neck, almost choking me.

"Hey, it's okay. I know you're scared, but once we get outside the city, everything will be okay. You just gotta run," I say, my words a little softer now as I hug him back. He feels so breakable in my arms.

"I ain't scared of what we're doin', I ain't! Me and Cat can run swift like the wind." His arms twine tighter. "What I'm most scared of is losin' you or Tater or Jax for good. I don't wanna lose anybody else that I love."

He sobs then, and it feels like my heart is being torn from my chest. Tears swim in my own tears as I bury my lips in his hair.

"I love you, too, you little stink turd," I whisper, finally admitting what I know now to be true. This annoying little pest has wormed his way into my heart just as much as any of my other kin, and the thought of possibly losing him fills me with the darkest of despair. We just hug each other tight, neither of us wanting to be the first to let go. We stay like this for a bit before Cat's big head forces its way between us. Her smell makes me wrinkle my nose, but I don't push her away.

"Speakin' of stink turds," I say as I kiss the top of her cold nose, and Finn lets loose this sound that's part sob, part laughter. He rubs her ears to appease her, and she purrs loudly.

"I'll be right behind you. I promise. You won't lose any of us. See ya on the other side, kiddo," I say as I finally let him go and stand up. Tater was watching the exchange, and he gives me a halfhearted smile as he and Duchess hold each other's hands tightly. I search for the right words to convey how I feel.

"Tater, Duchess, I'm sorry—"

"No need for maudlin apologies, girl. The hand of fate will weave our destiny this evening, and the indisputable fact is we are incapable of molding the outcome no matter what you say or do. As my dear mother would have said, 'What will be, will be.'"

His words jumble in my head as usual, and I try to filter

through them. I think he's actually trying to tell me no matter what happens tonight, it isn't my fault. I think. But it still doesn't lessen the wave of guilt that flows over me at the obvious fear on their faces. They all have that same look, right down to Jonas' group all huddling in the corner with their meager bags of possessions.

As if sensing my agitation, Ben steps in fronta me, blocking all their fearful faces. He takes both my hands in his.

"Hey, it's gonna be just fine," he says, and I nod adamantly, trying to convince myself.

"They all look so scared though," I whisper, my attempt to convince myself failing miserably.

"Aye," he says. "You'd be a fool not to be. What we're attempting tonight is damn scary. But you know what else I see in their faces? I see hope and promise. None of 'em know what their futures are gonna hold or even if they're gonna live through the night, but they all carry the hope that whatever is gonna happen to 'em is better than livin' here under his rule. You gave 'em that hope, Tara."

I shake my head at him. "No, you're wrong, Ben. I don't give 'em hope. If it weren't for me, none of you would be in this situation right now, on the run for your lives."

He drops my hands, grabs my shoulders instead, and gives me a little shake.

"If it weren't for you, I'd still be a prisoner in the Prezedant's dungeon along with Busher and Kell. If it weren't for you, Jonas and Belle and the rest of 'em would be still living every day as his slaves with no hope of escape. And as for Finn and Cat, well, I ain't sure what woulda happened to them if you hadn't found 'em, but I bet ya the boy would agree that he's damn thankful you did come along. So stop beating yourself up, okay?"

He smiles at me then and touches my necklace lightly, trying to distract me.

"Still cain't believe you have this. If only we knew what that day was gonna bring ..."

"Of course I still have it." My nervous laugh sounds a little unbalanced even to my own ears. "I wasn't about to let anything happen to this. Was all I had left of you and Grada and Rivercross." I break off as my words catch in my throat. He pulls me tight against his chest and rests his chin on top of my head.

"Whatever happens tonight, Tara, know this. None of what happened was your fault. It was destiny, and none of us can stop that. I'm just so grateful that you came for me and that I didn't die in that hell hole. And you are gonna get us out of here just the same. I believe in you. Few days from now, we are all gonna be together, you and me and Jane and Thomas and Finn. Just keep believin' that, okay?"

I nod my head against his chest as I sigh. He always could make me feel better.

"How'd you get to be so smart?" I mumble into his tunic.

"I was always smart," he says. "You were just so blinded by my good looks you never noticed."

He laughs at his words, and I suddenly feel like all that time we'd been forced apart just melts away. Like it was just us back at the swimming hole again, planning some stupid folly to break up our day and laugh about later. Like my best friend was back and everything was still the way it used to be. I know it isn't the same. I know that we're not doing something silly like hiding Lou's handcart all over the village and driving him plum crazy out of his mind. Instead, we're about to make a run for our lives. But looking into Ben's trusting eyes makes me think that just maybe everything *is* going to be okay.

"Hate to break you two kids up, but it's time." Jax's ice-blue stare cuts me through to my core, and I move out of Ben's arms like I'm guilty of something.

I didn't even hear him and Zoe come back in from their watch. Even though I have nothing to be ashamed of, his look raises my hackles, and I glare back.

Zoe steps between us, breaking our contact.

"Okay, everyone, listen carefully." Almost as one, the entire room steps closer, surrounding her.

"The patrol tank has passed on. We counted fifteen guards on the wall, plus six at the gate. Once the raiders begin their attack on the wall, Beanie, Talbert, Riven, and Busher will take out the gate guards. Flip and the others up on the roof will take care of the guards on the wall. We clear the way for Mack to get into that booth, so he can open the gate. Once the gate starts opening and the guards are taken down, Talbert will give the signal. At that signal, you all go. We won't have much time. The next patrol will be around at one on the hour. We have to all be out of the gate and the tunnel blown before the next patrol manages to get a target on our asses. Everyone got it?"

A bit of mumbling and head nodding follows her remark.

"Good. Now, be ready; it should be any time now."

Almost on cue with Zoe's words, we hear the attack

begin. The raiders start shooting on the wall. The group of five designated to take out the guards at the gate move out as one as the onslaught begins. I want to go with them so badly, and I know Jax is itchin' too, but we have our own jobs. We're to make sure the rest of the crew get to the gates at the signal, so we stand silently at the door, one on either side, waiting to herd the rest to their fates.

The shooting outside echoes in my head like a heartbeat. Maybe it is my heartbeat. I can't tell the difference. All I know is that every shot seems to take a day off my life. My eyes frantic, I search out Ben and Finn and Jax as if I'm trying to remember every detail of their faces. Like somehow, my mind is telling me this may be the last time I will ever see them. *Stop thinkin' that way,* I scold myself in my head.

Seems like an eternity passes; time has no meaning. What's happening? Why are they still shooting? Are they being captured, hurt … or worse? My hands holding my shooter sweat like crazy, and I wipe them on my trousers. Blood rushes to my head, and I shake my head to clear it. *Oh gods, it ain't gonna work,* I think. There's still so much shooting. There shouldn't be so much shooting. There are too many guards at the gate and on the wall. We had counted wrong, and now my people are all captured or dead. I know it. The terrible thoughts jump through my head, one after another, and it's all I can do to keep myself from running out into the street to see what's happening with my own eyes.

And just like that it stops. Silence descends, bringing with it a whole new set of fears. The shooting has stopped, but why? Had our plan worked? We wait, scared to even breathe, but still the silence drags on.

There's no signal. There's nothing but silence, which is much worse than any shooter fire we had just heard. No signal. Where is the damned signal? I stare across at Jax in dawning horror, his face mirroring my own deep fears. They failed. They hadn't made it. They were probably all lying dead in the street. Oh, gods, oh gods, oh gods!

Suddenly, three sharp whistles ring through the night air, freezing me in place.

"Go!" Jax yells, pushing open the door, bringing me out of my stupor. We stumble into the street, me and him, checking for any sign of Army. Whatever other souls that had been hanging about the streets at this hour have rightly disappeared at the shooter fire. I check up and down the streets, but there's not one single person milling about in the deserted section of city, not even a soldier. Good, but I know they'll be here soon. I stand off to the side, Jax on the other as we rush the others out the door.

"Don't stop for anything. Run straight to the gate!" Jax yells as they rush past us.

Finn shoots me a frantic look as he and Cat brush by, and for a split second, I think he's going to stop. I scream at him, "Get to the gate!" as Ben grabs him by the scruff of the neck, dragging him along. Finally, the last person is out of the cellar, and Jax and I hurry to bring up the rear.

We run, all eyes fixated on the gate. It looms in front of us, barring our way to freedom and still locked tight. My heart falls to my gut in terror. We're not getting out. But then I notice the rumbling underneath my feet at the same time realization kicks in. The gate is opening. Mack had done it.

The closer we get to the wall, though, the more evidence

we see of the earlier fight. Bodies litter the ground. We step over the ones in our way, and I'm glad for the darkness hiding their wounds from us, from Finn. As much as I know this part was necessary to save our own lives, he doesn't need to see this.

Please let 'em all be Army lying there, I think desperately as my eyes search for the familiar faces of my people through the gloom. I finally spot Mack in the little booth that operates the gate with Riven outside keeping watch. Beanie and Talbert stand at the widening gate, ushering the others through, and I almost cry in relief as I watch Finn and Cat pass out of sight through the opening. Ben is right there too, but he stops and looks back. Looking for me, I know. I keep running as I yell to him, "Go. I'm right behind you."

This is it. The plan had worked. We're finally going to make it out of this damn city. Once we get through that tunnel and the raiders blow it, we'll be safe.

I stifle a scream as a shadow looms up in front of me, and I skid to a stop. I raise my shooter in defense, but hands grab the barrel before I can fire, and it almost gets yanked from my hands. A tug of war ensues as the soldier in front of me tries to wrestle my shooter away. Where the hell had he come from? Why isn't he down with the rest of them?

I hang on for dear life, two sets of hands pulling the shooter back and forth in the silent tug-of-war.

"No. You. Ain't. Gettin'. It!" I snarl as I pull with all my might, but the soldier is strong.

He gives one more forceful tug pulling me off balance, and I stumble into him. We're so close now I can see the frenzied glint in his eyes, and I know his intention. Only one of us is gonna walk away from this alive. My knee impacts into his groin, and he loosens his grip. I pull the shooter away and slam the stock of it into his forehead with a sickening crunch, his wild eyes glazing over before he falls to the ground. *Please don't let there be more,* I pray, but my fears are painfully justified as I look around. The brown robes are all I can see, swarming us through the darkness. No. There's not supposed to be this many.

I hear Jax's angry growl as two of them tackle him at the same time. He manages to take one down with a solid uppercut, but the other jumps on his back and gets him by the throat. I run at them, determined to help, but a painful kick to my knee from behind sends me face planting the ground, and my shooter skitters across the stones. Without a moment to lose I flip onto my back to fight off my attacker, but already he's on top of me, his hands closing around my throat.

I kick and buck like a madwoman, trying to dislodge him from my chest, but his hands stay strong, and I'm soon gasping for air. He's leaving nothing to chance. He doesn't seem to give one lick about taking me alive.

Desperate now, I move my hands in underneath his arms, trying to knock them away, but my strength is waning quickly along with my air. I can't breathe. My vision grows fuzzy. Everything is turning dark, and I know I'm about to black out completely. No, it can't end like this. It can't.

Shooter fire explodes at my head and stuns me for a moment, but I still have sense enough to roll out of the way as my attacker's hands leave my neck. He falls on the ground beside me with unseeing eyes, and I shimmy away on my elbows, gasping for air and trying to suck it into my starving lungs. Already, I can feel the pain and swelling of my bruised throat.

"Tara, hide!" Zoe's voice is almost drowned out by the ringing in my ears as she yanks me to my feet. Shizen. Why are my ears ringing so badly? I shake my head, trying to clear the confusion before I realize the sound isn't my ears at all. It's an alarm. The Army had sounded the alarm. There's going to be a horde of them here any minute now. White light erupts, nearly blinding me as the whole area comes ablaze from the electric torches on the wall.

"Move. You cannot be captured," Zoe yells again as she grabs my arm, and we stumble back into the street. I let her drag me to cover behind the burned-out husk of a veacal, hiding us from the Army now ascending from the darkness of the city. I can hear the yells of the soldiers as they pass.

"Find the New Blood. She has to be taken alive."

It wasn't supposed to be this way.

I need to help the others. Jax. Mack. Beanie and Talbert. I have to help them. They have to get out of here with the rest of them. I stand, holding my damaged throat and looking for my people. I hear Zoe yelling at me to get back down. I do, but I don't heed her. I watch Jax lose his battle as the two soldiers now become five, and they beat him down to the ground with the force of their blows, his face almost unrecognizable under the blood. Mack and Riven are fighting heroically, but they too disappear under the soldiers swarming the gate booth. One of the soldiers makes his way inside the booth and starts closing the gate again, trying to lock the rest of us in. Busher barrels through the mob covering Mack and

Riven, sending some of them flying into the air. Mack claws his way out from the jumble, stumbling into the booth, and shoots the soldier inside point-blank. His blood-spattered, crazed face finds me where I stand, and I hear his roar from across the distance as clear as if he's standing next to me.

"TARA! GET OUT NOW!"

Even with his own life hanging in the balance, he's still trying to protect me.

I don't move. I can't. I'm rooted in spot, but Zoe's not as stupefied. Grabbing me again, she drags me across the road towards the gate, her intention to follow Mack's order. No. I dig in my heels, stop her from pulling me. I can't leave. I have to help the others.

Beanie and Talbert stand strong at the gate, trying to keep the soldiers from following our people that had already made it through, a couple of stacked water barrels their only protection from the slugs zipping past them. They spot us, and Talbert stops firing long enough to wave wildly with his arm.

"Run, Mistress. Come on!"

He tries to duck back behind his flimsy shelter again, but a slug sends him spinning backwards and his shooter flying through the air. Beanie runs to help, screaming Talbert's name, but his yell is cut short as a soldier smacks him in the back of the head, sending him to his knees. They go down quick and soon get surrounded with shooters pointing at them from every direction. Oh, Gods. The soldiers are gonna kill them.

Flip runs toward them, screaming like a lunatic, shooting as he goes. He manages to take out a few of the soldiers holding them down before his heads explodes in a hideous shower of gore and blood, killed instantly by the slug that hits him. My scream is lost in the roar of the onslaught of more brown robes.

It wasn't supposed to be this way.

A black blur sails through the gate at that moment, attacking the remaining soldiers surrounding Beanie and Talbert, taking down five or six with one swipe of massive paws. The soldiers left standing are rattled at the sight of the crazed, black beast, some of them opting to run while others raise their weapons.

Cat! No, she was already past the gate. Why had she come back? Fear courses through me, making me stagger under its weight because right away I know what that means. He would never let her come back on her own, not without him. The scream leaves my lips as I spot the red head squeeze back through the opening, frantic eyes searching for his beloved beast.

"Finn, no. Go back. Go back!"

He doesn't hear me over the shouting, the shooting, or the alarm. I watch in horror as he finds Talbert's shooter and picks it up, his intention obvious: to protect his beast.

"What are you doin'?" I scream at him. "Stop it. Get back outta that gate."

I have to get to him. He has to drop that weapon. The soldiers won't care that he's just a boy.

My body finally responds to my fear. Shaking off Zoe's hand, I run toward Finn. I have to reach him, get him to safety. My eyes don't leave his face as he finally sees me running at him, screaming his name.

I don't see where the shot comes from. I don't even see it hit him. One minute, he's staring at me with such defiant bravery and the next; he's looking down at himself in wonder as the red blossoming on his tunic causes the world to tilt around me. His little hand touches his chest; his face turns to me quizzically as if to say, "What is this, Tara?" before he slumps to his bony knees and falls face first into the dirt.

My heart stops beating. I feel it stop. I feel it break, shattering into a thousand tiny pieces.

It wasn't supposed to be this way.

There's no small flickering of flame or gradual buildup of my Chi like before. It hemorrhages, bursting through every fiber of my being, searing me painfully into action. The scream that leaves my lips is one of primal grief and rage as I throw myself into a reckless attack on the soldiers coming at me, blocking my way to Finn. I have to get to him. I can save him like before.

I jump straight into the sea of soldiers and kick at the lead one, slamming my foot hard into his chest. He falls back into the others, knocking them down like dominoes. Whipping out my knives as I land, I ram them into the throats of the next two soldiers, spinning past their screams, attacking flesh wherever I see it.

Movement flickers at the corner of my eye, and I twist away just as a shooter barrel comes for my head. It slams into my raised forearm instead, but my other hand remains steadfast as my knife blade enters the soldier's neck, his lifeblood spurting into the air.

A blow from behind hits me in the shoulder, throwing me forward. I can feel blood running down my back, but it doesn't slow me down. I continue slashing and slicing, nothing breaking through my silent onslaught, although inside I'm screaming like a madwoman. Chest, throat, gut, no target is safe from my blades as I strike out with pure rage. I dispatch every soldier in my way with brutal precision.

I feel their hot blood splatter my face; I see their life spark fade from their startled eyes. It does nothing to penetrate my all-consuming need for vengeance. There is no room in my heart for anything else.

The last soldier falls from my blade, and I stand among the carnage, a strange sense of satisfaction flowing through my gut. Like what I'd just done was meant to be. I stand unmoving, knives gripped tight in blood-soaked hands as my Chi finally ebbs away, leaving me with one bone-chilling realization. My Chi is no gift like the others believed, not by any means. It *is* a curse. A terrible, dire weapon. Until this very moment, I hadn't understood that. Now everything is crystal clear.

"Finn!" His name explodes from my lips, forcing me to remember. Setting the pain free. I try to go to him, but the ebbing Chi is taking its usual toll on my body. My head spins dangerously, nausea boils in my gut, and my legs threaten to give way. Heat rushes over me so intense it feels like my eyeballs are roasting and the hair is sizzling off of my head at the roots. What's happening? I fight it, but I stumble forward and fall to the ground, the bloody knives still clutched in my hands.

Finn.

I pull myself to my hands and knees, start crawling towards the boy. I can still help him; I just have to get to him.

"Tara?" Jax calling my name breaks through my numbing grief.

I look up at him. He stumbles towards me crying, the tears mixing with the blood on his face and causing fat, red droplets to drip from his chin.

"Tara, stop," he pleads, but his voice sounds like it is echoing down a deep well.

My vision is blurring ... everything is hazy, but still I use every last remaining bit of strength to pull my useless body toward the boy.

"Finn," I whisper brokenly as my strength finally betrays me. The weakness takes over, and I collapse onto the ground. I lay there, my cheek pressed into the cold mud, and my eyes glued to the tiny, still body. *I'm sorry. It wasn't supposed to be this way.*

People are piling through the gate now with blurred faces and vague yelling. I want to scream in protest as someone picks up the boy and starts taking him away, but nothing leaves my damaged throat. It's the last thing I see before blackness swallows me.

Chapter Fifteen

The Reunion

———❦———

Birds. I hear birds singing. I can't remember the last time I heard that beautiful sound. It reminds me of being a young'un back in Rivercross and fills me with an odd sense of peacefulness. A light breeze flows from somewhere, stirring my hair and bringing with it the sweet smell of grass. I try to open my eyes, but they don't want to cooperate. Feels like they're sewn together, and the lids refuse to budge. So I keep them closed and lay there, letting the sounds and smells wash over me.

I reckon it must be daytime. The light shining on my face is so bright I can see the veins in my eyelids, thin, pink lines of blood. My serene mood lasts only a moment longer until I realize the reason I woke up in the first place. I can hear low murmuring that grows louder in urgency.

"… she will need to know..."

"... not yet … too weak … Chi nearly killed her …"

"… needs to understand..."

The voices sound close, but I still can't understand all of what they're saying. Are they talking about me? I fight with my eyes, prying them open.

It takes a minute of frantic blinking until my eyes adjust to the brightness and fall on the two shadows standing next to me, so close I could probably reach out and touch them. I notice the eyepatch right away. Mack is facing me, but the other person's back is to me, and all I can see are the tufts of gray hair, instantly making me think of Grada. But then reality sinks in, and I know it isn't him. Grada is dead. Gone. Just like—

"Finn!" the name bursts from me in a wail of pure grief, and the pain that shoots through my chest takes my breath away. I bolt up, hyperventilating, the pain making it impossible to draw a breath into my starving lungs.

"Hey, hey, calm down." Mack is on me in a flash, holding my shoulders. "It's okay, Tara. Finn is fine. He's alive."

I stare back in bewilderment, the words not making a bit of sense in my head. Why would Mack play such a cruel joke on me? I'd seen Finn shot; I seen him die in front of me. Why would Mack try to make me believe otherwise? I reckon he sees the disbelief on my face since he shakes me a little.

"I would never lie to you about that, girl. Finn is very much alive."

I start to tremble as my brain refuses to believe Mack's word even though my heart is already invested. Finn is alive?

"How ..." I begin as I fight the spark of rising hope. "That's impossible."

"See for yourself," Mack says, smiling as he stands aside and motions to the open window on the other side of the room. On shaky legs, I make my way from the bed and to the window, the smell of the grass much stronger now. My gaze is hesitant, almost afraid to look, afraid that Mack is lying to me after all. But then I hear that laugh. That silly, goofy laugh and I look out upon the sweetest sight my eyes have ever seen. Finn is sitting on a little hill across a green, grassy field covered in wild flowers. Flowers. One arm is in a sling while the other throws a stick for Cat, who takes off like a shot after the projectile.

"He's alive," I whisper, and I don't care that tears are squirting from my eyes now like some old gramma on her grandbaby's born day. I feel life slowly seeping back through my heart like much-needed rain seeping through the cracks of a dried-up riverbed. My legs feel like they're going to give out on me, and I have to lean against the windowsill to keep myself upright. It feels like my heart just may break from sheer joy as the reality finally dawns on me. Finn is okay. I keep staring at him, taking in his features like I can't get enough of him.

Mack comes up behind me, laying his hand gently on my shoulder.

"Finn, like his furry companion, truly does seem to have the proverbial nine lives."

"But I seen him shot," I whisper to Mack. "I saw the

wound. How did he survive that?"

"Some thanks goes to lady luck, the slug missed anything vital. But mostly because of our new friend here. He was the one who saved Finn's life."

New friend? I turn around then to finally acknowledge the other person in the room. He's old, older than even Orakel, I think. His hair is sparse and sticks up from his head in scraggly tufts. His face is so wrinkled and caved in it looks like crinkly paper. Like if you blew on it, it would just disintegrate into the wind. But despite all that, there's nothing feeble about him. He stands tall, his back straight and proud, and his gray eyes stare into me with fierce interest and something else I can't quite place.

"Tara, Ernst. Ernst, Tara."

"I am so happy to see you, child," he says with such a strong voice it surprises me. Then, without warning, he crosses the room in two strides and pulls me into his arms. I start at the familiar blood bond tingle that passes between us, but I don't pull away. Instead, I hug him back with all the thankfulness in my heart for saving Finn's life.

"You're a New Blood," I say, my voice muffled by his shoulder. He pulls away some but still holds me at arm's length, staring into my face.

"I was, at one time," he says.

"That's how you saved Finn."

"That was part of it," he says.

His words baffle me, but I don't question what he's saying. Not for the moment. Finn is alive, and it seems because of this stranger in front of me.

"Thank you," I whisper, and he simply smiles at me, his

hand brushing the side of my face like he can't truly believe I'm standing before him. Like somehow, he knew me. It unnerves me a little.

"Jax? Ben? Tater?" I question Mack, my fear renewed as my brain finally begins making all the connections, and I start remembering.

"They all made it out alive and well. Jonas and Belle and their people. Beanie and Talbert too, although they are a little worse for wear," he says, and I close my eyes, squeezing back more tears. But then the image of Flip pops into my head, and I can feel my heartbeat increase with sickening dread. I don't want to ask the question, but I need to know.

"Who ... who didn't make it?" I say hoarsely.

Mack sighs and rubs the back of his neck.

"Maybe this isn't the best time, Tara—"

"Who, Mack? I need to know," I plead, and I guess hears the desperation in my voice because he don't argue no more.

"Flip ... two of Zoe's men ... and Riven."

Flip I remember, but another little piece of my soul dies at Riven's name. His big, burly frame lingers in my mind, and I'm glad I didn't see it happen, not like Flip. I don't want to remember him any other way. Zoe's men. I don't even remember their names, yet they had died trying to get us out of the city, and I send a silent prayer of thanks to them, to all of them who died and for all that they sacrificed for us.

"There would have been more casualties for certain if you hadn't done what you did—"

"Mack, don't try to justify ..." I whirl in anger, attempting to cut off the line of bullshite he's about to lay on me, but I'm startled into silence as the door bursts open and hits the wall.

Two bodies fighting for position, pretty much fall into the room. Two pairs of eyes, one brown and one sky blue, gaze upon my face with happiness.

"Told ya I heard her voice," Ben says over his shoulder as he strides across the room and pulls me into his arms with years of familiarity. I hug him back, so glad to see him alive and in one piece. But it's the blue eyes that I stare at with yearning. Those are the arms that I want to feel around me. The still-bruised face is the one I ache to touch. But Jax doesn't come to me like Ben had done, even though I'm wishing with all my might. Instead, he just stares at me ravenously, like he hasn't laid eyes on me in years. That look makes my legs weaken, and I stumble back to the cot I'd been laying on earlier.

"Nice of you to join us, boys," Mack says at their unruly interruption, his tone implying anything but.

"Nice of you to let us know she was awake," Jax's comment is filled with sarcasm, and I look back and forth between them, puzzled at their tone. "You said you would let us know as soon as she woke up. Have you told her anything?"

"No, we have't had the opportunity—"

"Told me what?" I interrupt right away.

"All in good time," Mack says, still glaring at Jax, but my irritation begins to sprout at their evasiveness.

"Told me what?" I insist. "And while we're at it, someone mind tellin' me where the hell we are?"

I've finally noticed my surroundings. The room is … odd to say the least. The walls are half built from stone, looks like, and the wall the cot rests against seems to be made of solid rock. Like the place was built into the side of a mountain.

The old man answers my question, confirming my belief.

"We are deep in the mountains. Safe. My home, and far away from his prying eyes."

The mountains? The mountains were days of travel from Skytown, possibly weeks.

"How did we get here? I don't recall any traveling. How long was I out?"

Mack and Jax exchange a look.

"I think it is too soon; she just woke up," Mack says.

"She has a right to know everything, Mack," Jax says.

"I agree with Mack. Give her more time," the old man says.

"She's strong enough to handle it." Even Ben? And he is agreeing with Jax. What the hell is going on here?

"You know I can hear y'all, right? I mean, I'm sittin' right here," I say. Ben and Jax don't seem to take any notice of my anger, but I can tell I've startled the old man. He scrutinizes me with his watery, gray eyes.

"Are you sure the time is right?" His question is meant for Mack, but it annoys me to no end.

"For the love of gods. If someone don't tell me somethin' soon, I'm gonna knock some heads together."

Mack finally nods at the old man, like he's giving permission for something. Ernst pulls up a chair and sits, studying my face over his clasped hands.

"Fine. What is the last thing you remember?"

I think back.

"Finn gettin' shot, tryin' to reach him. But I couldn't because I was so weak. So weak and ... like I was burnin' up." I remember the feeling intensely. Like my eyes were gonna cook right in my head and my hair was gonna burn off. I reach up and touch my hair, amazed that I still have any left. "It felt like there was this fire inside of me, roastin' me alive. Then people comin' through the gate and takin' Finn then … then nuthin'.'"

Ernst nods at my words, like they somehow made sense to him. Well, at least it seems to make sense to one of us.

"That was your uncontrolled Chi. It knocked you out of commission for twelve days while your body healed itself. Lucky, really. I have never known of anyone to experience mercurial Chi and live to talk about it. You must be impressively strong."

He looks pleased by his words, like somehow I had done him proud. All it does is scare me something fierce.

"So my Chi nearly killed me? Is that what you're sayin'?" The story of Jax's sister, Jenna, pops into my head. Of how she had died from her not being able to control her Chi. My heart hammers against my ribs as I realize how close I had come to meeting that same fate.

"Unfortunately, yes. It is still not under your control, especially when your emotions run high. You will have to learn to discipline the force that pumps through your blood. Right now, your Chi is just raw, pure energy in its most powerful configuration. Energy that is constantly changing beneath the surface and flowing through your blood. You can control it with your powerful mind to use as much or as little as you desire. Releasing too much of this energy in one burst can have detrimental effects on your physical body as you clearly found out. I can help you with that. I will teach you—"

"Who the hell are you?" I cut off his ramblings. He may be excited by what I'm telling him, but I'm sure not the least bit pleased at how close I'd come to dying. "And where did you come from? How did you find us? How were you conveniently there at that exact moment to help Finn? And why should I even trust anythin' that comes outta your mouth?"

He sits back in his chair, taken aback.

"I told you she was a volatile firecracker," Mack says indulgently, and Ernst chuckles.

"Yes, she certainly is a bit headstrong. That's something we can use to our advantage though—"

"*Again*, I can hear you. Stop talkin' about me like I ain't here," I say, and Ernst pretends to smooth out his gray mustache with his fingers, but I know it's just to cover up his grin. "And you better start answerin' my questions to my likin' or else this conversation is done, understood?"

"Tara, let him talk. This is something you're going to want to hear." Jax is now leaning against the wall, arms folded, and the look on his face tells me something is definitely up. I can't help the feeling of dread in my gut as I nod at the old man to go ahead.

He clears his throat.

"Very well. Let's start at the beginning then, shall we? As I have already told you, this mountain village is my home … and home to my people. There are over two hundred of us living here; although that number has increased two-fold since the arrival of the raiders and the escapees from Skytown. And yes, the refugees that made it out with you are all here," he says in answer to the question forming on my lips. I snap my mouth shut.

"I arrived at Skytown with the raiders. Ever since I heard of you from them, I have been eagerly waiting to find you, to talk to you, and help you become what I know you can be."

"Heard of me from them? So you're a raider, too?"

"Oh, my heavens, no. But I have known Busher and his crew a very long time. We have what you would call a mutual agreement. We supply them with crops and whiskey, and they supply us with whatever needs we cannot grow ourselves. It works well for us."

"Does he know you're a New Blood?" I say, questioning why he hasn't tried to turn the old man in for a reward like he'd done with me.

"It's a bit more complicated than that, I'm afraid. And I'm really not a New Blood in the true sense," he says.

That's not an explanation. He doesn't give any more detail on the matter though; he just keeps talking.

"I made my way to Skytown as soon as I heard of your presence there and the escape plan. I had a feeling my assistance would be required. I was not wrong. We waited for you all to escape the tunnel, but when only about half of you made it through, we knew something had gone terribly wrong. Then when we heard the shooting start up again, we realized we had to intervene. The cat and the boy doubled back before any of us even realized he was gone, unfortunately, but we were not far behind."

"Far enough to let him get shot," I say bitterly, "and to let my Chi grow so outta whack that I became a … a monster," I whisper the last words, the horror at what I had done to the soldiers still fresh in my head. But he hears them.

"No, you're not a monster. Misguided, untrained, naïve even, but not a monster. You experienced something that, unless you have been trained to control, was more like a force of nature. Your response was instinctive, primal. Your Chi recognized a threat and eliminated it. Any untrained New Blood would have reacted in the same manner."

"Would you have?" I study his face at my words, wondering if he will speak the truth or just say something he thinks I want to hear.

"Yes and no. My response would probably have been less archaic—and damn well less effective. I'm nowhere near as powerful as you. Not anymore. But nevertheless, it would have ended with the same result. Threat annihilated. Although, unlike you, I would not have been wiped out by my show of strength. I have been around a long time. Long enough to know how to control Chi and use it safely."

"How?" I ask, and he stares at me in puzzlement. "How do you know so much? Do you know where we come from? How this weapon of ours came about? Because it is a weapon, ain't it? It's no gift from the gods or any of that other shite I've been told. When I was … doin' that to those soldiers, I knew. Deep in my heart, I knew my Chi was a terrible weapon." I look at him with beseeching eyes. "I'm right, aren't I?"

He doesn't even try to lie to me. "Yes."

I'm afraid to look at Jax or Ben. I don't want to see how they react to this bit of info.

"How do you know?" I question.

"Because I was there from the beginning," he says.

"The beginnin' of what?"

"Of the change in the world order after the Shift. Of human evolution. Of New Bloods."

I scoff at his words. "That's impossible. The Shift was well over a hundred years ago. Lily said New Bloods have been around since then, too. How in hell would you have been around then? That would have to make you more than—"

"A hundred and sixty-two born years," he finishes for me. At first I think he's pulling my leg, but he's not lying. I can tell. Not in the least. I don't know why I'm not more surprised.

"*Him*, too?" I don't have to explain who I'm asking about.

"Yes. I knew him as Max." His laugh is humorless. "Quite a humble name really, for someone who became known as the all-powerful Prezedant. We were associates once—scientists in our former lives." He sees my confusion at his words because he tries again. "We were researchers, healers, I guess you would call us now, assigned to protecting our leaders from exposure to the biological warfare. The world was at war, Tara. And it wasn't just from fire bombs like you have been told. Radiation, toxic gases, tainted air, and water, those were the biggest threats. With most of our soldiers dying off from these deadly biological toxins, we needed to come up with some way to fight it. To keep our people alive. To make them more resistant, so we engineered human blood with genetically modified cells to fight these toxins. To build up immunity and keep our enemies from wiping us out. The basis was to produce high-value red blood cells that would do more than just carry oxygen through our bodies. They would transport a bounty of genetically engineered proteins that would protect its host by targeting specific toxins. In other words, it would fight off the poisons that were killing us. It worked better than we could have ever imagined at first. Not only was the modified blood neutralizing the toxins the hosts had already been exposed to, but any other diseases or conditions they had before the blood transfusions were being affected as well. The test subjects were healing themselves. From the simplest of broken bones to cancerous tumors, these soldiers were healing at an accelerated rate. But then a few of the test subjects began to exhibit other side effects."

I'm not understanding everything he's saying, but I get the gist. Him and the Prezedant, they had added something to the soldiers' blood to make them stronger. Something that wasn't natural.

"What were the side effects?" I say.

"They were slight at first. Increased strength, especially when distraught. The ability to affect their surroundings just by concentrating on doing so. Nudge a table, move a chair. Nothing too alarming. But then we started noticing physical changes in these few. Their hair started turning white: systematic white stripes that seemed to exude an aura when the subject was agitated. This aura, it was like raw, pure energy just radiating from their bodies."

This I do understand.

"Lily called it bio-energy," I say. "She said some people were born with an abundance of it while others weren't. The ones with the stripes, the ones of the light, were the most powerful."

He leans forward in his chair, clasping his wrinkled hands loosely between his knees.

"A very basic explanation but essentially correct. Some

test subjects showed just slight advancement from the modified blood while others excelled. It was amazing what their capabilities were. We knew there was something astonishingly different about these few select subjects. Whatever was strong inside of them, call it bio-energy or Chi, it was reacting to the altered blood, mutating them. Making them almost, well, super human."

"The first New Bloods," I say.

"We studied them intensely. When we realized that over time their abilities seemed to wear off, we thought we had failed. The blood transfusions only seemed to last four or five months before their auras would wane. But then some of them produced offspring. The children of these few ... they were absolutely incredible. It was as if they inherited every modified red blood cell trait and naturally enhanced them. We had no need to inject them with the modified blood. They were born already altered, making them stronger than we could have even predicted. That was when we realized we had our first batch of super soldiers."

I was hanging onto his every word, concentrating hard to understand, but that one word makes me jerk upright.

"Super soldiers? You were creating soldiers outta the young'uns?" I say, stunned, and he shakes his head, dropping his gaze from me.

"That was our goal at first, yes. We were losing this war; we had to take drastic measures. But in the end, it didn't matter. The world as we knew it ceased to exist. Governments fell, society collapsed, anarchy ruled. But through it all, we didn't stop. At first, I guess we believed that if we continued with our testing, we could ... fix it all maybe? I mean, somebody had to try and do something."

Jax's angry "Shizen," coupled with the vein throbbing in his temple, tells me this is the first he's hearing of this as well.

"So these children were not willing subjects, were they? He was doing the same just like he does now. They were prisoners, experimented on and tossed down a chute if they should, gods forbid, slow down your testing by inconsiderately dying," Jax accuses.

Ernst at least has the decency to look ashamed at Jax's words.

"At first, no. The world was dying around us. These were volunteers, soldiers who wanted to stay alive and keep their families alive. But then we needed more than just soldiers. And once we realized that some of these people—these children—were special, we just couldn't let them go. Not if we were to save the world."

"So the young'uns that were born, the New Bloods, they were given life just to be fodder for your experiments?" I say slowly, the ugliness of the truth starting to dawn on me.

"They were born in captivity, yes. But you have to understand; they were the key to our survival! And I was a scientist. Finding a solution was all I was consumed with."

I don't understand. How does he expect me to understand that reasoning? What this old man is telling us is horrifying. But I still need to hear more. I need to know the truth, all of it.

"Then, I fell ill. Just like the rest of the world, I was dying. We tried infusing the genetically altered blood at first, but I was too far gone. It didn't work. I can't remember which one of us had the idea to transfuse the test subject's blood into my body; it was so long ago. And I had nothing to lose." He breaks off as if deep in thought or lost in remorse, I can't tell. Finally, he looks deep into my eyes, and I get the uneasy feeling I'm not going to like much else of what he's about to say

"It seemed to work. I was healed from my affliction. Not just healed but better than before, stronger. My body enhanced, and my mind empowered. A New Blood myself it seemed. But then, just a few months later, I fell ill again. Not terminally like before, but there was a malaise about me I could not explain away. The only way to feel normal again was to do another transfusion. And then another and another. Each time I transcended and became more than I was before. Before long, I needed the blood; I craved it even. Max soon noticed the benefits of the blood and joined in my obsession. I am ashamed to say what first began as a way to save humanity soon became our own personal agenda. The world was crumbling apart, no one left to rule what was left. Why shouldn't we? We were smart enough, and with the help of New Bloods, strong enough. We could bring about this new, better world we always talked of."

Wait. Is he actually telling me that he was in league with the Prezedant? That he was just as evil and immoral and callous? As if he can sense my growing anger, he hurries on.

"But then Max slowly changed over time. And time we had plenty of. Infusing the New Bloods' power into our bloodstream not only increased our strength, but our lifespan. We seemed to age differently than others, even the New Bloods themselves. Maybe it was the combination of the various blood traits and proteins, but we appeared to slow down the ravages of time. At first, it was an exhilarating breakthrough. I will admit I was seduced by this unexplainable ability. But while I looked at each new day as a gift, Max became colder, more jaded. It was as if the longer he lived, the less human he became. He no longer cared if the people in his experiments lived or died, only the blood mattered. It was all about the blood, draining them of every last drop. I saw things—" he pauses and drops his head in his hands, too overcome for anymore words.

I find it hard to feel sorry for him with what I've heard so far. I mean, he experimented on my kind. Drained them of their blood and used it for his own purposes, so I'm real surprised when Mack clasps his shoulder in comfort. Ernst seems to give himself a mental shake, then goes on.

"I should have stopped it. I should have stopped him. But I was weak. I let him gain more and more control while I hid myself in my lab, content to let him do all the dirty work. But one fateful day, it all changed. One day, his men brought in a fresh batch of prisoners. Kin to the original test subjects, I assume. Living relatives born of the mutated soldiers. All powerful New Bloods in their own rights. She was one of them, and that's how I met her. Rease, your mother."

The room falls dead quiet as if they're all holding their breath as one, waiting for my reaction.

"You-you knew my ma?" I whisper.

He nods as silent tears start to drip down his sunken cheeks, and all of a sudden I don't want to hear any more of what he's about to say.

"Knew her ... loved her ... and miss her more with each passing day."

Loved her? Like a daughter or granddaughter? He reaches over and takes my hand in his papery one, and I'm too stunned to pull away.

"She changed me, Tara. With her good heart and kindness, she made me human again. I loved her as I have never loved anyone before. And when we found out about you—"

"No," I pull my hand from his grasp. "You're lyin'. There ain't no way you and my ma … knew each other. Not in that way. You're an old man. It's impossible," I snarl, not wanting to accept what I know he's trying to say.

"Old now, yes, but twenty years ago, I still had my illusion of youthfulness because of the blood. Twenty years ago, we fell in love and she saved my soul. You were the product of that love, Tara. You are my daughter."

"Lies!" I scream at him as I push at his chest, and the chair topples over, nearly spilling him to the floor. Mack and Jax save him from hitting the floor while Ben tries to calm me.

"Tara, please. Listen to what he has to say," Ben pleads as he grabs my arms, but I yank them out of his grasp.

"I don't know what bullshite story he's told you people, but there ain't no way my *father*," I spit the word from my mouth, "is this killer sittin' right here. Y'all just heard him same as I did. He just admitted to experimentin' on and killin' New Bloods just so he could live longer and rule the lands. He ain't no better than the Prezedant himself, and I don't understand why you ain't already put a blade through his heart."

"Tara, calm yourself. Think about what you are saying. If it weren't for him, Finn would be dead," Mack throws at me, but I'm way past caring.

"If it weren't for him, hundreds, possibly thousands of New Bloods would be alive right now. How many did they kill over the years? How many? He's a monster and I'm not gonna listen to any more of that poison spewin' outta his mouth."

I head for the door, nearly barreling over Ben in the process, but Jax's voice stops me in my tracks.

"Tara, please listen to what he has to say. It's important for all of us. For our survival. Please."

The pleading is what gets me. I'm not used to that tone from Jax. Staring up at the ceiling, I let loose a huge sigh as the stubbornness raging in me gives in to Jax. Turning around slowly, I stare at Ernst with all the contempt I can muster.

"Say your piece, old man," I grumble.

He spreads his hands to me, pleading.

"I'm so sorry, Tara. I know how you must feel, and I'm not asking you to accept me as your kin. I will die soon, and I know my eternal soul will not join with your mother's in the afterlife, as much as I would wish it to. I will be judged and punished for my sins, and I'm ready to face that punishment. But that is not for you to decide. That is between me and my gods. What I do have for you, right now, is information of great importance. Information that I have risked my life and the lives of my people to bring you here to hear, for he will not let you live now. I know that to be a fact. He will hunt you down and anyone associated with you, and he will kill us all. To stop that from happening, you must carry out what I have been afraid to do all these years. I know how you can do it. To avenge your mother and the others you loved that he has taken from you. And with the gods as my witness, I will help you get your retribution. I will help you with your ascension into your power. I will help you kill the Prezedant."

Scarlet Oath

About the Author

I wish I could tell you I've climbed Mt. Everest or taken a hot air balloon ride around the world, but alas I lead a very quiet life in Nova Scotia, Canada. The only adventures I go on are in books. But what adventures they are! When I'm not reading or writing, I manage a chocolate shop. That's right; I work with both books and chocolate. Living the dream. The rest of my time is spent with my three favourite guys; my hubby, my son, and my crazy fur baby. We are a family of geeks. Fans of Game of Thrones and The Walking Dead, lovers of books of any genre, and players of video games. And I wouldn't have it any other way.

Other books by Michelle Bryan

Crimson Legacy series
Crimson Legacy
Scarlet Oath
Blood Desstiny
Bood Hunt (a short story)
The Waystation (a novella)

The Bixby series
Grand Escape (Prequel)
Strain of Resistance
Strain of Defiance
Strain of Vengeance

Legacy of Light series
A War for Magic
A War for Truth
A War for Love